Peter Tremayne is t[...]
authority on the ancient Celts, who utilises his knowledge
of the Brehon law system and seventh-century Irish society to create a new concept in detective fiction.

In addition to this collection of short stories, Sister
Fidelma has appeared in nine full-length novels: *Absolu-
tion by Murder*, *Shroud for the Archbishop*, *Suffer Little
Children*, *The Subtle Serpent*, *The Spider's Web*, *Valley of
the Shadow*, *The Monk Who Vanished*, *Act of Mercy* and
Our Lady of Darkness are also available from Headline.

'This collection is an essential canonical text for Sister
Fidelma acolytes'   *Publishers Weekly*

'Fidelma's fans will welcome this first-ever collection,
many stories of which are appearing here for the first
time'   *Kirkus Reviews*

'The Sister Fidelma books give the readers a rattling good
yarn. But more than that, they bring vividly and viscerally
to life the fascinating lost world of the Celtic Irish. I put
down *The Spider's Web* with a sense of satisfaction at a
good story well told, but also speculating on what modern
life might have been like had that civilisation
survived'   Ronan Bennett

'A treasure trove of small gems for historical mystery
fans'   *Booklist*

To discover more about the world of Sister Fidelma, visit
her own website at www.sisterfidelma.com

Hemlock
At Vespers
Volume 2

A Collection of Sister Fidelma
Mysteries

Peter Tremayne

HEADLINE

First published in 2000 by
HEADLINE BOOK PUBLISHING

First published in this edition in 2001 by
HEADLINE BOOK PUBLISHING

10 9 8 7 6 5 4 3 2 1

ISBN 0 7472 6784 7

Typeset by Letterpart Ltd
Reigate, Surrey

Printed and bound in Great Britain by
Clays Ltd, St Ives plc.

HEADLINE BOOK PUBLISHING
A division of Hodder Headline
338 Euston Road
London NW1 3BH

www.headline.co.uk
www.hodderheadline.com

For John Carson,
Fan and collector *extraordinaire*!
To celebrate twenty-one years of friendship.
May your shadow never grow less.

Table of Contents
∾

Introduction

The Sister Fidelma mysteries are set during the seventh century AD, mainly in her native Ireland.

Sister Fidelma is not simply a religieuse, a member of what we now call the Celtic Church, whose conflicts with Rome on matters of theology and social governance are well known; as well as differences in rituals, the dating of Easter and the wearing of a dissimilar tonsure, celibacy was not widely practised and many religious houses contained individuals of both sexes who raised their children to the continued service of God. Fidelma is also a qualified *dálaigh*, or advocate of the law courts of Ireland, using the ancient Brehon Law system, for in those days a woman could be equal with men in the professions, and many women were lawyers and judges. There is even a record of a female judge, Brig, correcting on appeal a judgement given by a male judge, Sencha, on women's rights.

Those who have followed Sister Fidelma's adventures in the series of novels, might be unaware that she made her debut in short story form. Four different stories featuring Fidelma appeared in separate publications in October, 1993, and it was the gratifying response to these stories which precipitated Fidelma into the series of novels but also created a demand for even more short stories. The fifteen stories in this volume comprise the complete set of those published at the time of writing this introduction.

To let you into a secret, there might not have been a Fidelma. Under my other hat, as a Celtic scholar, I decided to create the concept of an Irish female religieuse who was a lawyer, and who solved crimes under the ancient Brehon law system of Ireland, primarily to demonstrate to a wider audience both the fascinating system of law and the prominent role that women could and did play in that period. I drafted the first story back in 1993 and named her Sister Buan. It was an ancient Irish name meaning 'enduring'. Buan occurs in myth as a tutor to the hero Cúchulainn. When I showed the draft to my good friend Peter Haining, the anthologist and writer, he loved the story but threw up his hands in dismay at the name. He felt it did not trip easily off the tongue, in spite of its shortness.

As I reflected on this, suddenly, Fidelma was born. It was as if she had been waiting to catch my attention. The name is also ancient and means 'of the smooth hair'. Once Fidelma 'introduced herself' to me, everything fell into place. The name gave her an instant background and a family! The masculine and feminine forms of the name were popular among the royal dynasty of the Eóghanachta who ruled the kingdom of Munster from their capital of Cashel (Co. Tipperary). And it was an area that I knew very well, for my father's family had been settled sixty kilometres from Cashel for seven hundred years, so the records show. Cashel was always a special place, of magic, mystery and history for me.

Fidelma immediately identified herself as the daughter of the Cashel King Failbe Fland, who died c. AD 637–639 within months of Fidelma's birth. So before she became a religieuse and a lawyer, Fidelma was raised as an Eóghanachta princess.

Sharp-eyed readers will have realised that a strict chronology is followed in the novels. The stories have so far taken place between the spring of AD 664 and autumn of AD 666. In fact, AD 666 was a rather busy time for Fidelma, for it was the year in which four full-length mystery adventures occurred between January and October.

The adherence to a set chronology also applies to the short stories. Fidelma first appears at around the age of twenty-seven, having trained not only at an Irish ecclesiastic centre but at the secular college of the Brehon (Judge) Morann at Tara; there was, incidentally, a real Brehon Morann whose dictums still survive in ancient Irish literature. Fidelma achieved her qualifications in law to the level of *Anruth*, one degree below the highest that the ecclesiastical and secular colleges could bestow. While she was a student, she had an unhappy *affaire do coeur* with a warrior who was not her intellectual equal. She subsequently joined the community which had been founded by St Brigid at Kildare, and while there started to achieve a reputation by solving difficult legal mysteries, and her talents as a lawyer, a *dálaigh* in Old Irish, became much in demand.

Readers may be surprised that Brother Eadulf plays no part in any of the short stories. In the first novel, *Absolution By Murder* (1994), Fidelma, already with a reputation as an incisive inquirer and legal expert, was sent to advise the Irish delegation at the Synod of Whitby in AD 664. This Synod was the location of the famous historical debate between representatives of the Celtic and the Roman Church. It was there that Fidelma met the young Saxon monk named Brother Eadulf. He had been trained in Ireland but now wore the tonsure of Rome. He became her 'Doctor Watson' and has featured in every novel except one – *Suffer Little Children* (1995).

In the following stories, Fidelma solves the mysteries without Eadulf's good-intentioned but often critical assistance. This is because several of the stories, such as 'Murder in Repose' and 'Murder by Miracle', are set prior to Fidelma's meeting with Eadulf. Other early adventures include 'Tarnished Halo', 'Abbey Sinister' and 'Our Lady of Death'.

In the early stories Fidelma announces herself as 'Fidelma of Kildare'. A reader once wrote and asked me why she decided to leave that community, for after the events of *Suffer Little Children* (1995) she takes on the mantle of 'Fidelma of Cashel'. The reason why she began her break with Kildare is explained in 'Hemlock at Vespers'. At that point Fidelma set off to discuss her problems with her mentor, the chubby faced and kindly Abbot Laisran of the great abbey of Durrow where, in the mid-seventh century, young men and women from no fewer than eighteen nations were recorded as students. 'A Canticle for Wulfstan' is located at Durrow. While there Fidelma receives a cry for help from a close friend of her childhood, a girl she has grown up with, who has been accused of murdering her husband and her own child. The resultant adventure is told in 'At the Tent of Holofernes'. On her continued journey to the High King's court at Tara, she finds that the Yellow Plague, which devastated much of Europe at this time, had been instrumental in causing the death of the joint High Kings, Diarmuid and Blathmac. The new High King, Sechnasach, is about to be installed, but part of the ceremonial regalia has gone missing. Civil war and anarchy could result if Sechnasach cannot prove his right to the kingship by showing the sacred artefacts. The mystery is recounted in 'The High King's Sword'.

From there Fidelma is off to Whitby to attend the Synod, as previously mentioned. From Whitby she travels to Rome with a party which includes Brother Eadulf. In the autumn of that year, the newly appointed Archbishop of Canterbury is found murdered in the papal palace – an actual historical event – and Fidelma and Eadulf join forces to solve the mystery in *Shroud for the Archbishop* (1995). The short story, 'The Poisoned Chalice' is also set in Rome in this same period but, again, Eadulf is not in attendance. Fidelma and Eadulf part company in Rome, Fidelma to return home while Eadulf is to instruct the new Archbishop of Canterbury, Theodore of Tarsus, before accompanying him to England to assume his duties. Fidelma makes her journey home via the Abbey of Nivelles, an Irish foundation in the forest of Seneffe, in what is now Belgium, where 'Holy Blood' takes place.

Back in Ireland in AD 665 she returns to Tara, the setting for 'A Scream from the Sepulchre'. She then goes back to Kildare where she solves a race course mystery in 'The Horse that Died for Shame'. She is uncomfortable at Kildare, and when her brother, Colgú, sends her a message to return to Cashel because her help is urgently needed, she sets off eagerly.

It is still AD 665 and the King of Cashel, Fidelma's cousin, Cathal Cú Cen Máthair, is dying. His last request sends Fidelma into a harrowing adventure in an out-of-the-way Irish monastery featured in *Suffer Little Children* (1995). By the end of the story King Cathal has died and Fidelma's brother, Colgú, the heir-apparent, is now King of Munster. Indeed, Colgú was a great historical Munster King who ruled between AD 665–678/701.

Fidelma is reunited with Eadulf in extraordinary circumstances in the midwinter setting of a remote abbey in south-west Ireland featuring in the next book *The Subtle Serpent* (1996). The adventure culminates in January AD 666. From then on Fidelma and Eadulf join forces and Munster's capital, Cashel, becomes their base. They remain in partnership in *The Spider's Web* (1997), *Valley of the Shadow* (1998) and *The Monk Who Vanished* (1999). Only now and then does Fidelma find herself without Eadulf's assistance, for example in the short stories 'Invitation to a Poisoning' and 'Those That Trespass'.

Welcome, then, to a period which we mistakenly call 'The Dark Ages'. For Ireland, it was an 'Age of Golden Enlightenment', when law, order, literacy and the recording of knowledge created one of the most fascinating European civilisations; a time when missionaries from Ireland, singly and in groups, set off to spread learning and literacy as far east as Kiev in the Ukraine, north to Iceland and the Faroes, and south to Spain and across the Alps into Italy, to Taranto where an Irish monk named Cathal became St Cataldus, patron saint of the city. It was a time of high artistic achievement, the production of the great illuminated Gospel books, of breath-taking metal-working, the fabulous reliquaries, book shrines, chalices and crosses; of a native literature that is second to none and, of course, a fascinating law system and social order that in many ways, was as advanced in its philosophy and application as our own.

But, and there is always a 'but', in the affairs of mankind, it was a very human age, encompassing all the virtues and vices that humans are prey to; virtues and vices that we can recognise and understand today. The motives for crime have remained unaltered over the centuries, and in seventh-century Ireland there was still a need for a keen-eyed examiner with an analytical mind, yet often with a humane interpretation of the law for, as Fidelma herself once remarked, 'law is not always justice'. So we can now follow the good Sister into a world which may be one in which the superficial surroundings are unfamiliar to us but in which we still recognise the same fears, envies, loves and hates that have and do exist in all ages and in all civilisations.

Peter Tremayne

Tarnished Halo

Father Allán looked up with a frown from his interrupted devotions as Sister Fidelma opened the door of his *cubiculum* unannounced.

'I am told that you have urgent need of a lawyer,' she said without preamble.

As he scrambled from his knees, making a hasty genuflection to the crucifix that hung on the wall and before which he had been praying, she noticed that his face was graven in lines of anxiety. Once on his feet he turned and surveyed the young religieuse who stood poised within the door frame. From the surprise on his face, she was clearly not what he had been expecting. She was tall, with rebellious strands of red hair escaping from her *cabhal* or head-dress; her figure, lithe and vital, clearly indicated a joy in living, scarcely concealed by her habit.

'Are you the *dálaigh* whom I was told to expect?' Father Allán's voice held an incredulous tone.

'I am Fidelma of Kildare, an advocate of the courts,' affirmed Fidelma. 'I am qualified to the rank of *Anruth*.'

The Father Superior blinked. The qualification of *Anruth* was only one degree below the highest qualification obtainable either at the ecclesiastic or secular universities of the five kingdoms of Ireland. He swallowed as he eventually

1

remembered his etiquette and thrust out a hand to invite the religieuse in.

'Welcome, Sister. Welcome to our community of piety and peace . . .'

Fidelma interrupted the ritual greeting with a slight cutting motion of her hand.

'Not so peaceful, I am told,' she observed drily. 'I was informed by the Abbot of Lios Mór Mochuda that murder has been committed within these walls and that you have need of the services of a *dálaigh*. I came as soon as I could.'

Father Allán's lips compressed into a thin line.

'Not exactly within these walls,' he countered pedantically. 'Come, walk with me in our gardens and I will endeavour to explain matters.'

He led the way from the tiny grey monastic building which was perched on a rocky outcrop thrusting itself above a forest, and beside which a winding river meandered. The small religious community had a breathtaking view across the green vegetation towards distinct blue-hazed mountain peaks.

There was a small enclosed garden at the back of a dry-stone-built oratory. A young Brother was hard at work hoeing in a far corner. Father Allán led the way to a granite wall, well out of earshot of the young man, and seated himself. It was midday and the sun was warming and pleasant on the skin. Fidelma followed his example, perching herself on the wall.

'Now . . .?' she prompted.

'There has, indeed, been murder committed here, Fidelma of Kildare,' confirmed Father Allán, his tone heavy with sorrow.

'Who was killed, when and now?'

Father Allán waited a moment, as if to gather his thoughts before he spoke.

'Brother Moenach was killed. Perhaps you have heard of him?'

'We are many miles from Kildare,' observed Fidelma. 'Why would I have heard of this Brother Moenach?'

'He was a saintly youth,' sighed Father Allán. 'Yes, a veritable saint. He was a lad of eighteen summers but so steeped in wisdom, in poetry and in song; so serene and calm of nature was he that he was surely blessed by the Living God. His charity and sweet disposition were renowned as much as his musical accomplishments. Abbots and chieftains, even the King of Cashel, sought his musical talent to create solace for their spirits.'

Fidelma raised a cynical eye at Father Allán's enthusiasm for the virtues of Moenach.

'So an eighteen-year-old member of your house, Brother Moenach, was killed?' she summarised.

The Father Superior of the settlement nodded.

'When?'

'It happened a week ago.'

Fidelma exhaled deeply. That meant that there was little evidence for her to see. And doubtless Brother Moenach had been decently buried many days ago. But she had promised the Abbot of Lios Mór Mochuda that she would investigate this affair, for the tiny community fell within his ecclesiastical jurisdiction.

'How?'

'It was a village woman named Muirenn who killed him. We have her locked up to be taken before the chieftain for summary justice . . .'

'After she has been given a proper hearing before the local Brehon,' interrupted Fidelma. 'But I ask "how" not "who".'

Father Allán frowned.

'I do not follow.'

Fidelma restrained her irritation.

'Tell me the facts about this incident as you know them.'

'One evening, Brother Aedo came running to find me. It was shortly before vespers, as I recall. He had been

3

returning through the forest from the village with some vegetables for the settlement when he saw a movement through the trees to one side of the path. Curiosity prompted him to investigate. To his horror, in a clearing, he came upon the body of young Moenach. Kneeling beside him was an old woman of the village, Muirenn. She was holding a rock in her hand. There was blood on the stone and on the head of young Moenach. Brother Aedo fled and came straightaway to tell me of this terrible thing . . .'

'Fled? Yet you tell me that Muirenn is an old woman? What put such fear into a man of God?'

The Father Superior wondered whether Fidelma was being sarcastic but could not make up his mind.

'Muirenn turned on his approach with such a ghastly look on her face that Aedo was afraid for his life,' Father Allán explained. 'If Muirenn could kill Moenach then she could equally kill Aedo.'

'Her guilt is supposition at the moment. Then what? What after Aedo reported the matter to you?'

'Some of us went to the spot. Moenach was still lying there. His skull had been smashed in from behind. A bloodstained rock was lying where Muirenn had apparently discarded it. We hunted for her and found her hiding in her *bothán* in the village . . .'

'Hiding? Why would she return to her own cabin and her own village? Surely she would have known that she had been seen and recognised? It would be the last place to hide. And how was she hiding? Was she concealed somewhere in the cabin?'

Father Allán shook his head with a soft breath of vexation.

'I do not pretend to understand the workings of her mind. We caught her in her *bothán*, seated before her own hearth. We have been holding her for your interrogation, pending trial before the Brehon.'

'Hardly "hiding", from what you tell me,' observed

Fidelma somewhat scornfully. 'And did she admit culpability for the crime and volunteer a reason why she killed Moenach?'

The Father Superior sniffed deprecatingly.

'She claimed to have no knowledge at all of the murder although we have an eye-witness.'

'An eye-witness?' Fidelma's voice was sharp. 'Who is your eye-witness?'

Father Allán looked pained as if dealing with a dim-witted pupil. 'Why, Brother Aedo of course.'

'But you told me that he was only an eye-witness to this woman kneeling by the side of Moenach and holding a bloody rock in her hand. That is not an eye-witness to the actual murder.'

Father Allán opened his mouth to protest and then, seeing the angry glint in Fidelma's eyes . . . were they green or light blue? . . . he fell silent. When annoyed, her eyes seem to dance with a curious ice-coloured fire.

'I don't pretend to be learned in law,' he said stubbornly. 'I have no time for such nuances.'

'The law text of the *Berrad Airechta* states clearly that a person can only give evidence about what he or she has seen or heard and what does not take place before a witness's eyes is irrelevant. Nor can hearsay evidence be accepted.'

'But it was obvious . . .' began Father Allán.

'I am here to deal with law, not supposition,' snapped Fidelma. 'And as a *dálaigh*, I would counsel you to be more careful with the words you choose. Tell me more about this . . . this saintly youth.'

Father Allán heard the slight sarcastic emphasis in her voice. He hesitated a moment, wondering if he should chide her mocking tone but finally decided to ignore it.

'He was the son of a chieftain of the Uí Fidgente. He displayed a rare gift as a musician, playing the *cruit* like an angel would play a harp. His poetry was sweet and pure. He was given to us for his fosterage when he was seven years of age and, after reaching the age of choice last year, he decided to stay on with us as a member of our community.'

'So he had a reputation as a musician?'

'He would be invited to attend the feastings of chieftains and abbots for miles about here,' Father Allán repeated.

'But what sort of person was he?'

'A pleasing person. Kind, wise, considerate of his brethren and of all who met him. He would always go out of his way to please his superiors and attend their needs. He was especially fond of animals and . . .'

'Was he beyond all human frailties, then?'

Father Allán took her question seriously and shook his head. With a sniff, Fidelma stood up. The set smile on her face was somewhat false. Father Allán was too full of angelic visions of his acolyte to be of further use to her.

'I would now speak with the woman, Muirenn,' she said. 'After that, I wish to see Brother Aedo.'

The Father Superior slid reluctantly from his seat on the wall and indicated that she should follow him to a corner of the settlement buildings.

Muirenn sat in a corner of the small *cubiculum*, perched on the edge of the cot which she had been provided for a bed. She looked up defiantly as Fidelma entered. She was a small, reed-like woman, with angry dark eyes, a thrusting jaw and a tumble of greying black hair. She was not really old but it could not be rightfully claimed that she was of middle age.

'I am Fidelma, a *dálaigh* of the courts,' announced Fidelma as she entered. She had asked Father Allán to leave her alone with the prisoner.

The woman, Muirenn, snorted.

'You have come to punish me for something I did not do,' she growled. There was anger in her voice, not fear.

'I am come here to discover the truth,' Fidelma corrected her mildly.

'You whining religieux have already decided what is the

truth. You should return from whence you came if you mean simply to confirm Allán's prejudices.'

Fidelma sat down instead.

'Tell me your story,' she invited. 'You are from the village below this settlement?'

'God curse the day that the religieux started to build here,' muttered the woman.

'I am told that you are a widow? That you have no children but help the village apothecary. Is this the truth?'

'It is so.'

'Then tell me your story.'

'I was in the forest, gathering herbs and other plants for medications. I heard a cry nearby. I pushed forward to see what I could see. In a small clearing I saw a young religieux lying face down on the ground. On the far side of the clearing the bushes rustled, marking the passage of someone leaving the clearing. I thought I might help the young boy. I knelt down and I saw that it was too late. His skull had been smashed in beyond repair. I automatically picked the rock up that lay near his head; it was covered in blood.

'It was then that I heard a gasp behind me. I turned and saw another young religieux standing at the edge of the clearing staring at me. I scrambled to my feet and fled in terror back to my *bothán*.'

Fidelma raised an eyebrow.

'Why would you run in terror when you beheld a young Brother standing there? Surely the natural thing would have been to seek his help?'

Muirenn scowled in annoyance.

'I ran in terror because I thought he was the murderer come back.'

'Why would you think that?' demanded Fidelma. 'He was clearly a member of this community.'

'Exactly so. When I first entered the clearing and saw the bushes closing over the retreating figure, I caught a glance of his back. He was wearing the brown robe of a religieux. Moenach was killed by a member of his own community. I did not kill him.'

Outside the cell Father Allán glanced expectantly at Fidelma.

'Do you still wish to see Brother Aedo or have you concluded your investigation?'

Was there eagerness in his voice? He seemed so anxious that she simply endorse his claim that Muirenn was guilty. Fidelma pursed her lips and gazed at him for a moment before replying.

'I have just begun my investigation,' she replied softly. 'Tell me, how many Brothers reside in this community?'

'What has that to do . . .?' Father Allán bit his tongue as he saw the furrows on her brow deepen and caught the angry flash of fire in her eyes. 'There are ten Brothers altogether.'

'Did Brother Moenach have any special companions here?'

'We are all companions of each other,' sniffed the Father Superior. 'Companions in the service of Christ.'

'Was he liked equally by everyone in the community?' she tried again.

'Of course,' snapped Father Allán. 'And why wouldn't he be?'

Fidelma suppressed a sigh.

'Has his *cubiculum* been cleared?' she asked, deciding to try another tack.

'I believe so. Brother Ninnedo would know. He is tending the garden there.' He pointed to where the fair-haired young monk was trimming a bush across the grassy slopes. 'Come, I will . . .'

Fidelma held up a hand.

'I can see him. You need not trouble yourself, Father Allán. I will speak to him. I will find you when I am ready. Alert Brother Aedo to my intention to see him after I have spoken to Brother Ninnedo.'

She turned and made her way towards the young man, who was bent industriously to his work.

'Brother Ninnedo?'

The young man glanced up. He looked uncomfortable. His eyes darted towards the disappearing figure of Father Allán behind her.

'I am a *dál*—' Fidelma began to introduce herself.

The young man interrupted before Fidelma could explain.

'You are a *dálaigh*. I know. The community has been expecting you for some days since.'

'Good. And do you know why I am here?'

The young man simply nodded.

'I understand that you shared a *cubiculum* with Brother Moenach. I suppose you knew him well?'

Fidelma was surprised when she saw a positive expression of repugnance cross the young man's face.

'I knew him well enough.'

'But you did not like him?' she asked quickly.

'I did not say so,' replied Ninnedo defensively.

'You did not have to. Why didn't you like him? According to Father Allán, this Brother Moenach was little short of a saint.'

Ninnedo laughed bitterly.

'I did not like him because he was an evil person and not fit to serve the Living God. He could fool Father Allán. He could fool many people who were so complacent in office that they did not recognise a fawning sycophant who purposely flattered their vanity. But I and Brother Fogartach had to share a *cubiculum* with him and knew his evil ways.'

Fidelma stood with her head slightly to one side, slightly surprised at the young man's articulate vehemence.

'How long did you know him?'

'We were fostered together, Sister. A long time.'

'And did you hate him all that time?'

'Mostly.'

'So, tell me, in what way did he manifest evil? You accuse

9

him of being a fawning sycophant. Well, we are all, in some ways, flattering to those in power over us. That hardly constitutes evil.'

Ninnedo pressed his upper teeth against his lower lip, frowning a little, before he spoke.

'Father Allán would have Moenach as a saint. It would do me little good to speak plainly.'

'You are not speaking to Father Allán but a *dálaigh* of the courts. Speak only the truth and by truth you shall be rewarded.'

Ninnedo shifted uneasily at her sharp tone.

'Very well, Sister. Moenach was a liar, a thief and a lecher.'

Fidelma raised her eyebrows.

'If so, how could he disguise such vices from Father Allán?'

'He had the look of a cherub and could speak sweetly when the need arose. Often people cannot see beyond appearances. And he had an ability to make sweet music. He could fool people. But now and then that mask of innocence would slip. He was evil.'

'Can you cite proof, for hearsay evidence is inadmissible under the law.'

'Proof? He would steal anything he coveted. He stole from me and he stole from Brother Nath. Why, there used to be a Brother Follamon in our community until a few months ago. Moenach coveted a bejewelled cup belonging to Father Allán. He could not control his desires and he stole it. Father Allán launched a search for it. Moenach realised that he could not get away with the theft so he planted it in the cot of Brother Follamon so that it would be found and blame placed on him.'

'What happened?'

'Father Allán simply had Follamon expelled from the community.'

'Why wasn't Moenach reported to the Father? If you knew and Brother Nath knew, why didn't Father Allán accept your evidence?'

Ninnedo laughed again. There was no humour in his voice.

'You do not realise just how entrenched is the good Father's belief in Moenach. Nath told him, for Nath knew what had happened. Father Allán simply accused Nath of jealousy and threatened his expulsion as well.'

'But Moenach's position could not be maintained simply by Father Allán's prejudice alone? There must be others who agreed with Father Allán's views?'

Ninnedo sniffed bitterly.

'Oh yes. Moenach fooled some of the Brothers. That fool Aedo, for example.'

'Aedo who discovered the body with the old woman Muirenn kneeling by it?'

'The same. He was so shocked and prostrate by grief that, when he arrived back here with the news of what he had seen, he took to his bed for several days.'

'So? Aedo did not accompany Father Allán and the Brothers in search of Muirenn?'

'He did not.'

'And apart from some of these Brothers, Moenach fooled other people as well?'

'He had the same influence with many local chieftains and even abbots.'

'But you and Nath recognised him as evil?'

'We knew his ways, Sister. In fact, he seemed to delight in our knowing how he was fooling people like the Father Superior. He would challenge us to report him, knowing full well that we would not be believed.'

'Did you not support Nath against Father Allán?'

'Little use that was,' sniffed Ninnedo.

There came the sound of a distant bell.

'I must go,' Ninnedo said and moved off rapidly.

Fidelma stood for a moment watching him stride away and then she turned in search of Father Allán.

'You did not tell me that Moenach was not well liked by everyone.'

The Father Superior stared angrily.

'Who did not like him?' he demanded. 'Ninnedo, I suppose?'

'I also speak of Brother Nath.'

'Nath!' Father Allán's mouth drooped. 'So Ninnedo told you of that matter?'

Fidelma did not reply.

'Sister Fidelma, you know as well as I, that in spite of our vows and dedication to the service of the Living God, we do not suddenly become more than human, nor do we become incorrupt.'

'What are you saying?'

'That I am aware of the accusations of Nath and Ninnedo. I have known them for many years, ever since they came here to be fostered with Moenach. They all grew up together but as men sometimes take a dislike to each other, so too with boys. I knew of their jealousies and dislike of Moenach.'

'Yes? And to what reason did you attribute it?'

'Who knows? When a boy is as talented and pure as Moenach, he will have many enemies.'

'And are you so sure that their accusations were unfounded?'

'I knew Moenach since he was seven years old. He was beyond reproach.'

'Although you do admit that none of us is incorruptible?' Fidelma could not help the sarcastic thrust.

Father Allán did not rise to the bait.

'Moenach was someone special. It was a great pain for me to see Nath's jealousy.'

'I want to talk to Brother Nath.'

Father Allán gestured awkwardly.

'But he . . . he has absconded. Did Ninnedo not mention this to you?'

Fidelma gazed blankly at him for a moment.

'Nath has disappeared?'

'Yes. No one has seen him for the last week.'

Fidelma caught her breath to suppress a surge of anger.

'Are you telling me that Brother Nath disappeared a week ago? And it was a week ago that Brother Moenach was murdered. Why was I not informed of this before?'

Father Allán's face whitened.

'But Muirenn slew Moenach. Why would you be interested in a headstrong young man who has slunk away from the community?'

'Why was I not informed about this?' repeated Fidelma. 'Has any investigation been made into what has happened to Nath?'

Father Allán shrugged helplessly.

'He broke his vows and absconded. That is all.'

'Tell Brother Ninnedo to join me at once.'

Father Allán blinked, hesitated and moved off.

Ninnedo arrived with surly face. Father Allán stood behind him, watching anxiously.

'I want the full truth, Ninnedo,' Fidelma told him. 'And I want it now.'

'I have spoken the truth.'

'Yet you did not tell me that your friend Nath has been missing since the day of the killing of Moenach.'

Ninnedo blanched but contrived a stubborn expression.

'Are you accusing him of killing Moenach and running off?' he muttered. 'Everyone says Muirenn slew Moenach.'

'It is my role to find out the truth. Do you know where Nath is?'

Ninnedo stared at her. It was the young Brother who dropped his eyes first. He shook his head.

'Speak to Ainder, the daughter of Illand,' he muttered.

'Who is Ainder?' Fidelma asked.

Father Allán moved uneasily from one foot to the other.

'Ainder is a young girl of the village who washes the clothes of the community. She lives with her father, Illand, who oversees our gardens.'

Fidelma turned her gaze back to Brother Ninnedo.

'Why should I speak with this Ainder?'

'It is not my place to anticipate what she will say to you,' the young man replied spiritedly, attempting to copy Fidelma's style.

Fidelma stared at Ninnedo's stubborn features and sighed.

'Where will I find this Ainder?'

'The *bothán* of Illand is at the bottom of the hill,' interrupted the Father Superior. 'Seek her there, Sister Fidelma.'

She decided to ask Brother Aedo to accompany her in order to show her the spot where Moenach was killed and to confirm his story of the finding of the body. He was a simple ingenuous youth and had nothing else to add. He confirmed that he had been so distressed on his return to the community that he could do no more than report the matter to the Father Superior before becoming incapacitated by a surfeit of emotion. Father Allán and three other Brothers had left immediately to find Moenach and search for the woman Muirenn. Fidelma, looking round the small clearing, did not expect to find anything to assist her at the site. Nevertheless, it helped to fix the location of the crime in her mind. Without Brother Aedo's help, it would have been impossible to pinpoint the exact spot for there were many such little clearings amidst the great forest. She bade Aedo return to the hilltop community and continued on down the hill.

There was a small cabin at the bottom of the hill as Father Allán had said. A line of freshly laundered clerical robes were hanging to dry on a rope line strung between two trees. An elderly but sturdily built man was picking apples from one of the trees. He turned and watched suspiciously as Fidelma approached.

'Is this the home of Ainder, daughter of Illand?'

'I am Illand,' replied the man. 'My daughter is inside.'

'I am Fidelma of Kildare. I wish to speak with your daughter.'

The man hesitated before gesturing towards the cabin.

'You are welcome, Fidelma. But my daughter is not well . . .'

'But well enough to see the Sister,' interrupted a soft soprano voice.

A young girl, fair-haired and slim, and no more than fourteen years of age, stood framed in the doorway of the cabin.

'Please, father,' the girl said with hurried insistence before he could argue. 'I am at the age of choice.'

Fidelma glanced carefully at her, wondering why the girl had to point out her right to make her own decision.

Illand shrugged expressively.

'I have things to attend to,' he muttered in a surly tone and, picking up his basket of apples, moved off.

The girl turned to Fidelma with a pale face but determined chin.

'You must be the *dálaigh* whom Father Allán was waiting for,' she said. 'Why do you seek me out?'

'I am told you are laundress for the community,' returned Fidelma. 'Do you live here with your mother and father?'

A scowl flitted across the girl's face.

'My mother is many years in the place of truth,' she replied, using the Irish euphemism meaning that her mother was dead.

'I am sorry.'

'No need for sorrow,' said the girl.

Without another word, Ainder turned and went into the *bothán*, beckoning Fidelma to follow. She sat in the chair which Ainder indicated. The young girl sat opposite her and examined her carefully.

'I am glad that you are a woman and a young one.'

Fidelma raised her eyebrows in surprise.

'Why so?'

'I think you are here to ask me about Nath.'

'What do you know of Brother Nath?'

15

'He wishes to marry me.'

Fidelma blinked and sighed.

'I see.' Members of religious communities could and did get married under the Law of the *Fenechus*. 'So Nath is in love with you?'

'He is.'

There was a slight emphasis in her voice which contained a hidden 'but'.

'But your father disapproves?' hazarded Fidelma.

'Oh no!' The words were ejaculated hurriedly. 'He does not know.'

'You know that Nath has disappeared?'

Ainder nodded, eyes on the ground.

'You knew that Brother Moenach was murdered and that Brother Nath disappeared on the same day? Things look bad for him.'

Ainder seemed bewildered.

'But didn't the old woman, Muirenn, kill Moenach?' she demanded.

'That is what I am here to find out. What do you know of Nath's disappearance?'

The girl hesitated and then sighed deeply.

'Nath was frightened when Moenach was killed. You see, no one believes how evil Moenach really was. He had caused Brother Follamon to be expelled by his deception.'

'How did you know of this?'

'I grew up here, under the shadow of Father Allán's community. My father tends their garden and, after my mother died, I am laundress for the community. I knew most of the brothers. Follamon, Nath, Ninnedo and Moenach were all fostered together and when they reached the age of choice last year they all decided to stay on in the community of Father Allán. They all knew each other well enough. Follamon, Nath and Ninnedo became my friends.'

'But not Moenach?'

The girl shuddered.

'No!' Her voice was emphatic. Too emphatic.

'Why did you dislike Moenach?'

The girl raised her eyes to Fidelma. Two bright red spots coloured her cheeks. Then she lowered her gaze and spoke with studied care.

'I will not keep the truth from you, Sister. The day before Moenach was killed, he attacked me.'

Fidelma started.

'He attacked you?'

'He raped me.'

Fidelma noticed that she used the word *forcor* which indicated a forcible rape, a physical attack, distinguished in law from *sleth*, which covered all other forms of sexual intercourse with a woman without her consent.

'Explain to me the circumstances, Ainder. And let me warn you that this is a serious allegation.'

Ainder's face hardened.

'It is serious for me, for who now will pay my *coibche*?'

A husband gave a *coibche* or 'bride-price' which was shared between a bride and her guardian in law, usually her father. The 'bride-price' was related to the virginity of the bride and if the bride was not a virgin then humiliation and financial loss resulted.

'Very well. Tell me your story,' invited Fidelma.

'I was taking a basket of laundry up to the community. Moenach came upon me. He hated me because he knew Nath loved me. He insulted me and then knocked me to the ground and raped me. Afterwards . . . he said if I spoke of the matter no one would believe me for it was well known in the community that he was trusted of abbots and kings.'

'Was it an actually physical assault?' Fidelma pressed. 'You realise the differences between *forcor* and *sleth*?'

'Moenach was strong. I could not prevail against him. It was a physical attack.'

'And you told Nath about this?'

The girl paused a moment, examining Fidelma's face from under lowered eyelids, and then nodded quickly.

'I see. And Nath was angry, of course?'

'I have never seen him so angry.'

'When was this? How long before Moenach was killed?'

'He did not kill Moenach.'

Fidelma smiled thinly.

'I did not make such an accusation. But what makes you so emphatic?'

'He would not. It is not in Nath's nature.'

'It is in the nature of all men given the right motive. Answer my question then, how long before Moenach was killed did you tell Nath of this attack?'

'It was on the same afternoon that Moenach died. Scarcely an hour before.'

'When did you learn of Moenach's death? ' Fidelma asked.

'Why . . .' the girl frowned, 'it was when Father Allán and some others of the community came searching for the old woman Muirenn. But Father Allán said that Muirenn had been seen with the murder weapon in her hand.'

'Did you see Nath afterwards?'

Ainder appeared reluctant to speak and so Fidelma pressed the question again.

'That very evening,' the girl replied unwillingly. 'He came to me and was frightened. He had heard the news but was afraid for himself.'

'He must have known Muirenn was suspected. What made him run away?'

'Because he thought that he would be suspected. His dislike of Moenach was well known. And Nath believed that should the news of Moenach's attack on me come out, whether it was believed or not, he would be singled out as a suspect in the murder.'

Fidelma looked at the girl sadly.

'Certainly, Nath is now more of a suspect than the old

woman, Muirenn. Which makes me ask, why have you told me this story so readily, Ainder, when it makes things look so bad for Nath?'

The girl looked aggrieved at the question.

'I tell it because it is the truth and are we not taught that the truth stands against all things? Nath cannot continue to hide forever. I cannot marry with an outlaw forever hiding in the fastnesses and shadows of this land. I have urged Nath to surrender himself many times and rely on truth as his shield.'

Fidelma sat back and regarded the girl thoughtfully.

'You realise just how bad the situation is for Nath if he does not return to be heard before me?'

'I do. I believe that he should do so and that the truth will free him.'

'If that is so, will you tell me where Nath is hiding?'

The girl dropped her eyes to the ground. She did not speak for a long while. Then she sighed, as if making up her mind.

'Can I bring Nath to you?'

'It is all the same to me,' Fidelma replied indifferently. 'Just so long as he presents himself before me.'

'Then I will bring him to Muirenn's *bothán* at dusk.'

Fidelma did not really expect Brother Nath to turn up that evening. Somehow she did not really trust the credulous attitude of Ainder. She had been waiting in Muirenn's cabin for half an hour before she heard Ainder's voice call softly.

Fidelma was seated in a chair beside the grey remnants of the dead turf fire.

Ainder's shadowy figure stood for a while framed in the doorway.

Fidelma rose and lit a candle.

It was then she saw the pale young man in the robes of a religieux standing nervously behind the young woman.

'And so you are Nath?' she asked.

Ainder drew the young man into the cabin by her hand and quickly closed the door.

'I have told him not to fear you, Sister Fidelma, but only to speak the truth.'

Fidelma studied the young man. He was fresh-faced, tousle-haired and had a look of bemusement as if he were caught in a stream of events over which he had no control. Something maternal stirred in Fidelma for the youth had the vacant expression of a little boy lost and alone in a frightening forest. She shook herself to rid her mind of the emotion.

She gestured for him to sit down.

'Tell me your story, Nath,' she invited, also seating herself.

'Little to tell,' the boy said quietly. 'I love Ainder and wish to marry her. Moenach was always an enemy to me, to me and to my other brethren. He was a bully always, as a child and as a youth. He delighted in actions that harmed us but like most bullies he knew how to ingratiate himself to his betters. Father Allán would not hear a word against him. Moenach engineered the expulsion of Follamon . . .'

'I know about this. I have talked with Brother Ninnedo.'

Nath gave her an intense look.

'Then you know what Moenach was really like?'

'I know what I have been told. So when Ainder came to you and told you what had happened, you were in a great rage?'

Nath lowered his head and sighed.

'I rage still. Sister, I do not regret Moenach's death. We are taught to forgive our enemies, them that do us ill. I cannot find it in my heart to do so. I rejoice in his death. I approve his ultimate punishment. My heart is exuberant. My mind tells me, however, that this is not the law nor the path of the Living God.'

'Did you kill him?'

'No!' The word was ejaculated like a rasping breath.

'Then why did you run away? Muirenn had been taken prisoner and the rest of the community thought the guilt lay at her door. Why bring suspicion down on your head?'

Nath looked bewildered.

'There were many who did not believe in Muirenn's guilt and believed that Father Allán was using her as an easy scapegoat to protect Moenach's reputation.'

'If they knew Muirenn to be innocent, they must have known someone to be guilty. By running, you provided a suspect.'

Nath shook his head. 'Knowing that it is impossible for someone to kill does not mean that one must have knowledge of who committed the deed.'

'That is true,' conceded Fidelma. 'You, for instance, knew Muirenn not to be guilty of the deed. You claim that you, too, are innocent. Why should you be believed any more than Muirenn?'

'Father Allán said . . . I thought it for the best until I could make myself heard before a Brehon.'

'What did Father Allán say?' demanded Fidelma sharply.

Nath hesitated.

'When Ainder told me her story, I went straightaway to tell Father Allán. As before, he did not believe me. He fell into a terrible rage and it was some time before he calmed himself. He would not believe anything against his favourite. He told me to go away and never speak of it again. Later, when I heard Moenach was dead, I feared Father Allán would blame me.'

'So Father Allán knew that Ainder accused Moenach of rape?' mused Fidelma. 'And you, Nath, you blindly ran into hiding even though you must have realised that, in the meantime, your running away would compound any suspicions of your own guilt?'

'But there was no suspicion,' interposed Ainder, 'for everyone thought that Muirenn had committed the deed.'

Fidelma nodded thoughtfully.

'That is what puzzles me. On Brother Aedo's word, Father Allán had Muirenn imprisoned until my coming. You say that many did not believe her guilty but the entire community seemed apparently satisfied to have the old woman locked up and the assumption of her guilt left until my arrival. I still find it hard to understand why, knowing this, you, Nath, did not return to your community and await my arrival like the rest? Why draw attention to yourself by running away ... unless you had something to hide?'

Nath looked blank while Ainder was agitated and defiant.

'The truth, Nath!' snapped Fidelma when neither of them spoke. 'I no longer want to indulge in your games.'

The young man raised his shoulders in a shrug of helplessness.

'We thought it for the best . . .'

Fidelma glanced at Ainder. Her lips were compressed and she was staring at the ground. Abruptly, a thought dawned in Fidelma's mind.

'Ainder told you to go into hiding, didn't she?' She asked the question sharply, without warning.

Nath started nervously and raised his head to look at Ainder.

'Look at me, Nath!' Fidelma said sharply. 'Tell me the truth and you will have nothing to fear.'

The young religieux hung his head.

'Yes. Ainder advised it was for the best.'

'Why?'

'It was Ainder who came to me with the news that Moenach had been slain. When I told her that I had already told Father Allán about Moenach's attack on her, she felt that no one would ever believe her any more than they believed me when I told people that Moenach was the culprit who stole Father Allán's cup. But she feared that suspicion might fall on me for the killing because of what I had told Father Allán. He knew I hated Moenach. I agreed that I should hide until the whole affair was over or until a learned Brehon arrived who might view my case with sympathy.'

'That was stupid. If Muirenn had been found guilty, that would have weighed heavily on your conscience.'

'I would not have let that happen. I would have returned,' protested Nath.

'Returned? And what excuse would you have offered for your absence? You would have willingly returned to exchange places with Muirenn? That I find hard to believe.'

'Believe it or not, it is the truth.' The young cenobite looked defiant.

Fidelma turned reprovingly to Ainder.

'That was foolish advice which you gave to Nath.'

The young girl raised her chin pugnaciously.

'I thought it best at the time,' she answered.

Fidelma gazed thoughtfully at the girl.

'I believe you did.'

She rose and turned towards the door.

'I am returning to see Father Allán now. You should return to the community, Nath. You have told me the truth.'

Father Allán rose awkwardly as Sister Fidelma entered his *cubiculum*.

'Will you tell me why you killed Moenach, or shall I tell you?' she demanded with an abruptness that left him staring open-mouthed at her. Her voice was cold, impersonal.

Father Allán blinked and his jaw slackened at the unexpectedness of the question. Before he could protest innocence, Fidelma added with emphasis: 'I know you did it. It would save time if we dispensed with any false protestations. I first suspected when I heard that after Brother Aedo had arrived here with the news, he was so distraught that he could not lead you to the spot. Yet you unerringly led the way to where Moenach's body was, in spite of the fact that there are many similar glades and dells in the forest; even if Aedo had given you the best directions in the world, you might have hesitated before you found the body.'

A bewildering variety of expressions chased one across the face of the Father Superior. Then, as he realised that

Fidelma was coldly determined, he sat down abruptly and spread his hands helplessly.

'I loved Moenach!'

'Hate is often simply the other side of love,' observed Fidelma.

The Father Superior hung his head.

'I raised Moenach from a boy. I was his foster father before the law. He had everything a young man could want, good looks, talent and a way of bending everyone to his will, of deceiving everyone into believing his goodness and piety . . .'

'Not quite everyone,' Fidelma pointed out.

'I know. I know,' sighed Father Allán, his shoulders hunched. 'I should have listened to his fellow cenobites a long time ago. I should have listened. But I was prejudiced and stopped up my ears when they told me the truth.'

'What changed you?'

'I tried to deceive myself for a long time about Moenach. Then Nath came to me with the terrible news of what Moenach had done to Ainder. I could not allow the evil that I had nurtured to continue. If he were capable of this as a boy, what evil lay in store in the future?'

'What happened?'

'I dismissed Nath, pretending that I did not believe him. I knew that Moenach had gone down to the village and so I hurried immediately down the path and waited for him. The rest was simple. He had no suspicions. I drew his attention to something on the ground and while he was bending to examine it, I picked up a rock and hit him, again and again until . . .'

'Then Muirenn happened to come on the scene . . .?'

'I heard someone coming along the forest path. I hurried away as quickly as I could.'

'And poor Muirenn saw the form of a religieux hastening away from the scene. You left the old woman there to be blamed for Moenach's death.'

'I did not wish that. My soul has been in purgatory ever since.'

'Yet you did not speak up when Brother Aedo claimed that she was the murderess? You went along with it and added to the evil of your deed by arresting her and calling for a Brehon to try her.'

'I am a human being,' cried Father Allán. 'I am not beyond sin if self-preservation is a sin.'

Fidelma pursed her lips as she gazed at him. 'Your attempt to shift the blame to the innocent and stand by while the innocent suffered is a sin.'

'But my deed was not evil. I have cleansed the world of an evil that once I nurtured in the mistaken belief of its goodness.' Father Allán had recovered his composure. His features were scornful, almost boastful now. 'I believed that Muirenn might prove her innocence. But if Muirenn was innocent then suspicion should not fall on me. Nath had foolishly been persuaded to disappear. He might have been blamed. Everyone knew how he hated Moenach.'

Fidelma felt troubled. There was something about this puzzle that did not fit exactly together. A piece of the puzzle was still missing. She accepted that Father Allán had struck the blows that killed Moenach. However, why would Father Allán, who had not previously accepted Brother Nath's word about Moenach, nor, indeed, the word of any of those who had tried to warn the Father Superior about Moenach, suddenly accept Nath's story of Ainder's rape to the extent that he went straightaway and killed Moenach? Something did not fit.

Suddenly Fidelma's mouth split into an urchin grin of satisfaction.

An hour later she presented herself at the cabin of Illand.

Ainder greeted her at the doorway.

'I will not keep you long, Ainder,' Fidelma said. 'I want to clarify one point. You told me that Nath loved you?'

Ainder nodded with a frown of curiosity.

'But you did not return his love,' Fidelma continued calmly. 'You never returned it. You only used him.'

Ainder flashed an angry glance at Fidelma. She saw the grim signs of knowledge in the eyes of the religieuse.

'Father Allán is under arrest for the murder of Moenach. Muirenn is released and no suspicion falls on Nath whose only crime was that he was easily led.'

For a while Ainder said nothing. Then she seemed to explode in emotion.

'Nath was weak, untalented. Allán was a chieftain's son with position and a reputation. I, we . . .'

She suddenly realised the implication of what she had confessed to. Her shoulders hunched and then she said in a small-girl voice: 'What will happen to me now?'

Fidelma did not feel pity for this child-woman. Ainder did not love Father Allán any more than she had loved Nath. She had been using Father Allán simply as a means of changing her station in life. It had been Father Allán who had become infatuated with the girl. So besotted with her that when he heard that Moenach had raped the girl, and had it confirmed from her lips, he had waylaid the young man and killed him. The rage that Nath had witnessed had not been for his accusation against Moenach but for Moenach's crime against Ainder. It was a rage born of jealousy.

That much might have been understandable as a justification for killing Moenach. But Father Allán and Ainder together had conspired to lay the blame on two innocent people. Muirenn might well have proved her innocence and so they had plotted to use the guileless fascination of Nath for Ainder and manipulate him into guilty behaviour. Ainder had cynically deceived and exploited the enamoured youth.

'You will be tried for complicity in the murder of Moenach,' replied Sister Fidelma.

'But I am only a . . .'

26

'A young girl?' finished Fidelma drily. 'No. As you have previously remarked, you are at the age of choice and considered responsible in law. You will be tried.'

Fidelma gazed a moment at the hatred on the girl's face. She was thinking of the infatuated Brother Nath and the love-sick Father Allán. *Grá is gráin* – love or hate, even the words came from the same root. What was it that the great poet Dallán Forgaill once wrote? Love and hatred were hatched from the same egg.

The Horse that Died for Shame

'Horse racing,' observed the Abbot Laisran of Durrow, 'is a cure for all the ills of humankind. It is a surrogate for people's aggression and for their greed. We would find the world a harsher place without its institution.'

The abbot was a short, rotund, red-faced man with an almost exuberant sense of humour. In fact, the abbot's features were permanently fixed in a state of jollity for he was born with that rare gift of fun and a sense that the world was there to provide enjoyment to those who inhabited it.

Sister Fidelma of Kildare, walking at his side, answered his philosophical pronouncement with an urchin-like grin which seemed to belie her calling as a member of the religieuses of the community of Kildare.

'I doubt that Archbishop Ultan would agree with you, Laisran,' she responded, raising a hand to her forehead in a vain attempt to push back the wisps of red hair which escaped beneath her head-dress.

The abbot's lips quirked in amusement as he gazed at his one-time protégée, for it had been Laisran who had urged Fidelma to study law under the renowned Brehon, Morann of Tara, and, when she had reached the qualification of *Anruth*, one degree below the highest rank of learning, becoming an advocate of the courts of law, he had persuaded her to join the community of Brigid.

'But the Bishop Bressal would agree with me,' he countered. 'He has two horses which he races regularly and he is not averse to placing wagers on them.'

Sister Fidelma knew that Bressal, who was bishop to Fáelán of the Uí Dúnlainge, king of Laighin, was a keen supporter of the sport but, then, there were few to be found in the five kingdoms of Éireann who were not. Even the ancient word for a festival in Éireann, *aenach*, meant 'the contention of horses', when people came together to discuss weighty matters, to race their horses, to place wagers, to feast, to make merry and generally indulge in celebrations. Only recently had Ultan of Armagh, the archbishop and primate, begun to denounce the great fairs as contrary to the Faith for, so he claimed, the fairs were merely an excuse for the people to indulge in idolatry and pagan dissoluteness. Mostly, his denouncements were ignored, even by his own clergy, for the ancient customs were so instilled in the people's lives that it would take more than one man's prejudice to alter or dilute them.

In fact, Ultan's pronouncements were being ignored that very day by Abbot Laisran and Sister Fidelma as they strolled through the crowds gathering for the Aenach Lífé, the great annual fair held on the plain which, since the days of the High King Conaire Mór, had been called the Curragh Lífé, or 'the race course of the Lífé', after the name of the broad river flowing close by, twisting under the shadow of Dún Aillin. Indeed, was it not recorded that the saintly Brigid, who had founded Fidelma's own community at nearby Kildare, had raced her own horses on this very plain? The Curragh was now the most celebrated race course in all the five kingdoms and the Aenach Lífé attracted people from all the corners of Éireann. Each year, the King of Laighin himself would come to officially open the proceedings as well as to race his own champion horses there.

Fidelma, smiling, waved away a youth trying to sell them hot griddle cakes, and glanced at her elderly companion.

'Have you seen Bishop Bressal this morning?'

'I heard that he was here earlier,' Laisran replied, 'but I have not seen him. He is racing his favourite horse, Ochain, today. However, I have seen the bishop's jockey, Murchad, laying heavy wagers on himself to win with Ochain. At least Murchad shares the bishop's faith in himself and his horse.'

Fidelma pursed her lips reflectively.

'Ochain. I have heard of that beast. But why name a horse "moaner"?'

'I understand that Ochain utters a moaning sound as it senses that it is about to win. Horses are intelligent creatures.'

'More intelligent than most men, oftimes,' agreed Fidelma.

'Between ourselves, certainly more intelligent than the good bishop,' chuckled Laisran. 'He is openly boasting that he will win the race today against Fáelán's own horse, which does not please the king. They say the king is in a sour mood at his bishop's bragging.'

'So Fáelán is also racing today?'

'His best horse,' confirmed the abbot. 'And, in truth, there is little doubt of the outcome, for the king's champion Illan is in the saddle and with Aonbharr beneath his thighs, no team in Laighin will even come near . . . not even Murchad and Ochain. And, indeed, the fact that Illan is riding the king's horse is doubtless a matter of displeasure for Bishop Bressal.'

'Why so?' Fidelma was interested in Laisran's gossip.

'Because Illan used to train and race Bressal's horses before the king of Laighin offered him more money to train and ride Aonbharr.'

'Aonbharr, eh?' Fidelma had heard of the king's horse. So fleet was it that the king had named it after the fabulous horse of the ancient god of the oceans, Manánnan Mac Lir, a wondrous steed which could fly over land and sea without missing a pace. 'I have seen this horse race at the Curragh last year and no one could best it. This horse of Bressal's

31

better be good or the bishop's boasting will rebound on him.'

Abbot Laisran sniffed cynically.

'You have been away travelling this year, Fidelma. Perhaps you have not heard that there is something of a feud now between the king and his bishop. Four times during the last year Bressal has presented horses at races to run against the king's champion horse and his jockey. Four times now he has been beaten. Bressal is mortified. He has become a man with an obsession. He thinks that he is being made a fool of, especially by his former trainer and jockey. Now he has one aim, to best the king's horse and Illan in particular. The trouble is that his very efforts are making him a laughing stock.'

Abbot Laisran raised an arm and let his hand describe a half circle in the air towards the throng around them.

'I reckon a goodly proportion of these people have come here to see Bressal humiliated yet again when Aonbharr romps past the winning post.'

Fidelma shook her head sadly.

'Did I not say that horses had more sense than men, Laisran? Why must a simple pleasure be turned into warfare?'

Laisran suddenly halted and turned his head.

Pushing towards them, and clearly hurrying to make contact with them, was a young man in the livery of the Baoisgne, the king of Laighin's élite warrior guard. There was anxiety on his youthful features. He halted before them awkwardly.

'Forgive me, Abbot Laisran,' he began and then turned directly to Fidelma. 'Are you Sister Fidelma of Kildare?'

Fidelma inclined her head in acknowledgement.

'Then would you come at once, Sister?'

'What is the matter?'

'It is the wish of the king, Fáelán himself.' The young man glanced quickly round before lowering his voice so that he would not be overheard by the surrounding crowds.

32

'Illan, the king's champion jockey, has been found . . . dead. The king's horse, Aonbharr, is dying. The king believes that there has been foul play and has caused Bishop Bressal to be arrested.'

Fáelán of the Uí Dúnlainge, King of Laighin, sat scowling in his tent. Fidelma and Laisran had been escorted to the veritable township of tents which had been set up for the king and chieftains and their ladies alongside the course. Often entire families would camp at the Curragh during the nine days of the meeting. Behind the tents of the nobles were the tents of the trainers, riders and owners of lesser status as well as the tents which served as stables for their horses.

Fáelán of the Uí Dúnlainge was a man approaching his fortieth year. His dark features, black hair and bushy eye-brows made his features saturnine. When he scowled, his face took on the appearance of a malignant spirit which caused many a person to quail in his presence and stand uneasy.

Abbot Laisran, however, who had accompanied Fidelma, stood imperturbably smiling at the king, hands folded in his robes. He was acquainted with Fáelán and knew his grim features disguised a fair and honourable man. At Fáelán's side sat his queen, the beautiful Muadnat of the burnished hair; tall and sensual, the tales of her amours were legend. She was richly dressed with a jewelled belt and dagger sheath at her waist, such as all noble ladies carried. But, Fidelma noticed curiously, the sheath was empty of its small ceremonial dagger. The queen looked dejected, as if she had been given to a recent fit of weeping.

Behind the king and queen stood the *tánaiste*, heir-presumptive, a nephew of Fáelán's name Énna; and beside him was his wife, Dagháin. They were both in the mid-twenties. Énna was a handsome, though morose man, while his wife was almost nondescript at first glance, fashionably dressed yet without the same care as her queen for Fidelma noticed that her dress was mud-stained and dishevelled.

Even the bejewelled belt and sheath looked scuffed and its ceremonial dagger fitted badly. She seemed ill at ease and impatient.

Fidelma stood before the king, waiting with her hands quietly folded before her.

'I have need of a Brehon, Sister,' began Fáelán. 'Énna, here,' he motioned with his head towards his *tánaiste*, 'Énna told me that you were on the course with the Abbot Laisran.'

Fidelma still waited expectantly.

'Have you heard the news?' Énna interrupted his king who controlled a look of annoyance at the breach of protocol. As Fidelma turned her gaze, Fáelán continued before she could reply to the question.

'My champion jockey has been murdered and an attempt has been made to kill my best horse. The horse doctor tells me that the beast is already dying and will be dead before noon.'

'This much your guard told me,' Fidelma said. 'Also, I am informed that Bishop Bressal has been arrested.'

'On my orders,' confirmed the king. 'There is no one else who benefits from this outrage but Bressal. You see . . .'

Fidelma stayed his explanation with a small impatient gesture of her hand.

'I have heard of your disputes over the matter of horse racing. Why do you send for me? You have your own Brehon?'

Fáelán blinked at her unceremonious address.

'He is not in attendance today,' explained the king. 'And it is only permitted that a Brehon should decide whether there are grounds to hold the bishop so that he may be taken before the law courts. In the case of a bishop, who better qualified to this task than a *dálaigh* who is also a member of the religious?'

'Then let me hear the facts,' Fidelma assented. 'Who discovered the body of your jockey?'

'I did.'

It was Dagháin who spoke. She was, now that Fidelma had time to assess her closely, a rather plain-looking girl, blonde of hair, and with features which seemed without animation. The eyes were grey and cold but they did not shy away from her level gaze.

'Let me hear your story.'

Dagháin glanced towards the king as if seeking permission and, after he had nodded approvingly, she turned to Fidelma.

'It was an hour ago. I had just arrived for the races. I went into Illan's tent. I found Illan's body on the floor. He was dead. So I hurried to find my husband, who was with the king, and told them what I had seen.'

Dagháin's voice was matter of fact, without guile.

Fidelma examined her closely.

'Let us go through this more carefully,' she smiled. 'You arrived from where?'

It was Énna who answered.

'My wife and I had been staying at Dún Ailinn. I came on here early this morning to meet with Fáelán.'

Fidelma nodded.

'And what made you go directly to Illan's tent instead of coming to find your husband?'

Did Dagháin blush and hesitate a little?

'Why, I went first to see the horse, Aonbharr. He was raised in my husband's stables before he was sold to the king. I saw that he looked unwell and went to tell Illan.'

'And found him dead?'

'Yes. I was shocked. I did not know what to do and so I ran here.'

'Did you fall in your haste?' asked Fidelma.

'Yes, I did,' admitted the girl with a puzzled expression.

'And that would explain the disarray of your dress?' Fidelma's question was more rhetorical, but the woman nodded in hasty relief.

'I see. What was the cause of Illan's death, were you able to see? And how was he lying?'

Dagháin reflected.

'On his back. There was blood on his clothing but I did not see anything else. I was too intent to inform my husband.'

A sob caused Fidelma to glance up quickly to where the king's wife, Muadnat, was sitting, dabbing at her eyes with a piece of lace.

'You will forgive my wife,' interposed Fáelán quickly. 'She has a horror of violence and Illan was one of our household. Perhaps she can withdraw? She has no knowledge of these events and so cannot help your deliberations.'

Fidelma glanced at the woman and nodded. Muadnat forced a small grimace of relief and gratitude, rose and left with her female attendant.

Fidelma then turned to Énna.

'Do you agree with this record thus far?'

'It is as my wife says,' he confirmed. 'She came into our tent, where I was talking with Fáelán, in a state of distress telling us exactly what she has now told you.'

'And what did you do?'

Énna shrugged.

'I called some guards and went to the tent of Illan. He lay dead on the floor as Dagháin has described.'

'He was lying on his back?'

'That is so.'

'Very well. Continue. What then? Did you look for the cause of death?'

'Not closely. But it appeared that he had been stabbed in the lower part of the chest. I left a guard there and went with a second guard to the stable tent and saw Aonbharr. As Dagháin had said, the horse was obviously distressed. Its legs were splayed apart and its head depressed between its shoulders. There was froth around its muzzle. I know enough of horses to know that it was poisoned in some way. I called Cellach, the horse doctor, and told him to do what he could for the beast. Then I came back to report to Fáelán.'

Fidelma now turned to the king.

'And do you, Fáelán of the Uí Dúnlainge, agree that this is an accurate account thus far?'

'Thus far, it is as Dagháin and Énna have related,' confirmed the king.

'What then? At what point did you come to believe that the culprit responsible for these events was your own bishop, Bressal?'

Fáelán gave a loud bark of cynical laughter.

'At the very point I heard the news. This year my bishop has become obsessed with beating my horse, Aonbharr. He has made vain boasts, has wagered heavily and, indeed, is deeply in debt. He has put forward a horse to race Illan in the main race of today, a horse named Ochain. It is a good horse but it would not have stood a chance against Aonbharr. It became obvious that Bressal could not afford to lose against me. If Illan and Aonbharr did not run, then Ochain would win. It is as simple as that. And Bressal hated Illan, who was once his jockey.'

Fidelma smiled softly.

'It is a well-conceived suspicion but there is not enough evidence here to arrest nor charge a man, Fáelán. If it is only this suspicion which has caused your action, then my advice is to free Bressal immediately lest he cite the law against you.'

'There is more,' Énna said quietly, and motioned to the warrior of the Baoisgne who stood at the flap of the tent. The man went out and called to someone. A moment later, a large man with a bushy beard and rough clothes entered and bowed to the king and his *tánaiste*.

'Tell the Brehon your name and station,' Énna ordered.

The big man turned to Fidelma.

'I am Angaire, hostler to Bishop Bressal.'

Fidelma raised an eyebrow but controlled all other expression on her features.

'You are not a member of Bressal's community in Christ,' she observed.

37

'No, Sister. The bishop employed me because of my expertise with horses. I train his horse Ochain. But I am no religieux.'

Angaire was a confident man, smiling and sure of himself.

'Tell Sister Fidelma what you have told us,' prompted Énna.

'Well, Bressal has often boasted how Ochain would beat Aonbharr at this race and he has laid heavy wagers upon the outcome.'

'Get to the main point,' pressed Fáelán irritably.

'Well, this morning, I was preparing Ochain . . .'

'You were to ride him in this race?' interrupted Fidelma. 'I thought . . .'

The big man shook his head.

'Bressal's jockey is Murchad. I am only Ochain's trainer.'

Fidelma motioned him to continue.

'Well, I told Bressal that it was my opinion, having seen Aonbharr in a trial run yesterday, that Ochain would have difficulty in catching the beast on the straight. Bressal went berserk. I have never seen a man so angry. He would not listen to me and so I withdrew. Half-an-hour later I was passing the tent of Illan . . .'

'How did you know it was Illan's tent?' demanded Fidelma.

'Easy enough. Each jockey has a small banner outside showing the emblem of the owner of the horse he rides. The insignia of owners are important at such gatherings as this.'

Fáelán interrupted: 'This is true.'

'As I passed the tent I heard voices raised in anger. I recognised Bressal's voice at once. The other I presumed to be that of Illan.'

'What did you do?'

Angaire shrugged.

'No business of mine. I went on to Murchad's tent to advise him how best to handle the race, though I knew he had little chance against Illan.'

'Then?'

'As I was leaving Murchad's tent I saw . . .'

'How much later was this?' interjected Fidelma again.

Angaire blinked at the interruption.

'Ten minutes probably. I can't recall. Murchad and I did not speak for very long.'

'So what did you see?'

'I saw Bressal hurrying by. There was a red welt on his cheek. His face was suffused with anger. He did not see me. Furthermore, he was carrying something concealed under his cloak.'

'What sort of something?'

'It could have been a long, thin knife.'

Fidelma drew her brows together.

'What makes you say that? Describe what you saw exactly.'

'He held something long and thin in one hand, hidden under his cloak, it was no more than nine inches long but I have no idea of the width.'

'So you cannot take oath that it was a knife?' snapped Fidelma. 'I am not here to listen to surmise and guesses but only facts. What then?'

Angaire looked aggrieved for a moment and then shrugged.

'I went about my business until I heard a guard telling someone that Illan had been found dead in his tent. I felt it my duty to tell the guard what I knew.'

'That guard came to me,' Énna agreed. 'I later verified Angaire's story with him.'

'And I had Bressal arrested,' confirmed Fáelán as if it ended the matter.

'What has Bressal replied to these charges?' Fidelma asked.

'He has refused to speak until a Brehon is sent for,' the king replied. 'When Énna told me that you were on the course, I sent for you. Now you know as much as we. I think

I have the right to hold the bishop for trial. Will you see Bressal now?'

Fidelma surprised them by shaking her head.

'I will see the body of Illan. Has a physician been in attendance?'

'None, since Illan is dead.'

'Then one needs to be sent for. I want Illan's body examined. While that is being done, I shall see the horse, Aonbharr, and this horse doctor . . . what name did you say?'

'Cellach,' the king said. 'He attends all my horses.'

'Very well. Your guard may escort me to the place where the animal is stabled.' She turned to Abbot Laisran, who had remained quiet during the entire proceedings. 'Will you accompany me, Laisran? I have need of your advice.'

Outside as they walked in the direction which the warrior of the Baoisgne conducted them, Fidelma turned to Laisran.

'I wanted to speak to you. I noticed that Queen Muadnat seemed to be very upset by the death of Illan.'

'Your perception is keen, Fidelma,' agreed Laisran. 'For example, I did not even notice the disarray of Dagháin's clothes until you mentioned it. But Muadnat has obviously been weeping. The death of Illan has upset her.'

Fidelma smiled thinly.

'That much I know. You know more of the gossip of the court, however. Why would she be so upset?'

'Muadnat is a handsome woman with, by all accounts, a voracious appetite in sexual matters. Perhaps I should say no more for Fáelán is a tolerant monarch.'

'You are still speaking in riddles, Laisran,' sighed Fidelma.

'I am sorry. I thought you might have heard of Illan's reputation as a ladies' man. Illan was only one of many lovers who has graced the queen's entourage.'

When Fidelma and Laisran reached the stable tent in which Aonbharr was, the horse was lying on its side, its great breath coming in deep grunting pants. It was clearly nearing the end. A few men were gathered around it and one of these was Cellach, the horse doctor.

He was a thin man with a brown weather-beaten face and he regarded the sister with large, sad grey eyes. He was obviously upset by the suffering of the animal.

'Aonbharr is dying,' he replied to Fidelma's question.

'Can you confirm that the horse has been poisoned?'

Cellach grimaced angrily.

'It has. A mixture of wolfsbane, ground ivy leaves and mandrake root. That is my diagnosis, Sister.'

Fidelma stared at Cellach in surprise.

The man sniffed as he saw her scepticism.

'No magic in that, Sister.'

He reached toward the horse's muzzle and gently prised it open. There were flecks of blood and spittle around the discoloured gums. Amidst this mucus Fidelma could see speckles of the remains of feed.

'You can see the remnants of these poisons. Yes, someone fed the horse on a potent mixture.'

'When would such feed have been administered?' she asked.

'Not long ago,' replied Cellach. 'Within the last hour or so. Such a mixture on this beast would have an almost instantaneous effect.'

Fidelma laid a gentle hand on the big animal's muzzle and stroked it softly.

The great soft brown eyes flickered open, stared at her and then the beast let out a grunting breath.

'Are there no other signs of violence inflicted on it?' she asked.

Cellach shook his head.

'None, Sister.'

'Could Aonbharr have eaten some poisonous plants by accident?' asked Laisran.

Cellach shrugged.

'While tethered in its stable here? Hardly likely, Abbot. Even in the wilderness, horses are intelligent and sensitive creatures. They usually have a sense of things that will harm them. Apart from the fact that one would not find mandrake root nor wolfsbane around these parts. And how could it crush ivy leaves? No, this was a deliberate act.'

'Is there no hope for the animal?' asked Fidelma sadly.

Cellach grimaced and shook his head.

'It will be dead by noon,' he replied.

'I will see Illan's body now,' Fidelma said quietly, turning towards the tent of the king's jockey.

'Are you Sister Fidelma?'

As Fidelma entered the tent of Illan she found a religieuse straightening up from the body of the man who lay on his back on the floor. The woman was big boned with large hands and an irritable expression on her broad features. On Fidelma's acknowledgement she went on: 'I am Sister Eblenn, the apothecary from the community of the Blessed Darerca.'

'Have you examined the body of Illan?'

Sister Eblenn made a swift obeisance to Laisran as he entered the tent before answering Fidelma.

'Yes. A fatal stabbing. One wound in the heart.'

Fidelma exchanged a glance with the abbot.

'Is there sign of the knife?'

'The wound was not made by a knife, Sister.' The apothecary was confident.

Fidelma controlled her irritation at the pause.

'Then by what?' she demanded, when there had been a sufficient silence and the religieuse had made no attempt to amplify her statement.

Sister Eblenn pointed to the table. A broken arrow lay on it. It was the front half of the arrow, about nine inches, of the shaft and head. It was splintered where the shaft had been snapped in two.

42

Fidelma reached forward and took up the section of arrow. She could see that it was covered with blood and it was clear that Sister Eblenn had taken it from the wound.

'Are you telling us that Illan was stabbed in the heart with this arrow?' intervened Abbot Laisran. 'Stabbed, you say, not shot with the arrow?'

Sister Eblenn pursed her lips and regarded him dourly.

'Have I not said so?' she asked petulantly.

Fidelma's voice was brittle.

'No; so far you have not explained matters at all. Tell us what you have discovered and be specific.'

Eblenn blinked. She was obviously unused to people questioning her. She was given to assuming knowledge on the part of others and did not explain herself clearly. She flushed angrily at the rebuke.

'The dead man,' she began slowly, speaking in wooden but distinct tones, like a child explaining the obvious, 'was stabbed in the heart. The instrument was this arrow. Whoever killed him thrust the arrow under the rib cage, avoiding the sternum and thrusting with some force upwards so that it entered the heart. Death was instantaneous. There was little bleeding.'

'Why do you discount the arrow being shot into the body?' insisted Abbot Laisran.

'The angle of incision is of such a degree that it would be impossible unless the archer was standing five feet away and shooting upwards at a forty-five degree angle at least five feet below the target. There is also the fact that the arrow snapped in two. I believe the impact of the blow, the arrow gripped hard in the hand of the attacker, was the cause of its breaking.'

'I presume that you cut out the arrowhead?'

Eblenn pursed her thin lips and shook her head.

'The head is part of the shaft, simply a carved wooden point. I did not cut the arrow out at all but merely pulled it out. As it went in, so it came out. It was easy enough.'

Fidelma sighed deeply.

'So that when you came to examine the body, the arrow was in two pieces? One in the body, the other . . . where was that exactly?'

Sister Eblenn looked suddenly startled and peered around as if seeking the answer.

'I do not know. I presume it is somewhere about.'

Fidelma bit her lip. Extracting information from Sister Eblenn was like fishing for trout. One had to cast about blindly.

For a moment or two she stood looking down at the arrow. She became aware that Sister Eblenn was speaking.

'What?'

'I said, I must return to my apothecary's tent. I have already had one theft this morning and do not want to chance another.'

Fidelma swung round with sudden interest.

'What was taken from your tent?'

'Some herbs, that is all. But herbs cost money.'

'And these herbs – were they mandrake root, wolfsbane and crushed ivy?'

'Ah, you have spoken to the lady Dagháin.'

Fidelma's eyes rounded slightly.

'What has the lady Dagháin to do with this matter?'

'Nothing. She was passing my tent just after I discovered the theft. I asked her to inform her husband as the *tánaiste* has charge of the royal guards.'

'When exactly was this?'

'Just after the breakfast hour. Early this morning. Queen Muadnat had come by requesting a balm for a headache. It was soon after that I noticed the herbs were gone. Then, as I was going to breakfast, I saw the lady Dagháin and told her.'

After Sister Eblenn had left, still showing some bewilderment, Laisran grimaced.

'So now we know where the killer obtained the poison from.'

Fidelma nodded absently. While Laisran watched silently, she lowered herself to her knees and began to examine the body. Then she motioned Laisran to join her.

'Look at the wound, Laisran,' she said. 'It seems our Sister Eblenn is not as perceptive as she should be.'

Laisran peered closely to where Fidelma indicated.

'No pointed arrowhead made that wound,' he agreed after a moment. 'It is more of a gash, such as a broad-bladed knife would have made.'

'Exactly so,' agreed Fidelma.

For a while she searched all around the body in ever increasing circles to cover the whole floor of the tent. There was nothing on the floor except for a leather *cena*, a medium-sized bag, which she placed on a table top. She could not find what she was expecting to discover and climbed back to her feet. She took up the splintered arrow again and stared at it as if perplexed. Then she thrust it into the *marsupium* or purse which she always carried.

She gazed down to study Illan's features for a final time. Laisran was right; he had been a handsome young man. But his face was a little too handsome to attract her. She could imagine the self-satisfaction of his expression while he was in life.

Abbot Laisran coughed, as if to remind her of his presence.

'Do you have any ideas?' he asked.

She smiled at her old mentor.

'None that makes sense at this moment.'

'While you have been examining the corpse, I have examined this *cena* which you found in a corner of the tent. I think that you'd better look in it.'

Frowning, Fidelma did so. There was a mixture of herbs inside. She picked out a handful and sniffed suspiciously. Then she turned to Laisran with wide eyes.

'Are they what I suspect them to be?' she asked.

'Yes,' confirmed Laisran. 'Mandrake root, wolfsbane and ivy leaves. Moreover, there is a small insignia on the *cena* and it is not the same one as I noticed on Sister Eblenn's apothecary's bag.'

Fidelma pursed her lips as though to whistle but did not do so.

'This is a mystery that goes deep, Laisran,' she reflected slowly. 'We must discover the owner of the insignia.'

Énna suddenly entered the tent.

'Ah, there you are, Sister. Have you seen enough here?'

'I have seen all that I can see,' Fidelma replied.

She gestured down at Illan's body. 'A sad end for one who was so young and talented in his profession.'

Énna sniffed deprecatingly.

'Many a husband would not agree with you, Sister.'

'Ah? You mean the queen?' Laisran smiled.

Énna blinked rapidly and looked embarrassed. Many knew of the gossip of Muadnat's affairs but none in the court circle would openly discuss them.

'Doubtless,' he turned to Fidelma, 'you will want to see Bishop Bressal now? He is upset that you have not gone directly to see him.'

Fidelma suppressed a sigh.

'Before we do so, Énna, perhaps you can help. I believe, as *tánaiste*, that you have a knowledge of insignia, don't you?'

Énna made an affirmative gesture.

'What insignia is this?' Fidelma showed him the *cena* Laisran had discovered.

Énna didn't hesitate.

'That is the insignia of Bishop Bressal's household.'

Fidelma's lips thinned while Laisran could not hold back an audible gasp.

'I would not wish to keep the good bishop waiting longer than is necessary,' Fidelma said, with soft irony in her voice. 'We will see him now.'

'Well, Bressal, tell me your story,' invited Fidelma as she seated herself before the agitated portly figure of the king of Laighin's bishop. Bressal was a large, heavily built man, with pale, baby-like features and a balding head. One of the first things she noticed was that Bressal had a red welt on his left cheek.

Bressal frowned at the young religieuse before glancing across to acknowledge Abbot Laisran who had followed her into the tent and taken a stand with folded arms by the tent flap. The only other occupant of the tent was a tall warrior of Bressal's personal household, for the bishop's rank and position entitled him to a bodyguard.

'You have seated yourself in my presence without permission, Sister,' Bressal thundered ominously.

Fidelma regarded him calmly.

'I may be seated in the presence of any provincial king without permission,' she informed him icily. 'I am a *dálaigh*, an advocate of the courts, qualified to the level of *Anruth*. Therefore, I can sit even in the presence of the High King, though with his permission. I am . . .'

Bressal waved a hand in annoyance. He was well informed on the rules of the rank and privileges of the Brehons.

'Very well *Anruth*. Why were you not here sooner? The sooner I am heard, the sooner I can be released from this outrageous imprisonment.'

Fidelma eyed the bishop with distaste. Bressal was certainly a haughty man. She could well believe the stories that she had heard about him and this vanity of racing against the King of Laighin's horse.

'If you wish speed and urgency in this matter, it would be better to answer my questions without interpolating any of your own. Now, to this matter . . .'

'Is it not clear?' demanded the bishop with outrage in his voice. 'Fáelán is trying to blame me for something that I have not done. That much is simple. He has probably done this evil deed himself to discredit me, knowing my horse would have beaten his.'

Fidelma sat back with raised eyebrows.

'Counter accusations come better when you can demonstrate your own innocence. Tell me of your movements this morning.'

Bressal bit his lip and was about to argue, then he shrugged and flung himself onto a chair.

'I came to the race track with my personal guard, Sílán,' he gestured to the silent warrior. 'We came straightaway to see Ochain, my horse.'

'Who had brought Ochain here?'

'Why, Angaire, my trainer, and Murchad, my rider.'

'At what time was this? Tell me in relationship to the finding of Illan's body.'

'I do not know when it was discovered but I was here about an hour before that oaf Fáelán had me arrested.'

'And did you see anyone else apart from Angaire and Murchad in that time?'

Bressal sniffed in annoyance.

'There were many people at the track. Many who might well have seen me but who they were I cannot remember.'

'I mean, did you engage with anyone else in conversation; anyone in particular . . . Illan himself, for example?'

Bressal stared back at her and then shook his head. She could see that he was lying by the light of anxiety in his dark eyes.

'So you did not speak to Illan this morning?' pressed Fidelma.

'I have said as much.'

'Think carefully, Bressal. Did you not go to his tent and speak with him?'

Bressal stared at her and a look of guilty resignation spread over his features.

'A man of God should not lie, Bressal,' admonished Laisran from the entrance. 'Least of all, a bishop.'

'I did not kill Illan,' the man said stubbornly.

'How did you obtain that recent scar on your left cheek?' Fidelma demanded abruptly.

Bressal raised his hand automatically.

'I . . .' He stopped suddenly, apparently unable to think of an adequate reply. His shoulders slumped and he seemed to grow smaller in his chair, looking like a defeated man.

'Truth is the best refuge in adversity,' Fidelma advised coldly.

'It is true that I went to Illan's tent and argued with him. It is true that he struck me.' Bressal's voice was sullen.

'And did you strike him back?'

'Is it not written in the Gospel of Luke: "Unto him that smiteth thee on the one cheek offer also the other"?' parried Bressal.

'That which is written is not always obeyed. Am I to take it that you, who are obviously a man who is not poor in spirit, did not retaliate when Illan struck you?'

'I left Illan alive,' muttered Bressal.

'But you did strike him?'

'Of course I did,' snapped Bressal. 'The dog dared to strike me, a prince and bishop of Laighin!'

Fidelma sighed deeply.

'And why did he strike you?'

'I . . . roused his anger.'

'Your argument was to do with the fact that he had once been your rider and had left your service to ride for Fáelán?'

Bressal was surprised.

'You seem to know many things, Sister Fidelma.'

'So how did you leave Illan?'

'I hit him on the jaw and he fell unconscious. Our conversation had thus ended and so I left. I did not kill him.'

'How did the argument arise?'

Bressal hung his head shamefully but having embarked on the path of truth he decided to maintain it to the end.

'I went to his tent to offer him money to stand down from the race and return his allegiance to me.'

'Did anyone else know of your intention to bribe Illan?'

'Yes; Angaire did.'

'Your trainer?' Fidelma thought hard for a moment.

'I told Angaire that I was not happy with the way he was training my horse, Ochain. I told him that if I could persuade Illan to return, then he could look elsewhere for a job. In all my races this year, Angaire has failed to provide me with a winner.'

Fidelma turned to the silent warrior within the tent.

'How much of this story can you confirm, Sílán?'

For a moment the warrior stared at her in surprise. He glanced to Bressal, as if seeking his permission to speak.

'Tell them what happened this morning,' snapped Bressal.

Sílán stood stiffly before Fidelma, his eyes focused in the middle distance and his voice wooden in its recital.

'I came to the Curragh at . . .'

'Have you been personal guard to the bishop for a long time?' interrupted Fidelma. She disliked rehearsed speeches and when she sensed one she liked to interrupt and put the reciter out of stride.

'I have,' replied the surprised guard. 'For one year, Sister.'

'Go on.'

'I came to the Curragh not long after dawn to help set up the bishop's tent.'

'Did you see Illan at this time?'

'Surely. There were many people here already. The bishop, also Angaire, Murchad, Illan, even Fáelán and his queen and the *tánaiste* . . .'

Fidelma was not looking at his face. Her eyes had fastened thoughtfully on the quiver at the guard's side. One arrow seemed shorter than the others. Its feathered flight seemed to be sinking into the quiver among the other arrows.

'Turn out your quiver!' she suddenly ordered.

'What?'

Sílán was gazing at her, clearly amazed at her behaviour. Even Bressal was staring as if she had gone mad.

'Turn out the arrows in your quiver and place them on the table here before me,' instructed Fidelma.

Frowning, the warrior did so with no further hesitation.

Fidelma seized upon a shaft of an arrow. It was snapped off and only some six inches with its tail feathered flight remained. There was no need for Fidelma to look for the other half among the rest of the arrows.

They watched in silent fascination as Fidelma took from her *marsupium* the section of the arrow which had been found by Sister Eblenn in the body of Illan. She carefully brought the two pieces together before their fixed gaze. They fitted almost perfectly.

'You seem to be in a great deal of trouble, Sílán,' Fidelma said slowly. 'The head of your arrow was buried in the wound that killed Illan.'

'I did not do it!' gasped the warrior in horror.

'Is this one of your arrows?' Fidelma asked, holding out the two halves.

'What do you mean?' interrupted Bressal.

Laisran came forward with interest.

'The design on the flights are the same.'

Sílán was nodding.

'Yes, it is obviously one of my arrows. Anyone will tell you that it bears the emblem of the bishop's household.'

Fidelma turned to Laisran.

'Place the *cena* that we found in Illan's tent on the table, Laisran.'

The abbot did as she bid him.

Fidelma pointed to the insignia.

'And this emblem, being the same as on the arrow flight, is also the emblem of Bishop Bressal?'

Bressal shrugged.

'What of it? All the members of my household carry my insignia. Such bags as these are saddle bags, freely available among those who serve my stables.'

'Would it surprise you that this contains the mixture of poisonous herbs used to poison Aonbharr?'

Sílán and Bressal were silent.

51

'It could be argued that Sílán killed Illan and poisoned Aonbharr on the orders of his master, Bishop Bressal,' suggested Fidelma as if musing with an idea.

'I did not!'

'And I gave him no such order,' cried Bressal, his face turning white in horror.

'If you confessed that you were acting on the orders of Bressal,' Fidelma went on, speaking softly to Sílán, 'little blame would attach to you.'

Sílán shook his head stubbornly.

'I had no such orders and did not do this thing.'

Fidelma turned to Bressal.

'The evidence was circumstantial in the first place, Bishop. Yet, circumstantial as it is, it is against you. The evidence of this arrow and the *cena*, containing the poisons, now seems hard to refute.'

Bressal was clearly perturbed. He turned to Sílán.

'Did you slay Illan of your own volition?' he demanded.

The warrior shook his head violently and turned pleading eyes upon Fidelma. She could see the innocence in his face. The guard was clearly shocked at the evidence against him and his bishop.

'I am at a loss to explain this,' he said inadequately.

'Tell me, Sílán, have you carried your quiver of arrows all morning?'

Sílán paused to give thought to the question.

'Not all morning. I left my quiver and bow in the bishop's tent most of the morning while I had errands to run.'

'What kind of errands?'

'To find Murchad, for example. I found him talking with Angáire near Illan's tent at the time we saw the lady Dagháin come out, white-faced, and go running to her tent. I remember that Angáire passed some unseemly and lewd remark. I left Angáire and returned here with Murchad.'

'So the quiver of arrows was in this tent while you went to find the bishop's jockey at the bishop's request?' Fidelma summed up. 'The bishop was alone in the tent, then?'

Once more a look of indignation caused Bressal's face to flush.

'If you are saying that I took an arrow and went to kill Illan . . .' he began.

'Yet you were alone in this tent at that time?'

'Some of the time,' admitted Bressal. 'Sílán left his weapons most of the morning and we were constantly in and out of the tent. Also, there were visitors coming and going. Why, even Fáelán and his wife, Muadnat, were here for a moment.'

Fidelma was surprised. 'Why would he come here? You had become bitter rivals.'

'Fáelán merely wanted to boast about Aonbharr.'

'Was that before or after you had your argument with Illan?'

'Before.'

'And Muadnat was with him?'

'Yes. Then Énna came by.'

'What for?'

'To beg me to withdraw Ochain from the race, saying my argument with Fáelán was an embarrassment to the kingdom. This was pointless. Angaire and Murchad were here as well . . .'

'Was Énna's wife, the lady Dagháin, one of your visitors?' queried Fidelma.

The bishop shook his head.

'However, if you are looking for an opportunity to take an arrow and kill Illan, why, several people had that opportunity.'

'And what about the *cena* full of poison herbs?'

'All I can say is that it bears my insignia but I have no knowledge of it.'

Fidelma smiled thinly and turned to Laisran. 'Walk with me a moment.'

Bressal stared at her in outrage as she made to leave his tent.

'What do you propose to do?' he demanded.

Fidelma glanced across her shoulder towards him.

'I propose to finish my investigation, Bressal,' she said shortly, before stepping through the flap, followed by the bewildered Laisran.

Outside, Fáelán had posted several of his élite guards to keep the bishop a prisoner.

'You do not like the good bishop,' Laisran reflected once they were outside.

Fidelma gave her urchin-like grin.

'The bishop is not a likeable man.'

'And the evidence weighs heavily against him,' went on Laisran, as he fell into step with the religieuse. 'Surely that evidence is now conclusive?'

Fidelma shook her head.

'If Bressal or Sílán had used the arrow to kill Illan then neither would have kept hold of the incriminating half of the arrow so that it could be found so easily.'

'But, it makes sense. Either one of them could have stabbed Illan with the arrow. Then, realising that the design on the flight would betray them, they broke off the arrow and took the incriminating part away with them . . .'

Fidelma smiled gently. 'Leaving the *cena* with the poison and its insignia conspicuously in Illan's tent? No, my good mentor, if they were that clever then they would have simply destroyed the arrow. There are enough braziers in which to have burnt it. Why place it invitingly back in the quiver where it would easily be discovered? And they would have rid themselves of the *cena*. Also, my friend, in the excitement you have forgotten the very fact that neither Bressal nor Sílán appears to be aware of, and which demonstrates their innocence.'

Laisran looked bewildered.

'What fact?'

'The fact that the arrow was placed in the wound after Illan was dead in order to mislead us. The fact that Illan was

54

killed by a dagger thrust and not by stabbing with the arrow.'

Laisran clapped a hand to his head. He had forgotten that very point in the agitation of Fidelma's cross-examination of Bressal and Sílán.

'Are you suggesting that there is some plot to make Bressal appear guilty?'

'I am,' confirmed Fidelma.

Laisran looked at her thunderstruck.

'Then who . . .?' His eyes widened. 'Surely you are not suggesting that the king . . .? Are you saying that Fáelán might have feared that his horse would not win against Bressal's horse and so he contrived this intricate plot . . .?'

Fidelma pursed her lips.

'Your hypothesis is good but there is more work to be done before it can be used in argument.'

Énna was suddenly blocking their path.

'Have you seen Bressal, Sister?' he greeted, and when she nodded he smiled grimly. 'Has he now confessed his guilt?'

Fidelma regarded him for a moment.

'So you believe him to be guilty?'

Énna stood back in surprise.

'*Believe?* Surely there is no doubt?'

'Under our laws, one must be proven guilty of the offence unless one confesses that guilt. Bressal does not accept any guilt. My investigation must show proof against him.'

'Then that is not difficult.'

'You think not?' Énna looked uncomfortable at her mocking tone. 'I would have everyone concerned now gather in Fáelán's tent: Bressal, Sílán, Angaire, Murchad, Fáelán and Muadnat, yourself and Dagháin. There I will reveal the result of my investigation.'

As Énna hurried away, Fidelma turned to Laisran.

'Wait for me at Fáelán's tent, I will not be long.' At Laisran's look of interrogation, she added: 'I have to look for something to complete my speculation.'

At Fidelma's request they had all crowded into the tent of Fáelán of the Uí Dúnlainge, King of Laighin.

'This has been a most perplexing mystery,' she began when the king signalled her to speak. 'What seemed simple at first began to become mysterious and obscure. That was until now.'

Fidelma smiled broadly at them.

'And now?' It was Fáelán who prompted her.

'Now all the pieces of the puzzle fit together. Firstly, the evidence against Bressal is overwhelming.'

There was a gasp of outrage from Bressal.

'It is not true. I am not guilty,' he protested indignantly.

Fidelma raised her hand for silence.

'I did not say that you were. Only that the evidence against you was overwhelming. However, if you had been guilty, or, indeed, if Sílán had carried out the deed for you, then you would have known that Illan had not been stabbed with an arrow but with a dagger. Only the real killer knew this and the person who placed the arrow in the wound. The arrow was a false scent planted in an attempt to lay a path to Bressal. It was obvious, therefore, that someone wanted me to find that evidence and draw the inevitable but wrong conclusion.'

Bressal gave a deep sigh and relaxed for the first time. Sílán, behind him, looked less defensive.

'I first approached this matter from the viewpoint of the motive, which seemed obvious,' went on Fidelma. 'What immediately sprang to all minds was the idea that both Illan and the horse, Aonbharr, had been killed to prevent them taking part in the race today. Who would benefit by this? Well, Bressal, of course, for his horse, Ochain, and Murchad, his jockey, were the only serious contenders in the race other than Illan and Aonbharr. So if Bressal was not guilty, who could it have been? Who would benefit? Was it Murchad, who had laid a large wager on his winning? Laisran had already witnessed Murchad earlier this morning placing heavy wagers on himself to win.'

'No law against that!

Murchad had flushed angrily but Fidelma ignored him and went on: 'Obviously it was not Murchad for he did not have a motive. He would only have collected his winnings if he had won the race which essentially meant taking part in it. If he had murdered Illan, poisoned Aonbharr and left the trail of false clues to Bressal, then it would be obvious that Bressal would be arrested and his horse and Murchad would be disqualified from racing. That being so, Murchad would have forfeited his wager.'

Murchad nodded slowly in agreement and relief. Fidelma went blithely on.

'If not Murchad, what of Angaire, the trainer? He was not doing well for Bressal and had been told this very morning that Bressal was going to get rid of him. Bressal had made no secret of the fact that he had gone to see Illan in an attempt to persuade him to return to his stable and ride for him instead of Fáelán. Angaire had a better motive than Murchad.'

Angaire shifted uneasily where he stood. But Fidelma continued.

'You see, sticking to the line of argument about the horse race as the motive, there was only one other person with a motive who might benefit from putting the blame on Bressal.'

She turned towards Fáelán, the king. He stared at her in astonishment which swiftly grew into anger.

'Wait,' she cut his protests short. 'Such a plot was too convoluted. Besides everyone was of the opinion that Aonbharr could out-distance Ochain. There was no challenge there to be worried about. So there was no motive.'

She paused and looked around at their perplexed faces.

'It eventually became clear that the killing of Illan was not caused by rivalries on the race track. There was another motive for that crime. But was it the same motive as that for poisoning Aonbharr?'

They were all silent now, waiting for her to continue.

'The motive for Illan's death was as ageless as time. Unrequited love. Illan was young, handsome and his reputation among women was such that he had many lovers. He picked them up as one might pick up flowers, kept them until the affair withered and then threw them away. Am I not right?'

Fáelán was pale and he glanced surreptitiously at Muadnat.

'That is no crime, Fidelma. In our society, many still take second wives, husbands or lovers.'

'True enough. But one of the flowers which Illan had picked was not ready to be discarded. She went to his tent this morning and argued with him. And when he spurned her, when he said he would have no more to do with her, she, in a fit of rage, stabbed him to death. All it needed was one swift dagger blow under the rib cage.'

'If this is so,' said Énna, quietly, 'why would she go to such lengths to put the blame on Bressal? Why poison Aonbharr? The laws of our society allow leniency to those who perpetrate such crimes of passion.'

Fidelma inclined her head.

'A case could be made that any non-fatal injury inflicted by the woman in such circumstances does not incur liability. Our laws recognise the stirring of uncontrollable passion in such circumstances. In the matter of death she would be fined her victim's honour price only. No other punishment would be necessary.'

'Then why, if this were so, did the woman conceal her crime, for the concealment brings forth greater punishment?' repeated Énna.

'Because there were two separate villainies at work here and one fed off the initial deed of the other,' replied Fidelma.

'I don't understand. Who killed Illan?' Fáelán again glanced uneasily at his wife. 'You say it was a woman. By attempting to conceal the crime such a woman, no matter her rank, if found guilty would be placed into a boat with one paddle and a vessel of gruel and the mercy of God. Sister Fidelma,' his voice suddenly broke with passion, 'is it Muadnat of whom you speak?'

Fáelán's wife sat as if turned to stone.

Fidelma did not reply immediately but drew out of her *marsupium* a belt with a bejewelled ceremonial sheath. There was a small dagger in it. She took out the dagger and handed it to Muadnat.

'Does the dagger belong to you, my lady?'

'It is mine,' Muadnat replied grimly.

Fáelán gasped in horror, as if his worst fears were confirmed.

'Then . . .?' he began. Fidelma was shaking her head.

'No, Dagháin killed Illan.'

There was a gasp of astonishment from the company and all eyes turned on the flushed face of Énna's wife. Dagháin sat stunned for a moment by the revelation. Then, as if in a dream, she slowly rose to her feet and looked about her, as if searching someone out. 'Liar! Betrayer!' she hissed venomously. Fidelma glanced quickly in the direction of the woman's gaze and felt satisfied.

Dagháin now turned towards her and cursed her in a way which left no one in doubt as to her guilt. Énna had simply collapsed into a chair, immobile with shock.

After Dagháin had been removed to a place of confinement, Fidelma had to raise her hands to quell the questions that were thrown at her.

'Dagháin was seen coming to the Curragh early this morning. The apothecary, Sister Eblenn, saw her soon after she had been robbed which was just after breakfast. Dagháin therefore lied when she said that she had come later in the morning to the course. That lie alerted my suspicions. A suspicion which was increased when I realised that the arrow was not the murder weapon but the wound had been made by a dagger. When I first came before Fáelán, Muadnat had been wearing a ceremonial dagger sheath yet there was no dagger in it.'

'This I don't understand,' Fáelán said. 'Surely this would lay suspicion on Muadnat?'

'Indeed, I was suspicious for a while, that I admit. But it was obvious to my eye that the dagger in Dagháin's sheath was too small to fit comfortably. That I had to work out. Then I realised that she, at some stage, had put Muadnat's dagger in her sheath, is that not so?'

Muadnat spoke softly.

'She wanted an apple to calm her nerves and asked me for the loan of my dagger, saying she had mislaid her own. It was only a moment ago that I realised Dagháin had not returned it.'

'Dagháin,' Fidelma went on, 'in her description of the finding of Illan, said that she had run straight to tell Énna. Yet she was seen running from his tent directly to her own. I searched her tent a moment ago. Thankfully, she had discarded her ceremonial belt and sheath. I was confirmed in my suspicion that the dagger did not belong to her but was that of Muadnat.'

'Then where was Dagháin's own dagger?' demanded Laisran, intrigued.

'I found it where I suspected it would be, the blade still covered with Illan's blood. It was in Angaire's saddle bag.'

Angaire, with a cry of rage, made to jump to the tent door, but one of the Baoisgne, the king's guards, stayed him with a drawn sword to his chest. Fidelma continued without taking any notice of the drama.

'While Angaire did not kill Illan, he did poison Aonbharr, and then tried to place the guilt for both deeds on Bressal by planting the arrow and *cena* as evidence. Angaire's actions obscured the real murderer of Illan. You see Angaire knew that he was about to be discarded by Bressal. I have already given you his motive. Bressal had been quite open in his intention to replace Angaire. Indeed, even though Illan had refused Bressal's offer to return to his stable, Angaire's days as trainer were still numbered.

'Angaire had, I believe, already devised a plan to hurt Bressal. I believe his original intention was to poison Ochain. For that end, he stole some poisonous plants from the tent of Sister Eblenn early this morning. Then the mysteries of Fate itself took over. Angaire overheard Bressal arguing with Illan. But the plot did not occur to him then.

'It was only when he was with Murchad and Sílán a little while later that he saw Dagháin fleeing from Illan's tent. Her dress was dishevelled and the ceremonial dagger missing. She fled to her own tent. He made a lewd remark, an automatic remark. His companions, Sílán and Murchad, were leaving. Perhaps even before then the thought struck him that his unthinking remark might be true and what if . . . his mind was thinking about the missing dagger.

'He went to Illan's tent. There was Dagháin's knife buried in Illan's chest. His suspicion was right. He took out the knife with the idea growing in his mind. Here was his chance to get even with Bressal and to secure a future lucrative role for himself in the service of Dagháin. He hurried to her tent, showed her the knife, which he kept as a hold over her. He told her to wait a while before she should find her husband and tell him the story which she has subsequently told us. The reason for her to be in Illan's tent was that she had noticed that Aonbharr was ill. This was Angaire's addition, providing a perfect excuse and an essential part of his intrigue.

'Then he hurried to Bressal's tent, furtively took an arrow from Sílán's quiver, broke it in two, and left one half in the quiver. The other he took, together with his *cena* full of poisonous herbs, and hurried to his task. He fed Aonbharr the poison. Then he went into Illan's tent and thrust the forward section of the broken arrow into the wound. He left the *cena* in plain sight. The false trail was laid.

'Thus two separate villainies were at work, coming together over the one great crime. And who is the greater villain – Dagháin, a pitiful, rejected woman, or Angaire, petty and vengeful, whose spite might have led to an even greater crime? I tell you this, Fáelán, when the time comes for Dagháin to be tried before the courts, I would like to be retained as her advocate.'

'But what made you connect Dagháin with Illan?' demanded Fáelán.

'Énna himself indicated that his wife had had an affair with Illan by a chance remark. You knew of the affair, didn't you, Énna?'

Énna glanced up from his chair, red-eyed with emotional exhaustion. He nodded slowly.

'I knew. I did not know that she was so besotted with Illan that she would resort to such means to keep him when he finally rejected her,' he whispered. 'Fáelán, I will stand down as your *tánaiste*. I am not worthy now.'

The King of Laighin grimaced.

'We will talk of this, Énna,' he said, with considerable discomfiture, studiously ignoring his wife, Muadnat. 'I am not without sympathy for your situation. There are doubtless several victims in this terrible drama. Yet I still do not understand why Dagháin would do this thing. She was the wife of a *tánaiste*, heir presumptive to the throne of the Laighin, while Illan was merely a jockey. How could she behave thus simply because Illan rejected her for a new lover?'

The question was aimed at Fidelma.

'There is nothing simple about the complexity of human emotions, Fáelán,' replied Fidelma. 'But if we are to seek the real victim then it is the poor beast Aonbharr. Truly, Aonbharr was a horse that died in an attempt to conceal the shame of others.'

A trumpet sounded outside.

Fáelán bit his lip and sighed.

'That is the signal for me to open the afternoon's race . . . my heart is not in it.'

He rose and automatically held out his arm to Muadnat, his wife. She hesitated before taking it, not looking at her husband. There would be much to mend in that relationship, thought Fidelma. Then Fáelán turned and called to his bishop:

'Bressal, will you come with us? Stand alongside me while I open the proceedings so that the people will clearly see that we are together and are not enemies? As neither of our horses can now enter this race, let us show unity to our people for this day at least.'

Bressal hesitated before nodding his reluctant agreement.

'I'll send your fee to Kildare, Fidelma,' Fáelán called over his shoulder. 'I thank God we have Brehons as wise as you.'

After they had left the tent, Énna slowly rose. He stared at Fidelma and Laisran with sad eyes for a moment.

'I knew she was having an affair. I would have stood by her, even resigned my office for her as I will now. I would not have divorced nor rejected her had she come to me with the truth. I will continue to stand by her.'

Fidelma and Laisran silently watched him leave the tent.

'Sad,' remarked Fidelma. 'It is, indeed, a sad world.'

They left the tent and began walking through the shouting, carefree masses, milling towards the race course. Fidelma smiled thinly at Laisran.

'As you were saying, Laisran, horse racing is a cure for all the ills of humankind. It is a surrogate for people's aggression and for their greed.'

Laisran grimaced wryly but was wisely silent before the cynical gaze of his protégée.

At the Tent of Holofernes

S ister Fidelma halted her mare where the track curved
round the shoulder of the hill and gazed down at the
broad valley below. The placid light-blue strip of a river
wound its way through the valley, among the green culti-
vated clan lands of the Uí Dróna. She saw the grey granite
walls of the *ráth*, which was her goal, and her dust-stained
features formed into a tired smile of anticipation. She had
been four days on the road from the monastery of Durrow.
She was tired and uncomfortable with the dust of travel. Yet
it was not simply the prospect of the comforts of a bath,
fresh clothes, and a rest from being on horseback that caused
her to smile. It was the thought of seeing Liadin again.

Fidelma had been an only daughter with elder brothers,
and Liadin, her childhood friend, had been as a sister to her.
The bonding had been strong. They had reached the 'age of
choice' together when they had, under law, become women.
At that time Fidelma had become *anamchara*, the 'soul
friend', to Liadin: her spiritual guide according to the
practice of the faith in Ireland.

Now, in her pocket, there reposed an urgent message from
Liadin which had been delivered to Fidelma at Durrow a
week ago. It read: 'Come at once! I am greatly troubled.
Liadin.' Now as she reached her journey's end, Fidelma felt
both anticipation at the reunion and apprehension.

Fidelma had not seen her friend for several years. Their paths had eventually separated, for Fidelma had gone to Tara to continue her studies while Liadin had taken the path of marriage.

Fidelma remembered Liadin's trepidation at marriage, for it had been Liadin's father, a petty chieftain of Cashel, who had agreed to an arranged marriage as a matter of political expedience. Liadin's wish had been to become a teacher. She had a good knowledge of Greek and Latin and other studies. The marriage was to a foreign chieftain. He was a Gaul named Scoriath of the Fir Morc who had been driven into exile from his own lands. Scoriath had been granted sanctuary in the clan lands of the Uí Dróna in Laigin. It was the chieftain of the Uí Dróna who had interceded with Liadin's father and persuaded him of the political and financial advantage in marrying his daughter to the Gaulish warrior. He had made Scoriath captain of his bodyguard.

At the time, Fidelma's heart had been heavy for her unfortunate soul-friend, forced into such a marriage. Their paths continued on separate courses as Fidelma pursued her studies, eventually being admitted as a *dálaigh*, an advocate, of the law courts of Ireland.

After Liadin's marriage, Fidelma had met her friend only once and she was replete with happiness for she had, in spite of expectations, fallen in love with her husband. Fidelma had been astonished at her friend's transformation. Liadin and Scoriath's joining, so far as Fidelma could assess from her friend's enthusiasm, was that of a vine to a tree. Fidelma rejoiced in her friend's happiness and in the subsequent birth of her son. Then their paths separated again.

The child must be three years old now, Fidelma reflected, guiding her mount towards the fortress of the Uí Dróna. What could ail Liadin to make her send such a message?

Fidelma had observed that the man had been watching her approach for an hour, ever since she had rounded the shoulder of the hill and ridden carefully down into the valley towards the dark, brooding walls of the fortress. He lounged by the gate of the *ráth* with folded arms and made no attempt to change his position as she approached and halted her mount.

'What do you seek here?' he demanded gruffly.

Fidelma gazed down at him with irritation.

'Is this the *ráth* of the Uí Dróna?' she demanded.

The man motioned assertively with his head.

'Then I demand entrance.'

'On what business?'

'On my own business.' Her voice was soft but dangerous.

'I am Conn, *tanist* of the Uí Dróna. My business is to know your business here,' was the implacable response. A *tanist* was the heir-elect of a chieftain.

Fidelma was unperturbed. 'I am come to see Liadin. I am Fidelma of Kildare.'

Fidelma was aware of a momentary change of expression on the man's face. She had a curious feeling that it was a look of relief but it was gone before she was sure. The *tanist* shifted his weight upright.

'I regret, Sister, that Liadin is being heard before the Brehon Rathend even as we speak.'

Sister Fidelma's features re-formed into an expression of surprise.

'Being *heard*? Do you mean that she pleads a case in law before the Brehon?'

The *tanist* hesitated. 'In a way. She pleads her innocence.'

'Innocence? Of what is she accused?'

'Liadin is accused of the murder of her husband, Scoriath of the Fir Morc, and of her own son.'

The Brehon Rathend was tall and thin, with pale, bloodless-looking skin. The learned judge had hooded dark eyes with shadowy pouches under them which seemed to suggest that he was a man unused to sleep. The lines of his face certainly denoted that he was a man who had little sense of humour. His entire expression was one of controlled irritation. The whole measured up to an expression of ill-health and ill-humour.

'By what authority do you interrupt this trial, Sister?' he demanded querulously as he came into the chamber where Fidelma had been conducted. Fidelma told him of her qualification as a *dálaigh*.

'Is Liadin of the Uí Dróna represented by an advocate?' she demanded.

'No,' he replied. 'She refuses to plead.'

'Then I am here to plead her case for her. I would request a postponement of the hearing for twenty-four hours that I may consult with Liadin . . .'

Rathend grimaced diffidently.

'This will be difficult. Besides, how do you know she will accept your advocacy?'

Fidelma glared hard at the Brehon. Rathend tried to return her gaze but eventually dropped his eyes uncomfortably.

'Even if she accepts your advocacy, everyone has already gathered to hear the opening arguments,' he explained lamely.

'The purpose of the hearing is for justice to be done not for the convenience of an audience. The opening of the hearing can be delayed under law.'

A slight colour tinged the sallow cheeks of the thin Brehon. He was about to reply when the door of the room burst open abruptly and a young woman entered. Fidelma quickly appraised her and had to admit that she was attractive in spite of a prominent aquiline nose, sallow skin, and dark hair which made her rather foreign in appearance. Her dark eyes flashed vivaciously. That she was a woman of rank was obvious.

'What does this delay mean, Rathend?' The dark eyes fell on Fidelma and registered suspicion. 'Who is this?'

'Sister Fidelma is an advocate come to plead Liadin's case,' Rathend said obsequiously.

A flush of annoyance tinged the woman's cheeks.

'Then you are late in coming here, Sister.'

Fidelma let her gaze move almost languidly over the shorter woman's haughty features.

'And you are . . .?' she asked softly, reminding Rathend of his breach of etiquette and causing the woman's flush of annoyance to intensify.

'This is Irnan, chieftainess of the Uí Dróna,' Rathend supplied quickly. 'You stand in her *ráth*.'

Fidelma let a smile deepen the corners of her mouth and she inclined her head in acknowledgement of the woman's rank rather than in deference.

'Whether I am late or early, Irnan of the Uí Dróna, the point is that I am here and justice must be served.' A *dálaigh* of Fidelma's rank of *Anruth* could speak on equal terms with a provincial king and could even sit in the presence of the High King himself, though only at the latter's invitation. Fidelma turned back to Rathend. 'I shall need to consult with Liadin to arrange her defence. I need twenty-four hours' delay before the opening arguments.'

'Defence?' Was there a bitter humour in Irnan's interruption. 'What defence can there be for this woman?'

Fidelma barely glanced at her.

'I shall be able to inform the court of my defence once I have had access to Liadin.'

'The case is clear,' Irnan snapped. 'Liadin killed her husband and her son.'

'For what reason?' demanded Fidelma.

'It was an arranged marriage. Perhaps Liadin hated Scoriath?' the chieftainess sniffed. 'Who knows?'

'A weak reason when she could have sought the redress of law. And why kill the child? What mother would kill her own child? Why, indeed, kill after three and a half years of marriage if, as you say, it was in pique at an arranged marriage?'

Irnan's eyes flashed with uncontrolled anger. Her tone told Fidelma that here was a woman used to being firmly in control of a situation and obeyed without question. Opposition was something that Irnan was clearly unused to.

'I am not on trial here, Sister. I cannot answer your questions.'

'Someone will have to answer them,' replied Fidelma calmly. She turned to the Brehon again. 'To that end, will you grant the postponement?'

Rathend seemed to glance at Irnan before responding. Fidelma saw, from the corner of her eye, the chieftainess shrug. Rathend sighed and inclined his head in affirmative.

'Very well, Sister. You have twenty-four hours before the court sits to hear the charges. Be warned that the charge is that of *fingal*, kin-slaying, and is so grave in this instance that we are not talking of compensation in terms of an *eric* fine. If Liadin is judged guilty, so heinous is this crime that she will be cast adrift on the high seas in an open boat without oars, sail, food, or water. And if she survives, if she is cast ashore by the will of God, on whosoever's shore she lands, that person has the right of life and death over her. That is the judgement prescribed by law.'

Sister Fidelma knew well the penalty for extreme cases of murder.

'Only if she's found guilty,' she added softly.

Irnan let out a sharp bray of laughter.

'There is little doubt of that.'

She turned and swept from the room, leaving Rathend gazing in unhappy confusion after her.

The two women broke apart from their embrace. Fidelma's eyes were troubled as she gazed at the face of her friend. Liadin was shorter than Fidelma, with a shock of chestnut hair, pale skin, and dark brown eyes that seemed almost black from a distance. Her face was strained, the flesh under the eyes was dark with worry, the skin almost bloodless and etched with lines.

'Fidelma! Praise the saints that you have come at last. I

had given you up. I did not kill Scoriath nor my son Cunobel.'

'No need to convince me,' Fidelma replied quickly. 'I have succeeded in getting a postponement of your trial for twenty-four hours. You must now tell me everything so that I will know best how to defend you.'

Liadin let out a small sob.

'My mind has not worked since I heard the terrible news of Scoriath's death. I have been numbed with shock and could not believe that I was being accused. Somehow I thought I would awake from all this . . . that . . .'

Fidelma squeezed her friend's hand as her voice trailed off.

'I will do your thinking for you. Simply tell me the facts as you know them.'

Liadin wiped her tears and forced a smile.

'I feel such hope now. But I know so little.'

'When we last met, you told me you were very happy with Scoriath. Had anything changed since then?'

Liadin shook her head vehemently. 'We were blessed with contentment and a fine child.'

'Was Scoriath still commander of the bodyguard of the chieftainess of the Uí Dróna?'

'Yes. Even when Irnan succeeded her father, Drón, as chieftainess of the clan a month ago, Scoriath continued as her commander. But he was considering giving up war and simply working his own land.'

Fidelma pursed her lips. She could not help but recall the hostility which Irnan had displayed towards Liadin.

'Was there any conflict of personality? What of the *tanist*? Was there enmity with the heir-elect?'

'Conn? No, there was no animosity between Scoriath and Conn.'

'Very well. So let us turn to the facts of the death of Scoriath and your son.' Time enough to commiserate with her friend later.

'It happened a week ago. I was not here at the time.'

'Explain. If you were not here, on what grounds are you accused of carrying out the deed? Start at the beginning.'

Liadin made a little gesture of helplessness.

'On the day it happened I had left Scoriath and the child here and had ridden to visit a sick relative, my aunt Flidais. The illness was minor and when I reached her dwelling I found her past any danger and almost entirely well. It had been nothing but a slight chill. So I returned here, reaching the fortress in the late evening about an hour after sunset. As I made my way to our chambers Conn came out of our apartments and seized me.'

'Seized you? Why?'

'It is all so hazy now. He was shouting that Scoriath was slain along with my son. I could not believe it. He seemed to be accusing me.'

'For what reason?'

'He had found a bloodstained knife and clothing, my clothes hidden in my private chamber. Scoriath and my son had been found in our chambers – stabbed to death.'

'You immediately denied responsibility?'

Liadin nodded fiercely. 'How could anyone think a mother could slaughter her own child?'

Fidelma pursed her lips and shrugged.

'Alas, it has been known, Liadin. We have to look at things as logically as we can. Did they have any other grounds to accuse you?'

Liadin hesitated a moment.

'There came another witness against me. A house servant, Branar, came forward and said she had witnessed Scoriath and me in argument that very day.'

'Witnessed? And had she?'

'Of course not. I had not seen Branar that day.'

'So she lied? How could she claim to have seen this argument then?'

'She said that she had *heard* it,' corrected Liadin after a moment's thought. 'She said that she was passing our bedchamber door and she heard our voices raised in angry exchanges. She then thought it prudent to depart. I denied it but no one would believe me.'

'Who brought you the news of your aunt's illness?'

'A monk from the monastery of the Blessed Moling, which is not far from here. A Brother named Suathar.'

'And who saw you leave the *ráth* to visit your aunt?'

'Many people. It was midday when I left.'

'So it was well known that you had left the *ráth*.'

'I suppose so.'

'And who saw you arrive back that night?'

'Conn, of course, when he seized me.'

Fidelma frowned slightly.

'He saw you arrive through the gate, you mean? And then seized you later?'

Liadin shook her head in bewilderment.

'No. I meant that he saw me at the time he seized me at the door of my chambers.'

'So no one saw you actually arrive back? So far as people were concerned, you could have come back much earlier that evening. You travelled on horse. How about the stable boys?'

Liadin looked worried.

'Ah. I see what you mean. No one was about in the stable at the time. I unsaddled my own horse. I am afraid that no one saw me arrive back.'

'But your aunt will witness the time that you left her?'

'My aunt has come here already to testify but Rathend says this matters little. No one disputes that I went to see my aunt, nor that I returned that evening. They say, however, that I could have arrived back earlier, that I went straight to Scoriath, slew him, and then my child and was going to sneak back out into the night to feign a later arrival, hoping that the bodies would have been found before my return.'

Fidelma chewed her lower lip in thought.

'It seems indeed, that Branar is then central to the argument of your guilt, for she presents us with a motive; the motive being that your relationship with Scoriath was not what you claimed it to be. If the quarrel was not between Scoriath and yourself then either Branar is mistaken or lying. Was Scoriath seen by anyone after this alleged quarrel?'

'Of course,' Liadin said at once. 'Cunobel was with Branar all afternoon while Scoriath was attending Irnan at the assembly of the clan and while I was away from the *ráth*. The assembly rose at sunset. But what of the knife, and bloodied clothes in my chamber?'

'Anyone can plant such evidence. And there is an obvious contradiction there. You would hardly leave such evidence in your chamber and be sneaking back out into the night to gain an alibi, would you?'

Liadin paused to reflect on the logic and then she nodded with a faint smile.

'I hadn't thought of that.'

Fidelma gave her an encouraging grin.

'You see? Already we find a lack of logic in the arguments against you. The case against you seems so circumstantial. Has anyone put forward an argument as to why you should want to slay your own husband and your child? Have they ascribed a motive, a reason why you argued with Scoriath and why you would have killed him and your son?'

'Rathend believes I did it in some uncontrolled fit of jealousy.'

Fidelma looked hard at her friend.

'And did you have reason for jealousy?' she asked softly.

Liadin raised her chin defiantly, a hot colour on her cheeks.

'With Scoriath? Never!'

'So did he have enemies? As commander of the bodyguard, and as a foreigner in this land, he was surely bound to have created animosities. But was there anyone in particular that you know of?'

Liadin was frowning reflectively.

'None that I can name. But Scoriath became morose a few weeks ago and would not tell me what ailed him. All that Scoriath said was something I found very strange. We were talking about his giving up command of Irnan's bodyguard. As I said, he had decided to give up the profession of warfare and farm his own land. But he was brooding and depressed. As we were talking, he suddenly said, 'I will become a farmer unless the Jewess has plans to destroy our peace.'

Fidelma's eyes widened.

'The *Jewess*? Who did he mean?'

Liadin shrugged.

'I have no idea. I know of no Jewess in the kingdom.'

'You asked him to explain, of course?'

'I did, but he laughed it away and said it was nothing but a bad joke.'

'Can you repeat exactly what he said, and the manner in which he said it?'

Liadin did so. It did not make matters clearer.

Sister Fidelma rose to her feet, her brows drawn together. Then, she focused on her friend's worried features and smiled to reassure her.

'There is a mystery here, Liadin. Something curious that itches my mind, like a bug bite. I cannot yet scratch. I must investigate further. Do not worry. All will be well.'

Conn, the *tanist* of the Uí Dróna, stood awkwardly in front of Sister Fidelma, occasionally shifting his weight from one leg to another, trying to maintain an expressionless countenance. He was a fair-haired and handsome man.

Seated to one side was the Brehon Rathend, who, as the law ordained, had to attend any questioning of witnesses, excepting the questioning of the accused person, before the trial. His job was to observe and not to question nor even participate unless the *dálaigh* did not abide by the rules set forth for pretrial interrogations.

'Tell me about the events which led to your arresting Liadin.'

The young warrior cleared his throat and spoke woodenly, as if having learnt a lesson by rote.

'I found the weapon that killed Scoriath in the bedchamber of . . .'

'From the beginning,' Fidelma interrupted with annoyance. 'When did you last see Scoriath? See him alive, that is?'

Conn considered for a moment.

'On the evening of the day on which he was killed. It was the day of the clan assembly, the feast day of the blessed Mochta, the disciple of Patrick. That afternoon Scoriath, myself, and some other warriors were in attendance to our chieftainess, Irnan, at the assembly hall. An hour before sunset, the assembly dispersed so that each could return home before the hour of darkness.'

'Was that the last time you saw Scoriath alive?'

'It was, Sister. Everyone returned to their homes. Later Irnan's messenger came to me and said that he was looking for Scoriath, for Scoriath had been summoned by the chieftainess. The messenger said that he had gone to his chambers but could find no one.' The fair-haired young man paused and frowned, massaging his forehead with his fingers as if the act would conjure memory. 'I knew this to be strange for Scoriath had a child, and if he were not in his house then his wife and child or servant would be there.'

He paused as if seeking approval from Fidelma. She simply motioned him to continue.

'I went to the house with the messenger. No one answered in response to our knocking. I opened the door and went in. I cannot describe it. I felt something was wrong. A small oil lamp, whose light I could see through a crack in the door, burned in the bedchamber. I went to the door and pushed it open.' He genuflected hastily. 'There I found Scoriath face downward on the floor. Blood still gushed from a terrible wound in his neck.'

'*Still* gushed?' Fidelma interrupted quickly.

Conn nodded.

'Obviously he had not long been dead. I turned the body slightly and saw that his throat had been cut. Then, by the door of a small side chamber, was the body of Scoriath's child, Cunobel. He, too, was dead from several wounds in the chest. Blood stained the entire room.'

The *tanist* paused to swallow nervously.

'I saw that the side chamber door, a chamber where the child slept, and which Scoriath's wife used for her personal toilet, stood ajar. I noticed a trail of blood leading into the chamber. I followed this trail of droplets and it led me to a chest. Inside the chest was a knife, still sticky with blood, and a bloodstained outer garment which belonged to Liadin.'

He was silent for so long that Fidelma felt she had to prompt him. 'And then?'

'I sent the messenger back to Irnan to tell her what had been discovered. There was no doubt in my mind that Liadin was answerable for this foul deed.'

'Why?'

The fair-haired man blinked.

'Why?' he repeated as if surprised at the question being asked. 'Because, Sister, I found the knife and the garment. They were hidden in a chest in Liadin's room. The garment belonged to Liadin. I had often seen her wearing it.'

' "Hidden" is hardly an exact description, Conn,' Fidelma observed. 'A trail of blood led you to the chest.'

He shrugged. 'The bloodstains probably went unnoticed in Liadin's panic to hide the objects of her guilt.'

'Perhaps. But that is supposition. If you had done this deed, would you have gone into your personal chamber to hide the weapon and bloodstained garment? Even without the bloody trail, someone would surely be bound to examine that room later?'

Conn looked confused.

'Perhaps you are right, Sister. But surely no one else

could have done the deed, and that for a very good reason.'

Fidelma raised an eyebrow quizzically.

'What is that reason?'

'Scoriath was a warrior. A man of strength as well as full of a warrior's guile. Yet he turned his back on his murderer, allowed them to reach around his neck and slit his throat. The incision was made in the left side of the neck and the blade drawn along the throat to the right side. No one could have been placed in such a position to perform the deed unless Scoriath trusted them very well. Only a woman with whom Scoriath was intimate could be so trusted.'

For a few minutes Fidelma sat considering.

'Could the wound not have been made by a left-handed person, facing Scoriath?' mused Fidelma.

Conn blinked again. It was obviously a habit which signalled reflection on a question.

'But Liadin is right-handed.'

'Just so,' Fidelma remarked softly.

'And,' Conn continued, ignoring her point, 'if the murderer stood in front of Scoriath, he surely would have defended himself from the attack with ease.'

Fidelma mentally conceded the point.

'Continue, Conn. You say that you sent the messenger back to Irnan. What then?'

'I was surveying the scene when I heard a noise outside the building. I moved to the door, wrenched it open, and found Liadin attempting to sneak back into the building, presumably in an attempt to retrieve the knife and garment from her chamber.'

'That is surmise on your part,' Fidelma admonished.

Conn shrugged indifferently.

'Very well, I found Liadin outside the door and I arrested her. Irnan came soon afterwards with Rathend, the Brehon. Liadin was taken away. That is all I know.'

'Did you know Scoriath well?'

'Not well, save that he was captain of the guard.'

'Were you jealous of him?'

Conn appeared bewildered by the abrupt question.

'Jealous?'

'Scoriath was a foreigner,' Fidelma explained. 'A Gaul. Yet he had achieved high office among the Uí Dróna. Did it not annoy you to see a foreigner so well treated?'

'He was a good man, an excellent champion. It is not my place to question the decisions reached by the councils of the king nor those of my chief. He was a good warrior. As for high office . . . I am the heir-elect to the chieftainship, so why should I be jealous of him?'

'And what was your relationship with Liadin?'

Did a faint colour suffuse his cheeks?

'I have no relationship,' he said gruffly. 'She was Scoriath's wife.'

'A good wife, to your knowledge?'

'I suppose so.'

'A good mother?'

'I have no knowledge of such things. I am unmarried.'

'If she had murdered Scoriath as you suggest, do you not question the fact that she also murdered her own child . . . a three-year-old boy?'

Conn was stubborn.

'I can only state what I know.'

'Did Scoriath ever say anything about a Jewess to you?'

Conn was again apparently bewildered by this abrupt change of tack.

'Never. I have never heard of a woman of that religion in these parts, though it is said that many Jewish traders frequent the port of Síl Maíluidir on our southern coast. Irnan spent some of her youth there and may have an answer for you about such things.'

The servant, Branar, was a raw-boned, fresh-faced girl with wide guileless-looking blue eyes, and a permanent expression of confusion. She was no more than a year or two beyond the age of choice. Sister Fidelma smiled encouragingly at her and bade her be seated. Rathend sat in place, looking a trifle irritated. Branar had been escorted to the chamber by her mother but Fidelma had refused to allow the old woman to remain with her daughter during the interrogation, showing her to a side chamber. Rathend thought that Fidelma might have showed some compassion for the young girl and allowed the mother to remain. Branar was nervous and awed by the proceedings.

'How long have you been a servant to Liadin and Scoriath?' Fidelma opened.

'Why, not even a year, Sister.' The girl bobbed her head nervously as she sat. Her confused, somewhat frightened gaze travelled from Fidelma to the stony-faced Brehon and then back to Fidelma.

'A year? Did you enjoy working for them?'

'Oh yes. They were kind to me.'

'And you liked your work?' inquired Fidelma.

'Oh yes.'

'And you had no problems with either Liadin or Scoriath? Were there no arguments between them and you?'

'No, I was quite happy.'

'Was Liadin a caring wife and mother?'

'Oh yes.'

Fidelma decided to attempt another tack.

'Do you know anything about a Jewess? Did Scoriath know such a woman?'

For the first time Rathend raised an eyebrow in surprise and glanced at Fidelma. But he kept silent.

'A Jewess? No.'

'What happened on the day Scoriath was killed?'

The girl looked troubled for a moment and then her face lightened.

'You mean about the argument I heard? I went that morning to clean the house of Liadin and Scoriath as I usually did. They were in the bedchamber with the door closed, but their voices were raised in a most terrifying argument.'

'What were they saying?'

'I could not make out what was being said. The door was closed.'

'Yet you could clearly identify their voices and knew that they were engaged in a violent quarrel, is that it?'

'It is. I could hear only the tones of their voices raised in anger.'

Fidelma gazed at the ingenuous face of the house servant.

'You only heard Liadin's voice through a closed door but can identify it clearly?'

The girl's nod was emphatic.

'Very well. Do you think that you know my voice by now?'

The girl hesitated suspiciously but then nodded.

'And you would know your own mother's voice?'

The girl laughed nervously at the apparent stupidity of the question.

Sister Fidelma rose abruptly.

'I am going into the other room. I will close the door and will speak at the top of my voice. I want you to see if you can hear what I say.'

Rathend sighed. He clearly felt that Fidelma was pursuing too theatrical an approach.

Fidelma went into the next room and closed the door behind her. Branar's mother rose uncertainly as she entered.

'Is your questioning over, Sister?' she asked in a puzzled tone.

Fidelma smiled softly and shook her head.

'I want you to say anything that comes into your head, but say it as loud as you can. It is an experiment.'

The woman stared at Sister Fidelma as if she were mad but, at a nod from Fidelma, began talking a mixture of sense and gibberish as loud as she could until Fidelma signalled her to silence. Fidelma then opened the door and called to Branar. The girl rose uncertainly.

'Well,' smiled Fidelma, 'what did you hear?'

'Oh, I heard you speaking loudly, Sister, but I could not understand all you said.'

Fidelma smiled broadly now.

'But you did hear *my* voice?'

'Oh yes.'

'Clearly my voice?'

'Oh yes.'

Fidelma turned and pushed the door open. Branar's mother shuffled nervously forward, as perplexed as her daughter.

'The voice you heard was your own mother's voice, Branar. Are you still sure you wish to swear that it was Liadin who was arguing with Scoriath behind the closed door?'

The chambers where Liadin and Scoriath had dwelt were a set of rooms in the fortress not far from the stable buildings beyond the central gate. Three chambers constituted the dwelling; a living room, a bedchamber leading off it, and, with access from the bedchamber, a smaller chamber in which Liadin's young son had his bed and in which Liadin apparently stored her clothes.

The rooms now seemed cold and bleak, although they were filled with items which once spelt homeliness and comfort. Perhaps it was the lack of a fire in the hearth and the gloom of the day that enhanced the chill.

Rathend led the way, crossing the floor of the room in which meals were cooked and eaten; where an iron cauldron hung on a spit over the dead grey ashes.

'Scoriath was slain in this room,' Rathend explained, showing the way into the large bedchamber.

The granite blocks of the walls were covered with tapestries. There were no windows, and the room was dark. Rathend bent and lit a tallow candle. There was a large, ornately carved bed. The bedclothes, a jumbled mess of linen and blankets, were stained with what was obviously dried blood.

'Scoriath was lying there. The child, Cunobel, was found just by the door of the smaller chamber,' Rathend explained.

Fidelma noted the dark stains crossing the floor to the small arched door which led off the chamber. She saw, by the doorway, that there was a slightly larger pool of dried blood. But the stains also led beyond the chamber door.

She walked into the smaller chamber with Rathend, who held aloft the tallow candle, following her. The trail of dried blood led to a large wooden trunk as Conn had said it had. She noticed some footprints in the dried blood. They were large and must have been made by Conn during his investigation, obscuring the original footprints of the killer.

'That was the trunk in which Liadin's bloodstained garment was found together with the knife,' the Brehon said. 'Next to the trunk was a small cot in which the boy, Cunobel, must have slept. There are no bloodstains there so we can conclude that the child was slain where he was found.'

Fidelma did not reply but returned to the main bedchamber and examined it again.

'What are you looking for, Sister?' ventured Rathend.

'I do not know . . . yet.' Fidelma stopped suddenly, noticing a book satchel hanging from a peg. She reached into it and drew out a moderate-sized volume. She gazed with interest at the patterned binding, frowning slightly as she noted a few dark stains which spoilt the careful artistry of the leatherwork.

Reverently she placed it on a nearby table and motioned for Rathend to hold the candle higher.

'Why,' she said softly, opening the first page, 'it is a copy of the *Hexapla* of Origenes. What would Scoriath or Liadin be doing with this?'

The Brehon sighed impatiently.

'There is no law against the ownership of books.'

'But it is unusual,' insisted Fidelma as she turned the

pages. It was a collection of Hebrew religious texts which Origenes, head of the Christian school of Alexandria, had copied three centuries before. He had rendered the text in parallel columns, in Hebrew, Greek and then in Latin.

Fidelma frowned suddenly. Someone had marked a passage in a textual section entitled '*Apokrupto*'. Fidelma dredged her knowledge of Greek. It meant 'hidden texts'. She read the passage with a frown. The story told of how the Assyrian king, Nebuchadnezzar, sent his army against the Israelites. The army was commanded by an invincible general named Holofernes. As the Assyrian army lay encamped around the Israelite city of Bethulia a young Jewish maiden named Judith went to the Assyrian camp and was brought before Holofernes. She seduced him and then, afterwards, as he lay in a drunken slumber, she cut off his head and returned to her own people, who took heart by this sign, rushed upon the invading army, and routed them.

Fidelma smiled to herself. It was a story worthy of the ancient Irish bards, for it was once believed that the soul reposed in the head and the greatest sign of respect was to sever the head of one's enemy. Fidelma's eyes suddenly widened. Judith. Her eye travelled from the Hebrew text to the Greek and then to the Latin. She caught her breath as she realised the meaning of the name Judith – it meant Jewess.

Why had the passage been marked? What had Scoriath meant when he told Liadin that he would give up his warrior's role and become a farmer unless the 'Jewess' prevented him? Scoriath was a foreigner and, in a way, commander of an army as Holofernes had been. Also, Scoriath's head had nearly been severed. Was there some bizarre meaning to this?

Slowly she replaced the book under the puzzled gaze of the Brehon.

'Have you seen all you wish?'

'I wish,' Fidelma replied, raising her head, 'to see the genealogist of the Uí Dróna.'

★ ★ ★

'You now say that you wish to question the chieftainess of the Uí Dróna? What has she to do with this matter?'

It was an hour later and Rathend and Fidelma were seated in the great hall of the fortress.

'That is for me to discover,' replied Fidelma. 'I have the right to call Irnan for examination. Do you deny it?'

'Very well.' Rathend was clearly reluctant. 'But I hope you know what you are doing, Fidelma of Kildare.'

Irnan came in after a short, uneasy period of waiting. Rathend leapt to his feet as the chieftainess entered.

'Why am I summoned, Rathend?' Irnan's voice was irritable and she chose to ignore Fidelma. But it was Fidelma who replied to her.

'How long was Scoriath your lover, Irnan?'

A pin falling to the ground would have been heard for several seconds after Fidelma had spoken.

The face of the swarthy woman blanched, the lips thinned. An expression of shock etched her features.

Rathend was staring at Fidelma as if he could not believe what he had heard.

Suddenly, as if her bones and muscles would no longer support her, Irnan seemed to fold up on a nearby chair, her gaze, combining consternation and fear, not leaving Fidelma's imperturbable features. As she did not reply, Fidelma continued.

'Before your birth, I am told that your father, Drón, travelled to the port of Síl Maíluidir. His aim was to encourage some merchants of the clan to open trade there. While at the port he met a Phoenician merchant who had a beautiful daughter. Drón married her and they had a child. The child was yourself. Your mother was named Judith – the Jewess. She survived your birth by only a few months. When she died your father then brought you back here, where you were raised.'

'That story is no secret,' replied Irnan sharply. 'Molua, the genealogist, doubtless told it to you.'

'When did Scoriath tell you that he no longer loved you and wanted to resign his command and be a simple farmer?'

Irnan had apparently recovered her composure and chuckled drily.

'You do not know everything, *dálaigh* of the court. Scoriath did love me and told me as much on the day his wife slew him for jealousy.'

Fidelma found herself having to control her surprise at the sudden candour of Irnan's response.

'Scoriath loved me, but he was a man of honour.' Irnan's words were like acid. 'He did not want to harm Liadin nor his young son and so he told me that he would not divorce his wife. He would stay with them.'

'That provided you with a motive for killing him,' Fidelma pointed out.

'I loved Scoriath, I would never have harmed him.'

'So you would have us believe that you accepted the situation?'

'Scoriath and I were lovers from the first day that he arrived among us. My father, who was then chieftain, found out. While he admired Scoriath as a warrior, my father wanted me to marry an Irish prince of wealth. I think he was more determined that I should do so because of the fact that I was my mother's daughter and he wanted to compensate for my foreign blood. He then forced Scoriath into an arranged marriage with Liadin. Scoriath did not love her.'

Irnan paused and stared reflectively at the fire for a moment before drawing her dark eyes back to the graven features of Fidelma.

'When my father died, I became the Uí Dróna. I was then free to do as I willed. I urged Scoriath to divorce Liadin, making fair settlement on her and the child. He, however, was a man of honour and refused. He did not want to hurt Liadin. So we remained lovers.

'Then came the news of how Scoriath and his son were

slain. It was so obvious who did it and why. Liadin must have found out and killed him in jealous passion.'

Sister Fidelma gazed thoughtfully at Irnan.

'Perhaps it is too obvious a conclusion? We must take your word alone as to Scoriath's attitudes. You could just as easily have slain Scoriath because he rejected your love.'

Irnan's jaw came up pugnaciously.

'I do not lie. This is all I have to say.' Irnan stood up. 'Have you done with your questions?'

'All for the time being.'

The chieftainess turned and, without another glance at the unhappy Rathend or at Fidelma, strode from the room.

Fidelma sighed. There was something itching at the back of her memory.

Rathend was about to break the silence when the door of the hall opened and a nervous youth in the brown homespun robes of a religieux entered.

'Is the Brehon Rathend here?' he began nervously and then, catching sight of Fidelma, he bobbed his head nervously, '*Bene vobis*, Sister.'

'I am Rathend,' the Brehon said. 'What do you wish?'

'I am Suathar of the monastery of the Blessed Moling. I came to seek the return of the book we loaned to Scoriath. I was told that before I can reclaim the book, I must have your permission.'

Fidelma looked up swiftly.

'Scoriath borrowed the copy of Origenes's *Hexapla* from your monastery's library?'

'Yes; a week ago, Sister,' agreed the young man.

'Did Scoriath request the loan of this book in person?'

Suathar shook his head, puzzled by the question.

'No. He sent a message and asked that the book be delivered the next time someone came to the *ráth* of the Uí Dróna. I had to come here six days ago because the aunt of the lady Liadin was ill and requested me to bring her to nurse her. I gave the book to Liadin.'

Rathend had handed the book satchel to the monk.

'You'd best check to see whether all is in order,' Fidelma invited as the young man began his thanks.

The monk hesitated, pulled out the leather-bound book, turning it over in his hands. Then he opened it.

'Has someone made a mark on the story of Holofernes?' prompted Fidelma.

'The mark was not there when I left it,' agreed the young monk. 'Also,' he hesitated. 'The dark, brownish stains on the leather binding were not there before. They look like the imprint of the palm of a hand.'

Fidelma exhaled sharply, rebuking herself for her blindness. She took the book and, after a moment's examination, placed her hand palm down over the dark stain to assess the measurement of the imprint.

'I have been a fool!' she said softly, as if to herself. Then she drew herself up again. 'Suathar, is the work of Origenes one that is popular?'

'Not popular. As you must know, Sister, it is only of passing interest to we of the Faith because the Hebrew texts, which the great Origenes put together, are of a questionable nature, being the stories which we now call "The Apocrypha", from the Greek word.'

Fidelma raised a hand impatiently to silence him.

'Just so. Nowhere else is the story of Judith and Holofernes to be found?'

'None that I know of, Sister.'

'Has the lady Liadin ever visited your library at the monastery?'

Suathar pursed his lips in thought.

'Yes. Several weeks ago.'

Fidelma turned with a grave face to the Brehon.

'I have finished my inquiries, Rathend. I need only to see Liadin once more. The case may be heard tomorrow.'

'Then you will be entering a "not guilty" plea for the lady Liadin?' asked Rathend.

Fidelma shook her head at the startled Brehon.

'No. I shall be making a plea of "guilty". Liadin has been clever, but not clever enough.'

Before Sister Fidelma entered Liadin's small cell, she turned to Conn, the commander of the guard, whom she had asked to accompany her, and told him to remain outside the door in case he was needed.

As Liadin rose with bright expectation on her face, Fidelma positioned herself just inside the door with folded arms.

'I will defend you, Liadin,' she began coldly without preamble, 'but only to seek some mitigation for your guilt. It has been hard for me to believe that you would attempt to use me in this evil plot.'

When the horror of realisation at what Fidelma had said began to spread across her features, Liadin opened her mouth to protest.

'I know it all,' Fidelma interrupted. 'You appealed to my intellectual vanity with a number of false clues which you thought would lead me to suspect Irnan. Above all, you relied on my human weakness, that of my long friendship with you, to convince me that you could never have done this deed.'

Liadin's face was suddenly drained of emotion and she sat back on the cot abruptly.

'You learnt that Scoriath had never loved you,' went on Fidelma relentlessly. 'You learnt that he was having an affair with Irnan. The crime was well planned. If you could not have him, neither would Irnan. You hatched a cunning double plot. You decided to kill him and send for me, leaving me a false trail so that I would defend you by following that trail to Irnan.'

'How could I do that?' The girl was defiant.

'You had discovered the story of Irnan's parentage and it put you in mind of the story of Holofernes. You were always a good Greek scholar and decided to use that as the intellectual bait which you knew would appeal to my imagination.

You checked the story in the *Hexapla* by Origenes on a visit to the library of the monastery of Moling. When the time was right, you sent to ask Suathar, in Scoriath's name, to bring the book which would provide me with the next clue after you had dropped into your conversation with me that Scoriath was afraid of someone called the "Jewess".'

Fidelma paused and gazed sadly at her friend.

'You took the book and hung it in the chamber. One unexpected thing occurred. You were overheard by Branar having a row with Scoriath. But that turned out to be no problem because, having convinced myself so firmly of your innocence, I cleverly used a trick to dismiss Branar's infor-mation to my own satisfaction. Cleverness when used with prejudice is a formidable thing.

'You went off to your aunt. Later you returned unnoticed to the *ráth* and entered your chambers. There was Scoriath. He had no cause to suspect you, and you struck him from behind. Perhaps it was then that you remembered . . . in the row that morning you had neglected to plant the main piece of evidence needed for me to follow the trail. You had neglected to mark the passage about Judith and Holofernes. You did so then, for there was blood which stained the leather binding and went unnoticed.

'Then,' Fidelma went on remorselessly, 'then you went to hide in the stables and wait until Conn discovered the bodies. You appeared, pretending to have just returned from your aunt. You knew that you would be accused, but you had already sent for me and laid your false trail. The thing that was irritating my mind was the fact that you must have sent for me before the murder to allow me to reach here on time.'

'It is not true,' Liadin's voice was broken now. 'Even if I did kill Scoriath for jealousy, there is a flaw in your arguments and one I think you know in your heart.'

Fidelma raised her head and returned her friend's gaze. Did she detect a triumph in that gaze?

'And what is that?' she asked softly.

'You know that I would not be capable of killing my own son. While you have that doubt you will do all you can to argue my case and clear me of this crime.'

'You are right,' Fidelma admitted. 'I know that you could not have killed your son.'

Fidelma heard a movement outside the cell but did not take her eyes from Liadin's triumphant gaze.

'Come in, Conn,' she called quietly and without turning her head. 'Tell me why you had to kill Liadin's little son.'

The fair-haired young *tanist* entered the cell with his sword drawn.

'For the same reasons that I must now kill you,' he replied coldly. 'The plot was more or less as you have described it. There was a slight difference. I was the leading spirit. Liadin and I were lovers.'

Liadin had begun crying softly, realising the truth was finally out.

'I wanted my freedom from Scoriath to go with Conn. I knew Scoriath would not divorce me, for he was a man of principles. So there was no alternative. I had to make you believe that he was having an affair with Irnan . . .'

Fidelma raised an eyebrow in cynicism.

'Are you telling me that you did not know that Scoriath and Irnan were really lovers?'

Liadin's look of startled surprise told Fidelma that she did not.

'Then you did not know that Scoriath would have divorced you had you simply asked him? Or that he remained with you only because of what he considered was his duty to you and his son?'

Liadin stood frozen in horror. Then she stammered 'But Conn . . . Conn said . . . Oh God! If only I had known . . . then all this could have been avoided. Conn and I could have been together without guilt.'

'That would not be so, would it, Conn, *tanist* of the Uí Dróna?'

The young man's expression was sullenly defiant.

'You see,' Fidelma went on, speaking to Liadin, 'Conn was using you, Liadin. He persuaded you to work out the plan to implicate Irnan because if I followed your false trail and could demonstrate that Irnan was implicated, or at least was a suspect in Scoriath's death, then she would have had to relinquish the chieftaincy of the Uí Dróna. A chieftain must be without blemish or suspicion. Who would benefit from that but the *tanist* – the elected heir?'

Liadin had turned to Conn in disbelief.

'Deny it!' she cried. 'Say it is not so!'

Conn shrugged arrogantly.

'Why gamble just for love when one can take power as well? We laid out the plot as you have deduced it, Fidelma of Kildare. Except for one thing. I also slew Scoriath. And when the child stumbled into the room and saw me, I had to kill him as I must now kill you . . .'

Conn raised his sword.

Fidelma flinched, closing her eyes. She heard Liadin scream! The blow was not delivered. She opened her eyes to find that Liadin was clinging to Conn's sword arm while Rathend and two warriors crowded the cell to disarm and drag the struggling young man away.

Liadin collapsed into a sobbing heap on the cot.

Rathend was standing gazing at Fidelma with a look of admiration in his eyes.

'So you were right, Fidelma of Kildare. How could you have been so sure?'

'I was not sure. Only my instinct was sure. I was certain that Liadin could not have killed her son but that weighed against my certainty that it was Liadin who set the elaborate series of false clues for me to follow, knowing how they would appeal to my vanity for solving mysteries. I was faced with two conflicting certainties. That meant Liadin had an accomplice, and in that accomplice one could look for motive. I began to suspect Conn when he willingly provided me with the next link about Irnan and the Jewess connection.

'Poor Liadin, even when she knew that Conn had slain her child, she continued to go through with this plot for love of him. A strong thing, this blindness of love.'

She glanced compassionately at her friend.

'Only when I realised the width of the palm print on the book satchel was that of a male hand did things make sense. Conn, in setting the murder scene, had to make sure that Liadin had left the clue in its proper place and, in doing so, he left his own clue there. The plan needed my participation to follow the false clues. I was late in arriving here and found that Conn was looking for my coming. At the time I wondered why he was relieved when I arrived.'

Rathend sighed softly.

'So Conn persuaded his lover to participate in the crime, making her believe it was all for love while all the time he merely sought power?'

'Liadin is guilty, but not so guilty as Conn, for he played on her emotions as a fiddler plays upon his instrument. Ah, Liadin, Liadin!' Fidelma shook her head. 'No matter how well one thinks one knows someone, there is always some dark recess of the mind that even the closest of friends may never reach.'

'She saved your life, though. That will stand in mitigation when she is judged.'

'If only Scoriath had been honest with her,' Fidelma sighed. 'If Scoriath had confessed his affair with Irnan and told Liadin that he wanted a divorce, she would not have been led into this fearful plot.'

'It seems that Scoriath brought his own fate upon himself,' ventured Rathend.

'He was probably a coward to emotion,' agreed Fidelma as they turned from the cell, leaving the sobbing Liadin alone. 'Men often are. *Deus vult!*'

'God wills all things,' echoed Rathend hollowly.

A Scream from the Sepulchre

It was the evening of All Saints' Day and Tressach, a warrior of the guard of the royal palace of Tara, home of Sechnasach, High King of Ireland, was unhappy. That evening he had drawn the most unpopular duty, which was to act as sentinel in that area of the palace complex where generations of High Kings were buried. Rows of carved granite memorials marked the mounds where many of the great monarchs were interred, often with their chariots, armour, and such grave goods as were needed to help them on their journey to the Otherworld.

Tressach felt uncomfortable that this duty fell to his lot on this night of all nights. The evening of All Saints or All Hallows as some now named it, was an ancient observance which many still called the Samhain Festival even though the five kingdoms had long accepted the new Faith of Christendom. Samhain, according to ancient tradition, was the one night of the year when the mystic realms of the Otherworld became visible to the living and when the souls of the dead could enter the living world to wreak vengeance on anyone who had wronged them in life. So strong was this belief among the people that even when the new faith entered the land it could not be suppressed. The Christians therefore incorporated the ancient festival by creating two separate celebrations. All Saints' Day was set aside as a day when the saints, known and unknown, were glorified, and the following day, All Souls, was given to the commemoration of the souls of the faithful dead.

Tressach shivered slightly in the cold evening air as he approached the walled-off compound of graves, far away from the main palace buildings which made up the High King's capital. Autumn was departing with rapidity and the first signs of winter, the white fingers of a creeping evening frost, were permeating across the sacred hills of Royal Meath.

Tressach paused as he contemplated the path that he had to take between the darkened mounds with their granite stone portals. They called this 'the avenue of the great kings', for here were entombed some of the most famous of ancient rulers. There was the imposing tomb of Ollamh Fodhla, the fortieth king, who gathered the laws of Ireland and established a *féis*, or convention, which sat at Tara every three years at the feast of Samhain. This was when judges, lawyers, and administrators gathered to discuss the laws and revise them. Indeed, Tressach knew that hosts of judges and lawyers had already descended on Tara, for the convention fell this very year. They would start their deliberations in the morning.

Here, also, was the imposing tomb of Macha Mong Ruadh, Macha of the Foxy Hair, the seventy-sixth monarch and the only woman to have ruled all Ireland. Beyond were the tombs of Conaire the Great, of Tuathal the Legitimate, of Art the Solitary, of Conn of the Hundred Battles, and of Fergus of the Black Teeth. Tressach could reel off the names of those who inhabited the graves like a litany. How the mighty were laid low.

Yet, why a warrior needed to waste his time patrolling this resting place of the dead was a mystery to Tressach. What need was there to guard this desolate place and why this night of all the dark autumnal nights? Tressach would have preferred to be somewhere else . . . anywhere else.

At least he had a lantern, but its light gave him little comfort. He began to walk with a quick pace as he passed down the darkened aisle between the tombs. The quicker he completed his task so that – in good conscience – he could report to his commander that he had walked through the compound, the better. The thought that, at the end of his vigil, there would be a mug of *cuirm*, a strong mead, acted as an added incentive.

He turned a corner and conscience made him pause near a row of tombs for an inspection. He held his lantern before him. He owed it to his commander and his pride as a warrior to make a cursory check at each vantage point. His eyes fell on a newly dug grave and he found himself suppressing a shiver. He knew that Garbh, the keeper of the cemetery, whose duties included the maintenance of the graves and the digging of new tombs, had been working here over the last two days. Although the grave was unfinished and empty, Tressach felt a morbid fascination as he stared at the yawning black hole with its piled dark earth around it. His imagination began to run riot and fearful childhood fantasies clutched at his mind. Any moment something fearful could raise itself out of that black pit. He genuflected and turned abruptly away.

Here, at the end of the row of more modern tombs, stood a mound set slightly apart. This type of grave was ancient and called a *dumma*. It was surrounded by a circle of granite pillar stones notched in Ogham, the ancient Irish writing which was falling into disuse since the new faith had brought Latin script into the land. Had it not been so dark, Tressach knew that one would have seen that this tomb was more richly endowed than the others. Under its grey stone portals were heavy oak doors, panelled in copper and bronze and reinforced with iron. The panels were studded with patterning of gold and silver.

It was one of the oldest of the graves at Tara. In fact, according to the chroniclers, it was some fifteen hundred years old. It was the tomb of the twenty-sixth High King, Tigernmas, known as 'Lord of Death', for he was one of the most warlike of the ancient kings and had won thrice-nine battles in a single year. During his reign, so the old storytellers claimed, the first gold and silver mines were discovered and worked in Ireland. Tigernmas had become a rich and powerful king. It was he who had ordained that the people should wear clothes of varied colours to denote their clans and social status.

Of all the tombs that Tressach would have to pass this fearsome evening, he was most apprehensive of the tomb of Tigernmas. The old annalists had it that Tigernmas had forsaken the ancient gods and turned to worship an idol dedicated to blood and vengeance. Sacrifices were made at the feast of Samhain on the plain of Magh Slecht. Because of this, a terrible disaster had overtaken Tigernmas. He and all his followers died of a strange illness and his body was then returned to Tara to be interred in this last resting place of kings.

Tressach knew the story well and wished, for at least this night, that he could expunge it from his imagination. He clasped his sword hilt more firmly with one hand as he held the lantern high with the other. It gave him comfort. He was about to hurry on past the tomb of Tigernmas when a scream poleaxed him. His limbs lost all form of movement. It was a muffled cry, a strangled cry of pain.

Then an agonised voice distinctly cried: 'Help me! God help me!'

Tressach broke into a cold sweat, unable to move, unable to make a sound from his suddenly constricted and dry throat.

There was no question in his mind that the cry had come from the long-sealed tomb of Tigernmas.

The Abbot Colmán, spiritual adviser to the Great Assembly of the chieftains of the five kingdoms of Ireland, a thickset, ruddy-faced man in his mid-fifties, rose to greet the young religieuse who had just entered his chamber. She was tall, with grey-green eyes and strands of red hair escaping from under her head-dress.

'Sister Fidelma! It is always good to see you here at Tara. Alas, you do not often bless us with a visit.'

He came forward with both hands outstretched.

'*Dominus tecum*,' replied the religieuse solemnly, observing protocol. But the smiling abbot shook his head, gripped her hands warmly, and guided her to a chair beside the fire. They were old friends but it had been some time since their last meeting.

'I was wondering whether we should see you here this year for the convention. All the other judges and lawyers have already arrived.'

Sister Fidelma, of the house of Brigid of Kildare, grimaced wryly.

'It would have been remiss of me to fail to attend, for there are many contentious matters that I want to debate with the Chief Brehon.'

Abbot Colmán smiled happily and offered Fidelma a drink of mulled imported Gaulish wine. When she indicated her acceptance he took down a pottery amphora, emptying some of the red wine into a jug, then, taking a red-hot poker from the fire, he dipped it into the sizzling liquid. He poured a measure into a silver goblet.

The evening was chill and Fidelma appreciated the warm liquid.

'Is it really three years since you were last at Tara?' inquired the abbot, shaking his head in mock disbelief as he seated himself in the chair opposite her.

'It does seem a lifetime ago,' agreed Fidelma.

'The king still speaks with wonder of how you solved the mystery of his stolen sword.'

'How is Sechnasach, the king? Is he well? And his family, do they prosper?'

'They are all well, *Deo gratias*,' the abbot said piously. 'But I hear that much has happened to you since.'

He was interrupted by a sharp rap on the door.

The abbot made an apologetic glance towards Fidelma and bade the caller enter.

It needed no expertise to see that the warrior who stood there was in some state of shock. In spite of his sheepskin cloak, his body shook as if with intense cold and his face was white. The lips quivered almost uncontrollably. His dark eyes flickered from the abbot to the young religieuse and back again.

'Well, man,' Colmán said sharply. 'Out with it. What is it you seek?'

'Lord Abbot,' the man hesitated. His voice was a mumble.

Colmán heaved an impatient sigh.

'Speak up, man!'

'I am Tressach of the palace guard. My captain, Irél, has sent me to fetch you. There has been an incident . . .'

Tressach's voice trailed nervously away.

'An incident?' queried Colmán. 'What incident?'

'There has been an incident in the cemetery of the High Kings. Irél requests that you should attend immediately.'

'Why? What incident?' Colmán obviously did not enjoy the prospect of having to leave the warmth of his hearth and wine. However, the abbot was both an officer of the royal court and an ecclesiastical adviser, and any incident affecting spiritual matters at Tara, in which the upkeep of the cemetery was included, came under his jurisdiction.

Sister Fidelma had been examining the nervous warrior under lowered brows as she sipped her wine. The man was clearly in a state of extreme unease. The abbot's abrupt manner was not helping him. She placed her goblet on the table and smiled reassuringly up at him.

'Tell us what has happened and then we may see how best we can help.'

The warrior spread his arms helplessly as he turned to her.

'I was on guard. By the tombs, that is. This very evening, I was on guard. Abruptly there came a scream from the tomb of Tigernmas . . .'

'*From* the tomb?' queried Fidelma sharply.

'From inside the tomb, Sister.' The warrior lent emphasis to the statement by genuflecting. 'I heard a voice crying distinctly for God to help it. I was in mortal fear. I can fight with men but not with the wandering tormented souls of the dead.'

Colmán was tut-tutting. His face showed scepticism.

'Is this some mischievous prank? I am well aware what night this is.'

But Fidelma could see that humour was not in the fearful face of the warrior.

'Go on,' invited Fidelma. 'What did you do?'

'Do, Sister? I hastened away as fast as I could from that accursed place. I ran to report to my captain, Irél. At first, like the abbot, he did not believe me. He and another warrior took me back to the tomb. Oh, by my soul, Sister! The voice came again. It was fainter than before but still crying for help. Irél heard it and so did the other warrior who accompanied us.'

It was plain Colmán still did not believe him.

'What is it Irél wants me to do?' he demanded cynically. 'Go there and pray for the souls of the dead?'

'No. Irél is one not given to a belief in wandering spirits. My captain wants permission to open the tomb. He believes that someone is inside and hurt.'

The abbot looked aghast.

'But that tomb has not been opened in fifteen hundred years,' he protested. 'How could anyone be inside?'

'That's what Garbh told him,' agreed the warrior.

'Garbh?' queried Fidelma.

'The keeper of the cemetery. My captain, Irél, sent for him and requested that he open the doors of the tomb.'

'And did Garbh do so?' asked the abbot, irritably.

'No. He refused unless Irél obtained higher authority. That is why Irél sent me to you, to seek your permission.'

'Quite right. This is a matter of seriousness,' Colmán muttered. 'The decision to open tombs is not one a soldier – even the captain of the palace guard – can make. I'd better come along and see this Irél, your captain.' Colmán rose to his feet and glanced at Fidelma. 'If you will forgive me, Sister . . .'

But Fidelma was rising also.

'I think I will come with you,' she said quietly. 'For if a voice comes from a sealed tomb, then someone must have been able to enter it . . . or else, God forbid, it is indeed a spirit calling to us.'

They found Irél, the sombre-faced captain of the palace guard, standing outside the tomb with another warrior. There was a third man there, a stocky man with rippling muscles who was clad in a workman's leather jerkin and trousers. He had pugnacious features and was arguing with the captain. The man turned as they approached and, with relief on his face, greeted Abbot Colmán by name.

'I am glad that you have come, my lord Abbot. This captain is demanding that I break open this tomb. Such an act is sacrilege and I have refused unless ordered to do so by a churchman of authority.'

Irél stepped forward and saluted the abbot.

'Has Tressach explained the matter to you?' His voice was curt.

The abbot glanced disdainfully at him.

'Can we hear this voice?' Colmán's tone was sarcastic and he cocked an ear as if to listen.

'We have not heard it since I sent for Garbh,' replied Irél, keeping his irritation in check. 'I have been trying to get Garbh to open the tomb, for every moment is urgent. Someone may be dying in there.'

The man called Garbh laughed drily.

'Look at the doors. Not opened in fifteen hundred years. Whoever died in there, died over a millennium ago.'

'Garbh, as keeper of the cemetery, is within his rights to refuse your request,' Abbot Colmán explained. 'I am not sure that even I can give such permission.'

It was then that Sister Fidelma stepped forward.

'In that case, I shall give the order. I think we should open the tomb immediately.'

Colmán swung round and frowned at Fidelma.

'Do you take this matter seriously?'

'That an experienced captain of the guard and a warrior take it so should be enough reason to accept that they heard something. Let us see if this is so.'

Irél looked at the young religieuse in surprise while Garbh's features were forming into a sneer of derision.

Colmán however sighed and motioned to Garbh to start opening the doors of the tomb.

'Sister Fidelma is a *dálaigh*, an advocate of the law courts, and holds the degree of *Anruth*,' he explained to them in order to justify his action. 'She has the authority.'

Garbh's eyes flickered imperceptibly. It was the only indication that he made in recognition of the fact that the young religieuse held a degree which was only one below the highest legal qualification in the land. Irél's shoulders seemed to relax as if in relief that a decision had finally been made.

It took some time for Garbh to smash open the ancient locks of the door and swing them open.

As they pressed forward there were some gasps of astonishment.

Just inside the door was the body of a man.

They could see that this was no ancient body. It was the body of a man who was but recently dead. From his back there protruded a length of wood with which he had clearly been shot or stabbed. It was like the shaft of an arrow but without feathered flights. He lay face-down behind the doors, hands stretched out as if attempting to open the doors from the inside. They could see that his fingernails were torn and bleeding where he had scraped at the door in his terror. And his face! The eyes were wide with fear, as if he had been confronted by some evil power of darkness.

Tressach shivered violently. 'God look down on us!'

Garbh was rubbing his chin in bewilderment.

'The tomb was securely sealed,' he whispered. 'You all saw the seals on the door. It has been sealed for fifteen hundred years.'

'Yet this man was inside trying to break out.' Fidelma pointed out the obvious. 'He was apparently dying even as Irél was ordering the tomb to be opened. It was his dying cries, that Tressach and Irél heard.'

Irél glanced towards Sister Fidelma.

'This is hardly a sight for a Sister of the Faith,' he protested as he saw her moving forward.

'I am a *dálaigh*,' she reminded him. 'I shall take charge of this investigation.'

Irél glanced questioningly to Abbot Colmán, who nodded slightly and the captain stood aside to allow Fidelma to enter the tomb. She ordered the lanterns to be held up to illuminate the area.

Fidelma moved forward curiously. She had heard all the stories of Tigernmas, the infamous High King, who had ordered his druids to be put to death and turned to the worship of a gigantic idol. Generations of children had been frightened into obedience with tales of how the evil king's soul would ascend from the Otherworld and take them off unless they obeyed their parents. And now she stood at the door of his tomb, unopened since his body had been placed in it countless generations ago. It was not an inviting place. The air was stale, dank, and smelling of rotting earth and vegetation. A noxious, unclean atmosphere permeated the place.

The first thing she noticed, was that the body was of a man of middle years, somewhat plump, with well-kempt white hair. She examined the torn and bleeding hands and looked at the softness of the fingers and the palms. He was clearly someone not used to manual work. She examined his clothing. Apart from the dust and dirt of the tomb and the stains of blood from his wound, they were the clothes of someone of rank. Yet he wore no jewellery, no symbols of office, and when she examined the leather purse attached to the belt around his waist, she found only a few coins in it.

Only when she had conducted this scrutiny did she turn to examine his face. She tried to ignore the terrible mask of dread on it. Then she frowned and called for a lantern to be held more closely, studying the features with some dim memory tugging at her mind. The features seemed familiar to her.

'Abbot Colmán, please look at this man,' she called. 'I have a feeling that I should know him.'

Colmán moved forward somewhat unwillingly and bent down beside her.

'Christ's wounds!' exclaimed the abbot, forgetting his calling. 'It is Fiacc, the Chief Brehon of Ardgal.'

Fidelma nodded grimly. She knew that she had seen the man's features before. The chief judge of the clan of Ardgal was one of the learned judges of the country.

'He must have been here to attend the convention,' breathed Colmán.

Fidelma rose and dusted her clothing. 'The more important thing to discover is what he was doing here at all,' she pointed out. 'How did a respected judge come to be in a tomb which has never been opened in generations and get himself stabbed to death?'

'Witchcraft!' supplied Tressach in a breathless tone.

Irél glanced at his subordinate with a look of derision.

'Don't the teachings of Patrick's first council tell us there is no such thing as witchcraft?' he rebuked, before turning to Fidelma. 'There must be an explanation for this, Sister.'

Fidelma smiled appreciatively at the man's pedestrian approach.

'There is an explanation for everything,' she agreed, as she let her eyes wander into the interior of the tomb. 'Sometimes it is not easily seen, however.' Then she turned back to Colmán. 'Would you consult with the steward of the convention and see if Fiacc was in attendance and whether he was due to speak?'

Colmán hesitated only a moment before hurrying away on his task.

Fidelma bent again to the corpse. There was no disputing the cause of death. The shaft of wood, like an arrow, was stuck in the back of the corpse under the shoulder blade.

'The worst place to try to stab a man,' sniffed Irél. 'To stab him in the back,' he added when Fidelma glanced up questioningly at him. 'You can never be sure of inflicting a mortal wound. There are too many bones in the way of a vital organ, any of which might deflect the blow. It is better to stab from the front, in and up under the rib cage.'

He spoke with the relish of a warrior.

'So you would say that whoever delivered the blow was an amateur when it came to killing?' asked Fidelma drily.

Irél considered the point.

'Not necessarily. The implement has been inserted slightly to the side and with an abrupt thrust towards the heart. The killer knew what he was about. He was aiming to pierce the heart immediately. Nevertheless, the victim lived on for a while. If he had not we would never have heard his cries and discovered the body.'

'You are very observant, Irél. But why do you ascribe the killing to a man?'

Irél shrugged indifferently.

'It is logical. Look at the depth at which the wood is buried in the flesh. It would take strength to thrust it in so far.'

Fidelma could not fault the logic. But she was examining

the shaft of wood with more interest. It was a piece of aspen, some eighteen inches or more in length, and it was inscribed with Ogham characters. She ran her finger over the cut letters, feeling the faint stickiness of the sap. The words meant 'The gods protect us'. It was now obvious what it was. The aspen wand was called a *fé* – an instrument by which corpses and graves were measured. It was generally regarded as an unlucky object and no one would willingly touch a *fé* unless they had need to.

Even Fidelma felt that she had to summon a special courage before she reached over and yanked the piece of wood from the corpse of Fiacc. She immediately saw that it was no ordinary *fé*. Where the shaft had been driven in, it had been whittled into a sharp point and, when she'd wiped the blood on the clothes of the corpse, her eyes narrowed as she observed that this point had been hardened by fire.

Tressach, standing nearby, was gazing aghast at Fidelma's handling of the wooden *fé*.

'Sister,' he reproached, 'it is highly unlucky to handle that. And to handle the very *fé* that measured this tomb for Tigernmas . . .'

Fidelma did not reply. She rose to examine the rest of the tomb.

It was an oval-shaped chamber cut into a mound of earth with its floors flagged with stones while granite blocks lined the walls and were placed so that they formed a natural archlike structure across the entire roof. The length of the tomb was about fifteen feet, and its width a little more than twelve. Fidelma was thankful that the open doors of the tomb had allowed fresher, chill evening air to dispel the fetid atmosphere.

There was no need to ask where the remains of Tigernmas were. At the far end of the tomb, in a central position, stood an upright, rusting iron frame. In it, almost crumbled to pieces, were the remains of a skeleton. There were some fragments of clothing on it; a metal belt buckle and a rusty sword had fallen nearby. It had been the custom for the ancients to bury their chieftains and great rulers standing upright and facing their enemies, sword clasped in their dead hand. This iron cage had obviously been designed to keep the corpse upright in the burial chamber. By this method, it was said the aura of the dead was supposed to protect the living. The skull of the skeleton had fallen to one side in the cage so that its eyeless sockets appeared to be staring with malignant force in the direction of the dead Fiacc. The skeletal grin seemed to be one of satisfaction. Fidelma felt irritated at the way her imagination interpreted these images.

To one side of the tomb were the rotting remains of a chariot. This would be the king's most cherished vehicle, left there to help transport him to the Otherworld. Jars and containers of what had once been his favourite foods and drink stood nearby, large bronze and copper containers made by skilled craftsmen.

Fidelma moved forward and her foot caught at something. She bent down and picked up a small but weighty bar of metal. Having examined it closely by Irél's lantern, she realised that it was silver. She set it down carefully, and as she did so she saw a few brooches scattered about. They were of semiprecious jewels set in gold mountings. Again, it was the custom to bury a portion of wealth with a great chieftain, for he would also need some means to help him in his journey to the Otherworld. Frowning thoughtfully, Fidelma continued to examine the rest of the tomb.

By the beam of the lantern, Fidelma noticed that a small trail of blood led from a point before the iron cage of the skeleton to where the corpse of Fiacc lay before the doors. She could also see scratch marks on the granite floor.

Irél, standing beside her, articulated her thoughts.

'He was obviously stabbed while standing by the cage and then contrived to drag himself to the doors.'

Fidelma did not bother to glance at him.

'Obviously,' she replied shortly.

At the entrance of the tomb, Garbh, the keeper of the cemetery, was standing with Tressach and the other warrior, watching her progress with fascination.

'Speaking of things obvious, does it not surprise you that there is so little dust and dirt on the floor of this tomb?' she asked Irél. 'It is almost as if it had been recently swept.'

Irél stared at her, wondering whether she was making a joke. But she had passed on, examining the floor and looking carefully at one of the stone slabs that made up its surface. She pointed to the scratch marks across the floor.

'Bring your lantern closer,' she instructed. 'What do you make of those?'

The captain shrugged. 'It is probably where the floor stones were scored by ropes while they were being dropped into place.'

'Exactly so,' agreed Fidelma quietly. 'And have you noticed anything else that is curious about this sepulchre?'

Irél glanced quickly around but shook his head.

'Tigernmas, although he subsequently developed an evil reputation, is accredited as the king who first encouraged gold and silver to be smelted and works of great art to be produced in this land.'

'I have heard the stories,' replied Irél.

'And it was the custom of our people to place grave goods in the tombs, together with symbols of their wealth and power.'

'That much is well known,' acknowledged Irél, slightly irritated at Fidelma for not addressing the more urgent problem.

'Apart from a few golden brooches and a silver bar, which I see lying on the floor there as if they were hurriedly discarded, where are the riches that one would have expected to find in this tomb? It is singularly devoid of any such items.'

Irél tried to see some connection that Fidelma's remark might have with the murder of Fiacc but failed. He was not interested in the customs of ancients.

'Is that significant?' he asked.

'Perhaps.'

Fidelma walked back to the corpse and looked down at it once more. There was a movement outside and Abbot Colmán came hurrying back.

'Fiacc was certainly due to attend the convention tomorrow,' he confirmed. 'The steward says that Fiacc and his wife, Étromma, arrived in Tara a few days ago. However, and this is interesting, there was a problem, for, the steward says, Fiacc was to be heard before the Chief Brehon to answer charges which, if proved, would have debarred him from practice as a judge.'

'A special hearing?' Fidelma had heard nothing about such a contentious matter. She cast a final look around the tomb before returning her gaze to Colmán.

'Does the steward have details of the charges against Fiacc?'

'Only that it was something to do with malpractice. Only the Chief Brehon has the details.'

'Has Étromma been informed of her husband's death?'

'I took it upon myself to send word to her.'

'Then I think I should go and speak with her.'

'Is that necessary? She will be distraught. Perhaps tomorrow would be a more suitable time?'

'It is necessary to see her now in order to clear up this mystery.'

Abbot Colmán spread his hands in acquiescence.

'Very well. What about . . .?' He did not finish but gestured towards the tomb.

It was Garbh who finished the question. 'Shouldn't the body of this man be removed so that I can seal the tomb?'

'Not for the moment,' replied Fidelma. 'Irél, have a guard mounted outside the tomb. Everything is to be left as it is until I order otherwise. Hopefully, I shall have resolved the mystery before midnight. Then the tomb can be resealed.'

She left the tomb and began to walk slowly and thoughtfully back through the graves of the High Kings. She paused for a moment waiting for Abbot Colmán to catch up with her. He had stopped to issue final instructions to Irél. Her eyes flickered towards the yawning pit of a freshly dug grave and suppressed a shiver. Colmán came panting along a moment later and together they walked leisurely towards the lights of the main palace complex.

Étromma was surprisingly young to be the wife of a middle-aged judge. She was scarcely more than eighteen years old. She sat stiffly but in complete control of herself. There was little sign of anguish or of grieving on her features. The cold, calculating blue eyes stared with hostility at Fidelma. The lips were thinned and pressed together. A small nerve twitching at the corner of her mouth was the only sign of expression on her features.

'I was divorcing Fiacc. He was about to be disbarred and he had no money,' she replied coldly to a question Fidelma had asked her.

Fidelma was seated before her, while Abbot Colmán stood nervously by the fire.

'I do not see how the two things fit together, Étromma,' she commented.

'I do not want to spend my life in poverty. It was an agreement between us. Fiacc was an old man. I married him only for security. He knew that.'

'What about love?' queried Fidelma mildly. 'Had you no feelings for him?'

For the first time Étromma smiled, a humourless parting of her lips. 'Love? What is that? Does love provide financial security?'

Fidelma sighed softly.

'Why was Fiacc facing disbarment from practice as a judge?' Fidelma chose a new tack.

'During this last year he had made many wrong judgements. He was, as you know, judge of the Ardgal. After so many wrong judgements, he was no longer trusted by the people. He had made himself destitute from the continual payment of compensation.'

Fidelma knew that a judge had to deposit a pledge of five *séd*, or ounces of silver, for each case he tried as a surety against error. If, on appeal by the defendant to higher judges, a panel of no fewer than three more experienced judges, a judge was found to have made an error, then this pledge was confiscated and the judge ordered to pay further compensation of one *cumal*, the equivalent of the value of three silver *séd*.

'How many wrong judgements had your husband made this last year, then? How could he have become poverty-stricken?'

'There were eleven wrong judgements during this last year.'

Fidelma's eyebrows raised in surprise. Eighty-eight silver *séd*, which could buy nearly thirty milch cows, was a staggering sum to have to pay out in compensation in a single year. No wonder there was talk of disbarring Fiacc.

'He was to be heard before the Chief Brehon to answer the fact that he had gone into debt to pay fines and to answer for his competence as a judge,' Étromma added.

'Are you saying that he had borrowed money to pay?'

'That is why I was divorcing him.'

Fidelma realised that a judge who turned to moneylenders to support him would certainly be disbarred if he could not present a valid argument to endorse his actions. Clearly, Fiacc had been in considerable trouble.

'So your husband was worried about his situation?'

Étromma chuckled drily.

'Worried? No, he was not. At least not recently.'

'Not worried?' pressed Fidelma sharply.

'He tried to stop me divorcing him by claiming that it was only a temporary matter and that he was not really destitute. He said that he was expecting money shortly and, after that, if the people did not want him as judge, he would be rich enough to live without working.'

'Did he explain where the money was coming from? How would he pay off his debts and find the money to live for the rest of his life in any degree of comfort?'

'He did not explain. Nor did I care. I think he was just a liar or a fool. It was his problem. He knew that if he lied to me and he was disbarred and shown to be penniless then I would leave. It was as simple as that. I was not going to recall my application for divorce.'

Fidelma tried to conceal her dislike of the cold, commercial attitude of the young woman.

'You were not at all interested where your husband would suddenly obtain money, if he actually did so?'

'I knew he would not. He was a liar.'

'At what point did he become confident that he would manage to obtain money to pay his debts?'

The woman Étromma reflected for a moment.

'I suppose that he started to brag that he was going to overcome this problem a day or so ago. Yes, it was yesterday morning.'

'You mean that he was worried until yesterday morning?'

'Precisely so.'

'When did you both arrive here at Tara?'

'Four days ago.'

'And during that time, Fiacc was concerned? Then yesterday morning his attitude changed?'

'Yes, I suppose so.'

'Did he meet with anyone here?'

Étromma shrugged. 'He was known to many people here. I was not interested in his friends.'

'I mean, was there anyone in particular with whom he spent some time at Tara? Was there anyone who could be described as a close friend or confidant?'

'Not so far as I know. He was a solitary man. I do not think he met with anyone here. He kept to himself. The only thing that I know he did was go for walks on his own in the graveyard of the High Kings.' Étromma paused to sniff. 'I thought he was getting maudlin. But, as I said, yesterday he came back grinning like a cat who had found a dish of cream. He assured me that things would be all right. I knew he was a liar, so I was not going to alter my plans to leave him.'

Fidelma stood up abruptly.

'I will not express my condolences, Étromma,' she said with emphasis. 'Doubtless you do not expect them. You are obviously more concerned with the financial arrangements. Fiacc was still your husband when he met his death. Your husband was murdered. I think I now know who the murderer is and, if proven, the compensation due for the slaying of your husband, as a Brehon of lower rank, is three *séd* of silver. It is not a fortune but it will keep you momentarily from poverty, and doubtless you will soon find someone else to support you.'

Abbot Colmán followed her unhappily along the corridors of the palace towards his chamber. 'You were harsh, Sister. After all, she has just been widowed and is only eighteen years old.'

Fidelma was indifferent.

'I meant to be harsh. She felt nothing for Fiacc. He was merely a source of income for her. She proclaims her motto without shame – *lucri bonus est odor ex requalibet.*'

Colmán grimaced. 'Sweet is the smell of money obtained from any source. Isn't that from Juvenal's *Satires*?'

Fidelma smiled briefly.

'Send for Irél, Tressach, and Garbh to come to your chamber. I think I can now solve this problem.'

It was not long before the three men crowded curiously into the abbot's chamber.

Fidelma was seated in a chair before the fire while Colmán stood with his back to it, a little to one side. His hands were clasped behind his back.

114

'Well now.' Fidelma raised her head and regarded them each in turn before addressing the warrior, Tressach. 'How long have you been a guard at Tara, Tressach?'

'Three years, Sister.'

'And how long have you patrolled the compound containing the tombs of the High Kings?'

'One year.'

'And you, Irél? You are captain of the guards of Tara. How long have you been here?'

'I entered the service of the High Kings some ten years ago. Conall Cáel was still High King then. I have been captain here for the last year.'

She looked from one to another and shook her head sadly.

'And how long has Sechnasach been High King?' she continued.

Irél frowned, not understanding the logic of this question. He regarded Fidelma as if she were joking. But her expression was completely serious.

'How long? You must know that, Sister. Everyone does. It was three years ago when the joint High Kings, Diarmuid and Blathmac, died of the Yellow Plague within a week of one another. That was when Sechnasach became High King.'

'Three years ago?' pressed Fidelma.

'You must remember, Fidelma,' interrupted Colmán, wondering how she could have forgotten. 'You were in Tara on that occasion yourself.' But she ignored him and continued to direct her questions to Irél.

'And is the High King in good health?'

'To my knowledge, thanks be to God,' Irél replied, becoming slightly defensive.

'And his family?' continued Fidelma remorselessly. 'Are they in good health?'

'Indeed, the High King is blessed.'

'I told you as much myself when you arrived earlier,' frowned Colmán, wondering if Fidelma was losing her memory.

'So what is the purpose of the new grave being dug behind the tomb of Tigernmas?'

The question was asked so softly that it took a moment or two for its implication to sink in. Fidelma's fiery green eyes were fixed on the keeper of the cemetery.

Garbh's mouth dropped open and he began to stutter. Then he hung his head in silence.

'Hold him,' instructed Fidelma calmly. 'He is to be held for premeditated murder and grave robbery.'

With astonished expressions, Irél and Tressach moved close to the side of the keeper of the cemetery.

Fidelma now rose languidly to her feet and gazed sorrowfully at Garbh. 'There has been no death of a High King or any member of his family during the last three years. Sechnasach is still young and healthy. Why then dig a new grave in the cemetery of the High Kings? Will you explain, Garbh, or shall I?'

Garbh remained silent.

'You started digging the grave in order to construct a small passage into the tomb of Tigernmas, didn't you, Garbh?'

'For what purpose would one want to enter an ancient tomb?' demanded Colmán, chagrined that he had not spotted such an obvious matter as the new grave.

'To rob the tomb, of course,' replied Fidelma. 'Where were all the gold, silver, and jewels that would have been buried with Tigernmas? Only a single silver bar and some gold jewellery lay discarded on the floor of the burial chamber. Tigernmas was a king of many legends. But it was well known that he ruled a rich court. Following the custom of our ancestors, rich grave goods would have been placed there to serve him in the Otherworld.'

Irél was looking shamefaced. Fidelma had pointed out this very fact to him and it had not registered.

'But there is much to be explained,' he pointed out. 'How did the judge, Fiacc, come to be there? Had he spotted Garbh's intention and tried to catch him?'

116

Fidelma shook her head. 'It was Fiacc's idea to rob the tomb in the first place. Fiacc had married a mercenary young woman. He had also made several mistakes in judgement and had become destitute through the payment of compensation. He was desperately in debt. He needed money badly. He needed money prior to his hearing before the Chief Brehon tomorrow. Money to cover his debts and money to keep his capricious young wife. It was Fiacc's idea to rob the tomb of Tigernmas, which, according to the chroniclers, contained great riches. But how was he to do it on his own?'

'Do you have the explanation?' Colmán asked.

'When he arrived at Tara, Fiacc spent a day or so in the cemetery examining the tomb. He realised there was only one way to get access without attracting attention. He enlisted the aid of Garbh, the keeper of the graves. Once Garbh saw the simplicity of the plan greed took over. Money is always a great incentive.

'Garbh was always in the cemetery, repairing tombs. It was Garbh's job to dig the graves when a High King or his family died. No one was bothered when Garbh started to dig a grave near the sepulchre of Tigernmas. No one even thought to ask why he was digging a grave. Everyone saw Garbh at what was presumed to be his usual lawful task.

'Garbh and Fiacc broke into the tomb of Tigernmas this evening. When you come to examine the new grave which Garbh has dug and which he meant to fill in tomorrow, you will find traces of a short tunnel into the tomb. It will come up under the floor, under one of the granite slabs. One of those slabs, Irél, with the scratch marks on it which you so rightly observed had been made by ropes used to reset it into its proper place in the floor. The plan was that Garbh and Fiacc would extract the riches and reseal the passage so that no one would know that the tomb had even been entered. A few items were overlooked in the haste to extract everything. A bar of silver and some jewellery were left behind. But that was all!'

'How did Fiacc die?' demanded Irél, trying to follow the story.

'Was it the curse of Tigernmas that struck him down?' Tressach asked fearfully.

'Fiacc died,' replied Fidelma coldly, 'because Garbh decided that he did not want to share the easy money that had come his way. Having been shown the almost effortless way to gain riches, Garbh wanted those riches for himself. He waited until he and Fiacc had removed all the loot from the tomb and were cleaning up. Fiacc, you see, being a judge, was very meticulous about his planning. In case some accident caused the tomb to be opened, he had decided that the dust on the floor, which would show evidence of their activity and might provide a clue to their identity, should be swept away.'

Irél groaned. Again Fidelma had pointed this out to him and it had not registered as important.

'Go on,' he urged. 'You have told us why Fiacc died. Now tell us how exactly he died?'

'It was after the spoils had been removed and the cleaning finished that Garbh, using a *fé*, the measuring stick for graves, stabbed Fiacc in the back and thought he had killed him. He then left the tomb, resealed the entrance, and went back to the grave he was digging, perhaps filling in the tunnel after him. We shall see that later. I would imagine that he has stored his spoils in or near his cabin.'

Garbh shifted uneasily at this and Fidelma smiled in satisfaction.

'Yes, Irél, I think you will find the treasure of Tigernmas hidden at Garbh's cabin.'

'But Fiacc was not killed immediately,' Tressach interrupted. 'Garbh left him wounded in the tomb when he resealed it.'

'Garbh did not realise this. He thought he had killed Fiacc. The wound made Fiacc pass out. He was badly hurt. He was dying. But he came to consciousness and realised that he was sealed in the darkened tomb. He realised, in terror, that he himself was entombed. He gave a scream of dread, which you, Tressach, in passing the tomb, heard. He began to drag himself to the wooden doors, crying in desperation. Not knowing that Tressach had heard his scream, he began to scrabble at the doors until, in that fearful moment of horror, death overtook him.'

'I did not mean to kill him. It was an argument,' Garbh said slowly, speaking now for the first time and admitting guilt. 'It was Fiacc who wanted the greater part of the wealth for himself. He said that he would only give me a small portion of the spoils. When I demanded a fair and equal share, he attacked me. He picked up the old grave measure and attacked me and I defended myself. In the struggle, he was stabbed. I was not responsible for the murder. You cannot punish me for that.'

Fidelma shook her head.

'Oh no, Garbh. You plotted to kill Fiacc from the very beginning. As soon as Fiacc had explained the plan to you, you decided that you wanted all the spoils from the tomb. You kept Fiacc alive long enough for him to be of help in gaining entrance to the tomb and taking out the treasure. You planned to kill him and leave him in the tomb, hoping that no one would ever open the tomb again. Your mistake was twofold: firstly, not ensuring that he was dead when you left him, and secondly, vanity.'

'You cannot prove I set out to kill Fiacc!' cried Garbh. 'If I had meant to kill him I would have taken a weapon into the tomb. Fiacc was killed by an old grave measurement left lying in the tomb. Even Irél will bear witness to that.'

Irél reluctantly nodded in agreement.

'That seems so, Sister. It was a *fé* that killed Fiacc. You know that. And there was Ogham carved on it. I know the ancient script. It read, "May the gods protect us". The reference to the *gods* and not *God* shows that it belonged to the pagan tomb. It must have been lying in the burial chamber.'

'Not so. The grave measure was made by Garbh,' insisted Fidelma. She pointed to the table in the abbot's room on which she had already laid the *fé* taken from the tomb.

'That was not the *fé* that measured the tomb of Tigernmas. Look at it closely. The wood is new. The Ogham notches are clean-cut. Examine the cuts. There are traces of sap still drying. Whoever cut this, cut it within the last twenty-four hours.'

Colmán had picked up the stick, taking care to genuflect to keep himself from harm at the handling of such an unlucky instrument, and examined it carefully.

'The piece of aspen is still in sap,' he confirmed wonderingly.

'Garbh had burnt a point on it to ensure that it was hard and able to be used as a dagger. He carved some Ogham on it as an afterthought. That was his vanity. He had taken notice of Fiacc's exhortation to detail and thought of a great joke to play on him. If the tomb was ever excavated, they would find Fiacc with an ancient pagan *fé* stuck into his heart. Garbh was too clever for his own good. It was easy to see that the *fé* was new-cut. And it proves that Garbh premeditated the murder. He prepared his murder weapon before he entered the tomb. It was not a spur-of-the-moment argument.'

Garbh said nothing. The blood had drained from his features.

'You may take him away now,' Fidelma instructed Irél. 'And you may make the arrangements to reseal the tomb . . . but after the treasures of Tigernmas are replaced in it.' She grinned impishly. 'It would not do, this night of all nights, to provoke the spirit of Tigernmas by keeping back any of his gold or silver, would it?'

Abbot Colmán was pouring more mulled wine and handed the goblet to Fidelma. 'A sorry story, indeed,' he sighed. 'An avaricious official and a corrupt judge. How can such wickedness be explained?'

'You forget Étromma in that summation,' replied Fidelma. 'She was the catalyst who made Fiacc's need of money so desperate and who started this chain of events. It was her lack of love, her selfishness, and above all, her greed that caused this human tragedy. It is said in the book of Timothy: *radix omnium malorum est cupiditas.*'

'The love of money is the root of all evil,' translated Abbot Colmán and then bent his head in agreement.

Invitation to a Poisoning

T he meal had been eaten in an atmosphere of forced
politeness. There was a strained, chilly mood among
the diners. There were seven guests at the table of
Nechtan, chieftain of Múscraige. Sister Fidelma had
noticed the unlucky number immediately she had been
ushered into the feasting hall for she had been the last to
arrive and take her seat, having been delayed by the lure of
a hot bath before the meal. She had inwardly groaned as
she registered that seven guests plus Nechtan himself made
the unfavourable number of eight seated at the circular
table. Almost at once she had silently chided herself for
clinging to old superstitions. Nevertheless she conceded
that an oppressive atmosphere permeated the hall.

Everyone at the table that evening had cause to hate
Nechtan.

Sister Fidelma was not one to use words lightly for, as an
advocate of the law courts of the five kingdoms as well as a
religieuse, she used language carefully, sparingly and with
as much precision in meaning as she could. But she could
think of no other description for the emotion which Nechtan
aroused other than an intense dislike.

Like the others seated around the table, Fidelma had good
cause to feel great animosity towards the chieftain of the
Múscraige.

Why, then, had she accepted the invitation to this bizarre feast with Nechtan? Why had her fellow guests also agreed to attend this gathering?

Fidelma could only account for her own acceptance. In truth, she would have refused the invitation had Nechtan's plea for her attendance not found her passing, albeit unwillingly, through his territory on a mission to Sliabh Luachra, whose chieftain had sent for her to come and judge a case of theft. As one qualified in the laws of the Brehons to the level of *Anruth*, only one degree below the highest grade obtainable, Fidelma was well able to act as judge when the occasion necessitated it.

As it turned out, Daolgar of Sliabh Luachra, who also had cause to dislike Nechtan, had similarly received an invitation to the meal and so they had decided to accompany one another to the fortress of Nechtan.

Yet perhaps there was another reason behind Fidelma's half-hearted acceptance of the invitation, a more pertinent reason; it was that Nechtan's invitation had been couched in very persuasive language. He begged her forgiveness for the harm that he had done her in the past. Nechtan claimed that he sought absolution for his misdeeds and, hearing that she was passing through his territory, he had chosen this opportune moment to invite her, as well as several of those whom he had injured, to make reparation to them by asking them to feast with him so that, before all, he could make public the contrite apology. The handsomeness of the language was such that Fidelma had felt unable to refuse. Indeed, to refuse an enemy who makes such an apology would have been against the very teachings of the Christ. Had not the Apostle Luke reported that the Christ had instructed: 'Love your enemies, do good to them which hate you, bless them that curse you, and pray for them which despitefully use you, and unto him that smiteth thee on the one cheek offer also the other . . .'?

Where would Fidelma stand with the Faith if she refused

to obey its cardinal rule; that of forgiveness of those who had wronged her?

Now, as she sat at Nechtan's feasting table, she observed that her dislike of Nechtan was shared by all her fellow guests. At least she had made a Christian effort to accommodate Nechtan's desire to be forgiven but, from the looks and glances of those around her, from the stilted and awkward conversation, and from the chilly atmosphere and tension, the idea of forgiveness was not the burning desire in the hearts of those who sat there. A different desire seemed to consume their thoughts.

The meal was drawing to a close when Nechtan rose to his feet. He was a middle-aged man. At first glance one might have been forgiven for thinking of him as a jolly and kindly man. He was short and plump, his skin shone with a child-like pinkness, though his fleshy face sagged a little around the jowls. His hair was long, and silver in colour, but combed meticulously back from his face. His lips were thin and ruddy. Generally, the features were pleasant enough but hid the cruel strength of character which had marked his leadership of the Múscraige. It was when one stared directly into his ice-blue eyes that one realised the cold ruthlessness of the man. They were pale, dead eyes. The eyes of a man without feeling.

Nechtan motioned to the solitary attendant, who had been serving wine to the company, to refill his goblet from the pitcher which stood on a side table. The young man filled his vessel and then said quietly: 'The wine is nearly gone. Shall I have the pitcher refilled?' But Nechtan shook his head and dismissed him with a curt gesture so that he was alone with his guests.

Fidelma inwardly groaned again. The meal had been embarrassing enough without the added awkwardness of a speech from Nechtan.

'My friends,' Nechtan began. His voice was soft, almost cajoling, as he gazed without warmth around him. 'I hope I may now call you thus, for it has long been in my heart to seek you all out and make reparation to each of you for the wrong which you have suffered at my hands.'

He paused, looking expectantly around, but was met only with silence. Indeed, Fidelma seemed to be the only one to raise her head to meet his dead eyes. The others stared awkwardly at the remains of the meal on their plates before them.

'I am in your hands tonight,' went on Nechtan, as if oblivious to the tension around the table. 'I have wronged you all . . .'

He turned to the silent, elderly, nervous-looking man who was seated immediately to his left. The man had a habit of restively chewing his nails, a habit which Fidelma thought disgusting. It was a fact that, among the professional classes of society, well-formed hands and slender tapering fingers were considered a mark of beauty. Fingernails were usually carefully cut and rounded and most women put crimson stain on them. It was also considered shameful for a professional man to have unkempt nails.

Fidelma knew that the elderly man was Nechtan's own physician which made his untidy and neglected hands twice as outrageous and offensive in her eyes.

Nechtan smiled at the man. It was a smile, Fidelma thought, which was merely the rearrangement of facial muscles and had nothing to do with feeling.

'I have wronged you, Gerróc, my physician. I have regularly cheated you of your fees and taken advantage of your services.'

The elderly man stirred uncomfortably in his seat but then shrugged indifferently.

'You are my chieftain,' he replied stiffly.

Nechtan grimaced, as if amused by the response, and turned to the fleshy but still handsome middle-aged woman who sat next to Gerróc. She was the only other female at the table.

'And you, Ess, you were my first wife. I divorced you and drove you from my house by false claims of infidelity when all I sought was the arms of another younger and more attractive woman who took my fancy. By seeking to convict you of adultery I unlawfully stole your dowry and inheritance. In this, I wronged you before our people.'

Ess sat stony-faced; only a casual blink of her eyes denoted that she had even heard Nechtan's remark.

'And seated next to you,' Nechtan went on, still turning sunwise around the circle of the table, 'is my son, *our* son, Dathó. Through injustice to your mother, Dathó, I have also wronged you, my son. I have denied you your rightful place in this territory of the Múscraige.'

Dathó was a slim young man of twenty; his face was graven but his eyes – he had his mother's eyes and not the grey, cold eyes of his father – flashed with hatred at Nechtan. He opened his mouth as though to speak harsh words but Fidelma saw that his mother, Ess, laid a restraining hand on his arm and so he simply sniffed, thrust out his jaw pugnaciously but made no reply. It was clear that Nechtan would receive no forgiveness from his son nor his former wife.

Yet Nechtan appeared unperturbed at the reactions. He seemed to take some form of satisfaction in them.

Another of the guests, who was seated opposite Ess – Fidelma knew him as a young artist named Cuill – nervously rose from his seat and walked round the table, behind Nechtan, to where the pitcher of wine stood and filled his goblet, apparently emptying the jug, before returning to his seat.

Nechtan did not seem to notice him. Fidelma only half-registered the action. She continued to meet Nechtan's cold eyes steadily with her stormy green ones, and raised a hand to thrust back the wisps of red hair which crept from under her head-dress.

'And you, Fidelma of Cashel, sister of our king

Colgú . . .' Nechtan spread his hands in a gesture which seemed designed to extend his remorse. 'You were a young novice when you came to this territory as one of the retinue of the great Brehon Morann, chief of the judges of the five kingdoms. I was enamoured by your youth and beauty; what man would not be? I sought you out in your chamber at night, abusing all laws of hospitality, and tried to seduce you . . .'

Fidelma raised her jaw; a tinge of red showed on her cheeks as she recalled the incident vividly.

'Seduce?' Her voice was icy. The term which Nechtan had used was a legal one – *sleth* – which denoted an attempted intercourse by stealth. 'Your unsuccessful attempt was more one of *forcor*.'

Nechtan blinked rapidly and for a moment his face dissolved into a mask of irritation before resuming its pale, placid expression. *Forcor* was a forcible rape, a crime of a violent nature, and had Fidelma not, even at that early age, been accomplished in the art of the *troid-sciathagid*, the ancient form of unarmed combat, then rape might well have resulted from Nechtan's unwelcome attention. As it was, Nechtan was forced to lie indisposed for three days after his nocturnal visit and bearing the bruises of Fidelma's defensive measures.

Nechtan bowed his head, as if contritely.

'It was a wrong, good Sister,' he acknowledged, 'and I can only admit my actions and plead for your forgiveness.'

Fidelma, in spite of her internal struggle, reflecting on the teachings of the Faith, could not bring herself to indicate any forgiveness on her part. She remained silent, staring at Nechtan in ill-concealed disgust. A firm suspicion was now entering her mind that Nechtan, this evening, was performing some drama for his own end. Yet for what purpose?

Nechtan's mouth quirked in a fleeting gesture of amusement, as if he knew her angry silence would be all the response that he would receive from her.

He paused a moment before turning to the fiery, red-haired man seated on her left. Daolgar, as Fidelma knew, was a man of fierce temper, given to action rather than reflection. He was quick to take offence but equally quick to forgive. Fidelma knew him as a warm-hearted, generous man.

'Daolgar, chieftain of Sliabh Luachra and my good neighbour,' Nechtan greeted him, but there seemed irony in his tone. 'I have wronged you by encouraging the young men of my clan to constantly raid your territory, to harass your people in order to increase our lands and to steal your cattle herds.'

Daolgar gave a long, inward sniff through his nostrils. It was an angry sound. His muscular body was poised as if he were about to spring forward.

'That you admit this thing, a matter known to my people, is a step in the right direction towards reconciliation, Nechtan. I will not let personal enmity stand in the way of a truce between us. All I ask is that such a truce be supervised by an impartial Brehon. Needless to say, on behalf of my people, compensation for the lost cattle, the deaths in combat, must also be agreed . . .'

'Just so,' Nechtan interrupted curtly.

Nechtan now ignored Daolgar, turning to the young man who, having filled his goblet, had resumed his place.

'And now to you, Cuill, I have also made grievous injury, for our entire clan knows that I have seduced your wife and taken her to live in my house to the shame of your family before our people.'

The young, handsome man was sitting stiffly on the other side of Daolgar. He tried to keep his composure but his face was red with a mixture of mortification and a liberal amount of wine. Cuill was already known to Fidelma by reputation as a promising decorative artist whose talents had been sought by many a chieftain, bishop and abbot in order to create monuments of lasting beauty for them.

'She allowed herself to be seduced,' Cuill replied sullenly. 'Only in seeking to keep me ignorant of the affair was harm done to me. That matter was remedied when she left me and went to dwell in your house, forsaking her children. Infatuation is a terrible thing.'

'You do not say "love"?' queried Nechtan sharply. 'Then you do not concede that she loves me?'

'She was inspired with a foolish passion which deprived her of sound judgement. No. I do not call it love. I call it infatuation.'

'Yet you love her still.' Nechtan smiled thinly, as if purposely mocking Cuill. 'Even though she dwells in my house. Ah well, have no fear. After tonight I shall suggest that she returns to your house. I think my . . . infatuation . . . with her is ended.'

Nechtan seemed to take amusement from the young man's controlled anger. Cuill's knuckles showed white where he gripped the sides of his chair. But Nechtan seemed to tire of his ill-concealed enjoyment and now he turned to the last of the guests – the slim, dark-haired warrior at his right side.

'So to you, Marbán.'

Marbán was *tánaiste*, heir elect to Nechtan's chieftaincy. The warrior stirred uncomfortably.

'You have done me no wrong,' he interrupted with a tight, sullen voice.

Nechtan's plump face assumed a woebegone look.

'Yet I have. You are my *tánaiste*, my heir apparent. When I am gone, you will be chieftain in my stead.'

'A long time before that,' Marbán said, evasively. 'And no wrong done.'

'Yet I have wronged you,' insisted Nechtan. 'Ten years ago, when we came together before the clan assembly so that the assembly could choose which of us was to be chief and which was to be *tánaiste*, it was you who the assembly favoured. You were the clear choice to be chieftain. I discovered this before the assembly met and so I paid bribes to many in order that I might be elected chieftain. So I came to office while you, by default, became the second choice. For ten years I have kept you at my side when you should have ruled in my place.'

Fidelma saw Marbán's face whiten but there was no registration of surprise on his features. Clearly the *tánaiste* already knew of Nechtan's wrongdoing. She saw the anger and hatred pass across his features even though he sought to control the emotions.

Fidelma felt that she had no option but to speak up and she broke the silence by clearing her throat. When all eyes were turned on her she said in a quiet, authoritative tone:

'Nechtan of the Múscraige, you have asked us here to forgive you certain wrongs which you have done to each of us. Some are a matter for simple Christian forgiveness. However, as a *dálaigh*, an advocate of the courts of this land, I have to point out to you that not all your misdeeds, which you have admitted freely at this table, can be dealt with that simply. You have confessed that you should not legally be chieftain of the Múscraige. You have confessed that, even if you were legally chieftain, you have indulged in activities which did not promote the commonwealth of your people, such as encouraging illegal cattle raids into the territory of Daolgar of Sliabh Luachra. This in itself is a serious crime for which you may have to appear before the assembly and my brother, Colgú, King of Cashel, and you could be dismissed from your office . . .'

Nechtan held up his plump hand and stayed her.

'You had ever the legal mind, Fidelma. And it is right that you should point out this aspect of the law to me. I accept your knowledge. But before the ramifications of this feast of forgiveness are felt, my main aim was to recognise before you all what I have done. Come what may, I concede this. And now I will raise my goblet to each and every one of you, acknowledging what I have done to you all. After that, your law may take its course and I will rest content in that knowledge.'

He reached forward, picked up his goblet and raised it in salutation to them.

'I drink to you all. I do so contritely and then you may have joy of your law.'

No one spoke. Sister Fidelma raised a cynical eyebrow at Nechtan's dramatic gesture. It was as if they were watching a bad play.

The chieftain swallowed loudly. Almost immediately the goblet fell from his hand and his pale eyes were suddenly wide and staring, his mouth was open and he was making a terrible gasping sound, one hand going up to his throat. Then, as if a violent seizure racked his body, he fell backwards, sending his chair flying as he crashed to the floor.

For a moment there was a deadly stillness in the feasting hall.

It was Gerróc, the chieftain's physician, who seemed to recover his wits first. He was on his knees by Nechtan in a moment. Yet it didn't need a physician's training to know that Nechtan was dead. The contorted features, staring dead eyes, and twisted limbs showed that death had claimed him.

Daolgar, next to Fidelma, grunted in satisfaction.

'God is just, after all,' he remarked evenly. 'If ever a man needed to be helped into the Otherworld, it was this man.' He glanced quickly at Fidelma and half-shrugged as he saw her look of reproach. 'You'll pardon me if I speak my mind, Sister? I am not truly a believer in the concept of forgiveness of sins. It depends much on the sins and the perpetrator of them.'

Fidelma's attention had been distracted by Daolgar but, as she was turning back towards Gerróc, she noticed that young Dathó was whispering anxiously to his mother Ess, who was shaking her head. Her hand seemed to be closed around a small shape hidden in her pocket.

Gerróc had risen to his feet and was glaring suspiciously at Daolgar.

'What do you mean "*helped* into the Otherworld", Daolgar?' he demanded, his tone tight with some suppressed emotion.

Daolgar gestured dispassionately.

'A figure of speech, physician. God has punished Nechtan in his own way with some seizure. A heart-attack, or so it appears. That was help enough. And as for whether Nechtan deserved to be so stricken – why, who around this table would doubt it? He has wronged us all.'

Gerróc shook his head slowly.

'It was no seizure brought on by the whim of God,' he said quietly. Then he added: 'No one should touch any more of the wine.'

They were all regarding the physician with confusion, trying to comprehend his meaning.

Gerróc responded to their unarticulated question.

'Nechtan's cup was poisoned,' he said. 'He has been murdered.'

After a moment's silence, Fidelma rose slowly from her place and went to where Nechtan lay. There was a blue tinge to his lips, which were drawn back, revealing discoloured gums and teeth. The twisted features of his once cherubic face were enough for her to realise that his brief death agony had been induced in a violent form. She reached towards the fallen goblet. A little wine still lay in its bowl. She dipped her finger in it and sniffed at it suspiciously. There was a bitter-sweet fragrance which she could not identify.

She gazed up at the physician.

'Poison, you say?' She did not really need such confirmation.

He nodded quickly.

She drew herself up and gazed round at the disconcerted faces of her fellow guests. Bewildered though they were, not one did she see there whose face reflected grief or anguish for the death of the chieftain of the Múscraige.

Everyone had risen uncertainly to their feet now, not knowing what to do.

It was Fidelma who spoke first in her quiet, firm tone.

'As an advocate of the court, I will take charge here. A crime has been committed. Each one in this room has a motive to kill Nechtan.'

'Including yourself,' pointed out young Dathó immediately. 'I object to being questioned by one who might well be the culprit. How do we know that you did not poison his cup?'

Fidelma raised her eyebrows in surprise at the young man's accusation. Then she considered it slowly for a moment before nodding in acceptance of the logic.

'You are quite right, Dathó. I also had a motive. And until we can discover how the poison came to be in this cup, I cannot prove that I did not have the means. Neither, for that matter, can anyone else in this room. For over an hour we have been at this table, each having a clear sight of one another, each drinking the same wine. We should be able to reason how Nechtan was poisoned.'

Marbán was nodding rapidly in agreement.

'I agree. We should heed Sister Fidelma. I am now chieftain of the Múscraige. So I say we should let Fidelma sort this matter out.'

'You are chieftain unless it can be proved that you killed Nechtan,' interrupted Daolgar of Sliabh Luachra with scorn. 'After all, you were seated next to him. You had motive and opportunity.'

Marbán retorted angrily: 'I am now chieftain until the assembly says otherwise. And I say that Sister Fidelma also has authority until the assembly says otherwise. I suggest that we resume our places at the table and allow Fidelma to discover by what means Nechtan was poisoned.'

'I disagree,' snapped Dathó. 'If she is the guilty one then she may well attempt to lay the blame on one of us.'

'Why blame anyone? Nechtan deserved to die!' It was Ess, the former wife of the dead chieftain, who spoke sharply. 'Nechtan deserved to die,' she repeated emphatically. 'He deserved to die a thousand times over. No one in this room would more gladly see him dispatched to the Otherworld than I. And I would joyfully accept responsibility for the deed if I had done it. Little blame to whoever did this deed. They have rid the world of a vermin, a parasite who has caused much suffering and anguish. We, in this room, should be their witnesses that no crime was committed here, only natural justice. Let the one who did this deed admit to it and we will all support their cause.'

They all stared cautiously at one another. Certainly none appeared to disagree with Ess's emotional plea but none appeared willing to confess to the deed.

Fidelma pursed her lips as she considered the matter under law.

'In such a case, we would all need to testify to the wrongs enacted by Nechtan. Then the guilty one would go free simply on the payment of Nechtan's honour price to his family. That would be the sum of fourteen *cumal* . . .'

Ess's son, Dathó, interrupted with a bitter laugh.

'Perhaps some among us do not have a herd of forty-two milch cows to pay in compensation. What then? If compensation is not paid, the law exacts other punishment from the guilty.'

Marbán now smiled expansively.

'I would provide that much compensation merely to be rid of Nechtan,' he confessed without embarrassment. With Nechtan's death, Fidelma noticed, the usually taciturn warrior was suddenly more decisive in manner.

'Then,' Cuill, the young artist who had so far been silent, leant forward eagerly, 'then whoever did this deed, let them speak and admit it, and let us all contribute to exonerating them. I agree with Ess – Nechtan was an evil man who deserved to die.'

There was a silence while they examined each other's faces, waiting for someone to admit their guilt.

'Well?' demanded Daolgar, impatiently, after a while. 'Come forward whoever did this and let us resolve the matter and be away from this place.'

No one spoke.

It was Fidelma who broke the silence with a low sigh.

'Since no one will admit this deed . . .'

She did not finish for Marbán interrupted again.

'Better it was admitted.' His voice was almost cajoling. 'Whoever it was, my offer to stand behind them holds. Indeed, I will pay the entire compensation fee.'

Sister Fidelma saw Ess compressing her lips; her hand slid to the bulge on her thigh, her slender fingers wrapping themselves around the curiously shaped lump which reposed in her pocket. She had began to open her mouth to speak when her son, Dathó, thrust forward.

'Very well,' he said harshly. 'I will admit to the deed. I killed Nechtan, my father. I had more cause to hate him than any of you.'

There was a loud gasp of astonishment. It was from Ess. She was staring in surprise at her son. Fidelma saw that the others around the table had relaxed at his confession and seemed relieved.

Fidelma's eyes narrowed as she gazed directly into the face of the young man.

'Tell me how you gave him the poison?' she invited in a conversational voice.

The young man frowned in bewilderment.

'What matters? I admit the deed.'

'Admission must be supported by evidence,' Fidelma countered softly. 'Let us know how you did this.'

Dathó shrugged indifferently.

'I put poison into his cup of wine.'

'What type of poison?'

Dathó blinked rapidly. He hesitated a moment.

136

'Speak up!' prompted Fidelma irritably.

'Why . . . hemlock, of course.'

Sister Fidelma shifted her gaze to Ess. The woman's eyes had not left her son since his confession. She had been staring at him with a strained, whitened face.

'And is that a vial of hemlock which you have in your thigh pocket, Ess?' Fidelma snapped.

Ess gave a gasp and her hand went immediately to her pocket. She hesitated and then shrugged as if in surrender.

'What use in denying it?' she asked. 'How did you know I had the vial of hemlock?'

Dathó almost shouted: 'No. I asked her to hide it after I had done the deed. It has nothing to do—'

Fidelma raised a hand and motioned him to silence.

'Let me see it,' she pressed.

Ess took a small glass vial from her pocket and placed it on the table. Fidelma reached forward and picked it up. She took out the stopper and sniffed gently at the receptacle.

'Indeed, it is hemlock,' she confirmed. 'But the bottle is full.'

'My mother did not do this!' cried Dathó angrily. 'I did! I admit as much! The guilt is mine!'

Fidelma shook her head sadly at him.

'Sit down, Dathó. You are seeking to take the blame on yourself because your mother had a vial of hemlock on her person and you suspect that she killed your father. Is this not so?'

Dathó's face drained of colour and his shoulders dropped as he slumped back into his seat.

'Your fidelity is laudable,' went on Fidelma compassionately. 'However, I do not think that your mother, Ess, is the murderess. Especially since the vial is still full.'

Ess was staring blankly at Fidelma. Fidelma responded with a gentle smile.

'I believe that you came here tonight with the intention of trying to poison your former husband as a matter of vengeance. Dathó saw that you had the vial which you were attempting to hide after the deed was done. I saw the two of you arguing over it. However, you had no opportunity to place the hemlock in Nechtan's goblet. Importantly, it was not hemlock that killed him.'

She turned, almost sharply. 'Isn't that so, Gerróc?'

The elderly physician started and glanced quickly at her before answering.

'Hemlock, however strong the dose, does not act instantaneously,' he agreed pedantically. 'This poison was more virulent than hemlock.' He pointed to the goblet. 'You have already noticed the little crystalline deposits, Sister? It is realgar, what is known as the "powder of the caves", used by those creating works of art as a colourant but, taken internally, it is a quick-acting poison.'

Fidelma nodded slowly as if he were simply confirming what she knew already and then she turned her gaze back to those around the table. However, their eyes were focused towards the young artist, Cuill.

Cuill's face was suddenly white and pinched.

'I hated him but I would never take a life,' he stammered. 'I uphold the old ways, the sanctity of life, however evil it is.'

'Yet this poison is used as a tool by artists like yourself,' Marbán pointed out. 'Who among us would know this other than Gerróc and yourself? Why deny it if you did kill him? Have we not said that we would support one another in this? I have already promised to pay the compensation on behalf of the person who did the deed.'

'What opportunity had I to put it in Nechtan's goblet?' demanded Cuill. 'You had as much opportunity as I had.'

Fidelma raised a hand to quell the sudden hubbub of accusation and counter-accusation.

'Cuill has put his finger on the all-important question,' she said calmly but firmly enough to silence them. They had all risen again and so she instructed: 'Be seated.'

Slowly, almost unwillingly, they obeyed.

Fidelma stood at the spot in which Nechtan had sat.

'Let us consider the facts,' she began. 'The poison was in the wine goblet. Therefore, it is natural enough to assume that it was in the wine. The wine is contained in that pitcher there.'

She pointed to where the attendant had left the wine pitcher on a side table.

'Marbán, call in the attendant, for it was he who filled Nechtan's goblet.'

Marbán did so.

The attendant was a young man named Ciar, a dark-haired and nervous young man. He seemed to have great trouble in speaking when he saw what had happened in the room and he kept clearing his throat nervously.

'You served the wine this evening, didn't you, Ciar?' demanded Fidelma.

The young man nodded briefly. 'You all saw me do so,' he confirmed, pointing out the obvious.

'Where did the wine come from? Was it a special wine?'

'No. It was bought a week ago from a Gaulish merchant.'

'And did Nechtan drink the same wine as was served to his guests?'

'Yes. Everyone drank the same wine.'

'From the same pitcher?'

'Yes. Everyone had wine from the same pitcher during the evening,' Ciar confirmed. 'Nechtan was the last to ask for more wine from the pitcher and I noticed that it was nearly empty after I filled his goblet. I asked him if I should refill it but he sent me away.'

Marbán pursed his lips, reflectively.

'This is true, Fidelma. We were all a witness to that.'

'But Nechtan was not the last to drink wine from that pitcher,' replied Fidelma. 'It was Cuill.'

Daolgar exclaimed and turned to Cuill.

'Fidelma is right. After Ciar filled Nechtan's goblet and

left, and while Nechtan was talking to Dathó, Cuill rose from his seat and walked around Nechtan to fill his goblet from the pitcher of wine. We were all concentrating on what Nechtan had to say; no one would have noticed if Cuill had slipped the poison into Nechtan's goblet. Cuill not only had the motive, but the means and the opportunity.'

Cuill flushed. 'It is a lie!' he responded.

But Marbán was nodding eagerly in agreement.

'We have heard that this poison is of the same material as used by artists for colouring their works. Isn't Cuill an artist? And he hated Nechtan for running off with his wife. Isn't that motive enough?'

'There is one flaw to the argument,' Sister Fidelma said quickly.

'Which is?' demanded Dathó.

'I was watching Nechtan as he made his curious speech asking forgiveness. But I observed Cuill pass behind Nechtan and he did not interfere with Nechtan's goblet. He merely helped himself to what remained of the wine from the pitcher, which he then drank, thus confirming, incidentally, that the poison was placed in Nechtan's goblet and not the wine.'

Marbán was looking at her without conviction.

'Give me the pitcher and a new goblet,' instructed Fidelma, irritably.

When it was done she poured the dregs which remained in the bottom of the pitcher into the goblet and considered them a moment before dipping her finger in them and gently touching her finger with her tongue.

She smiled complacently at the company.

'As I have said, the poison is not in the wine,' she reiterated. 'The poison was placed in the goblet itself.'

'Then how was it placed there?' demanded Gerróc in exasperation.

In the silence that followed, Fidelma turned to the attendant. 'I do not think that we need trouble you further, Ciar, but wait outside. We will have need of you later. Do not mention anything of this matter to anyone yet. Is that understood?'

Ciar cleared his throat noisily.

'Yes, Sister.' He hesitated. 'But what of the Brehon Olcán? He has just arrived. Should I not inform him?'

Fidelma frowned.

'Who is this judge?'

Marbán touched her sleeve.

'Olcán is a friend of Nechtan's, a chief judge of the Múscraige. Perhaps we should invite him in? After all, it is his right to judge this matter.'

Fidelma's eyes narrowed.

'Was he invited here this night?' she demanded.

It was Ciar who answered her question.

'Only after the meal began. Nechtan requested me to have a messenger sent to Olcán. The message was to ask the judge to come here.'

Fidelma thought rapidly and then said: 'Have him wait then but he is not to be told what has happened here until I say so.'

After Ciar had left she turned back to the expectant faces of her erstwhile meal guests.

'So we have learnt that the poison was not in the wine but in the goblet. This narrows the field of our suspects.'

Daolgar of Sliabh Luachra frowned slightly.

'What do you mean?'

'Simply that if the poison was placed in the goblet then it had to be placed there after the time that Nechtan drained one goblet of wine and when he called Ciar to refill his goblet. The poison had to be placed there after the goblet was refilled.'

Daolgar of Sliabh Luachra leant back in his chair and suddenly laughed hollowly.

'Then I have the solution. There are only two others in this room who had the opportunity to place the poison in

141

Nechtan's goblet,' he said smugly.

'And those are?' Fidelma prompted.

'Why, either Marbán or Gerróc. They were seated on either side of Nechtan. Easy for them to slip the poison into the goblet which stood before them while we were concentrating on what he had to say.'

Marbán had flushed angrily but it was the elderly physician, Gerróc, who suffered the strongest reaction.

'I can prove that it was not I!' he almost sobbed, his voice breaking pathetically in indignation.

Fidelma turned to regard him in curiosity.

'You can?'

'Yes, yes. You have said that we all had a reason to hate Nechtan and that implies that we would all therefore wish him dead. That gives every one of us a motive for his murder.'

'That is so,' agreed Fidelma.

'Well, I alone of all of you knew that it was a waste of time to kill Nechtan.'

There was a pause before Fidelma asked patiently: 'Why would it be a waste of time, Gerróc?'

'Why kill a man who was already dying?'

'*Already* dying?' prompted Fidelma after the exclamations of surprise had died away.

'I was physician to Nechtan. It was true that I hated him. He cheated me of my fees but, nevertheless, as physician here, I lived well. I did not complain. I am advancing in years now. I was not going to imperil my security by accusing my chieftain of wrongdoing. However, a month ago, Nechtan started to have terrible headaches, and once or twice the pain was so unbearable that I had to strap him to his bed. I examined him and found a growth at the back of the skull. It was a malignant tumour for within a week I could chart its expansion. If you do not believe me, you may examine him for yourselves. The tumour is easy to discern behind his left ear.'

Fidelma bent over the chief and examined the swelling behind the ear with repugnance.

'The swelling is there,' she confirmed.

'So, what are you saying, Gerróc?' Marbán demanded, seeking to bring the old physician to a logical conclusion.

'I am saying that a few days ago I had to tell Nechtan that it was unlikely he would see another new moon. He was going to die anyway. The growth of the tumour was continuing and causing him increased agony. I knew he was going to die soon. Why need I kill him? God had already chosen the time and method.'

Daolgar of Sliabh Luachra turned to Marbán with grim satisfaction on his face.

'Then it leaves only you, *tánaiste* of the Múscraige. You clearly did not know that your chieftain was dying and so you had both the motive and the opportunity.'

Marbán had sprung to his feet, his hand at his waist where his sword would have hung had they not been in the feasting hall. It was a law that no weapons were ever carried into a feasting hall.

'You will apologise for that, chieftain of Sliabh Luachra!'

Cuill, however, was nodding rapidly in agreement with Daolgar's logic.

'You were very quick to offer your newfound wealth as chieftain to pay the compensation should anyone else confess. Had they done so, it would have solved a problem, wouldn't it? You would emerge from this without a blemish. You would be confirmed as chieftain of the Múscraige. However, if you were guilty of causing Nechtan's death then you would immediately be deposed from holding any office. That is why you were so eager to put the blame on to me.'

Marbán stood glowering at the assembly. It was clear that he now stood condemned in the eyes of them all. An angry muttering had arisen as they confronted him.

Sister Fidelma raised both her hands to implore silence.

'Let us not quarrel when there is no need. Marbán did not kill Nechtan.'

There was a brief moment of surprised silence.

'Then who did?' demanded Dathó angrily. 'You seem to be playing cat and mouse with us, Sister. If you know so much, tell us who killed Nechtan.'

'Everyone at this table will concede that Nechtan was an evil, self-willed man who was at war with life. As much as we all had reason to hate him, he hated everyone around him with equal vehemence.'

'But who killed him?' repeated Daolgar.

Sister Fidelma grimaced sorrowfully.

'Why, he killed himself.'

The shock and disbelief registered on everyone's faces.

'I had begun to suspect,' went on Fidelma, 'but I could find no logical reason to support my suspicion until Gerróc gave it to me just now.'

'Explain, Sister,' demanded Marbán wearily, 'for I cannot follow the same logic.'

'As I have said, as much as we hated Nechtan, Nechtan hated us. When he learnt that he was to die anyway, he decided that he would have one more great revenge on those people he disliked the most. He preferred to go quickly to the Otherworld than to die the lingering death which Gerróc doubtless had described to him. If it takes a brave man to set the boundaries to his own life, then Nechtan was brave enough. He chose a quick-acting poison, realgar, delighting in the fact it was a substance that Cuill, the husband of his current mistress, often used.

'He devised a plan to invite us all here for a last meal, playing on our curiosity or our egos by saying that he wanted to make public reparation and apology for those wrongs that he had done to us. He planned the whole thing. He then recited his wrongdoing against us, not to seek forgiveness, but to ensure that we all knew that each had cause to hate him and seek his destruction. He wanted to plant seeds of suspicion in all our minds. He made his recitation of wrongdoing sound more like a boast than an apology. A boast and a warning.'

Ess was in agreement.

'I thought his last words were strange at the time,' she said, 'but now they make sense.'

'They do so now,' Fidelma endorsed.

'What were the words again?' queried Daolgar.

'Nechtan said: "And now I will raise my goblet to each and every one of you, acknowledging what I have done to you all. After that, your law may take its course and I will rest content in that knowledge . . . I drink to you all . . . and then you may have joy of your law.'

It was Fidelma who was able to repeat the exact words.

'It certainly does not sound like an apology,' admitted Marbán. 'What did he mean?'

It was Ess who answered.

'I see it all now. Do you not understand how evil this man was? He wanted one or all of us to be blamed for his death. That was his final act of spite and hatred against us.'

'But how?' asked Gerróc, confused. 'I confess, I am at a loss to understand.'

'Knowing that he was dying, that he had only a few days or weeks at most, he set his own limits to his lifespan,' Fidelma explained patiently. 'He was an evil, spiteful man, as Ess acknowledges. He invited us to this meal, knowing that, at its close, he would take poison. As the meal started, he asked Ciar, the attendant, to send for his own judge, Brehon Olcán, hoping that Olcán would find us in a state of confusion, each suspecting the other, and come to a wrong decision that one or all of us were concerned in his murder. Nechtan killed himself in the hope that we would be found culpable of his death. While he was talking to us he secreted the poison in his own goblet.'

Fidelma looked around the grim faces at the table. Her smile was strained.

145

'I think we can now speak with the Brehon Olcán and sort this matter out.'

She turned towards the door, paused and looked back at those in the room.

'I have encountered much wrongdoing in this world, some of it born of evil, some born of desperation. But I have to say that I have never truly encountered such malignancy as dwelt in the spirit of Nechtan, sometime chieftain of the Múscraige.'

It was the following morning as Fidelma was riding in the direction of Cashel that she encountered the old physician, Gerróc, at a crossroads below the fortress of Nechtan.

'Whither away, Gerróc?' she greeted with a smile.

'I am going to the monastery of Imleach,' replied the old man gravely. 'I shall make confession and seek sanctuary for the rest of my days.'

Fidelma pursed her lips thoughtfully.

'I would not confess too much,' she said enigmatically.

The old physician gazed at her with a frown.

'You know?' he asked sharply.

'I know a boil which can be lanced from a tumour,' she replied.

The old man sighed softly.

'At first I only meant to put fear into Nechtan. To make him suffer a torment of the mind for a few weeks before I lanced his boil or it burst of its own accord. Boils against the back of the ear can be painful. He believed me when I pretended it was a tumour and he had not long to live. I did not know the extent of his evil mind nor that he would kill himself to spite us all.'

Fidelma nodded slowly.

'His blood is still on his own hands,' she said, seeing the old man's troubled face.

'But the law is the law. I should make confession.'

'Sometimes justice takes precedence over the law,'

Fidelma replied cheerfully. 'Nechtan suffered justice. Forget the law, Gerróc, and may God give you peace in your declining years.'

She raised a hand, almost in blessing, turned her horse and continued on her way towards Cashel.

Those that Trespass

'The matter is clear to me. I cannot understand why the abbot should be bothered to send you here.'

Father Febal was irritable and clearly displeased at the presence of the advocate in his small church, especially an advocate in the person of the attractive, red-haired religieuse who sat before him in the stuffy vestry. In contrast to her relaxed, almost gentle attitude, he exuded an attitude of restlessness and suspicion. He was a short, swarthy man with pale, almost cadaverous features, the stubble of his beard, though shaven, was blue on his chin and cheeks and his hair was dark like the colour of a raven's wing. His eyes were deep set but dark and penetrating. When he expressed his irritability his whole body showed his aggravation.

'Perhaps it is because the matter is as unclear to the abbot as it appears clear to you,' Sister Fidelma replied in an innocent tone. She was unperturbed by the aggressive attitude of the priest.

Father Febal frowned; his narrowed eyes scanned her features rapidly, seeking out some hidden message. However, Fidelma's face remained a mask of unaffected candour. He compressed his lips sourly.

'Then you can return to the abbot and report to him that he has no need for concern.'

Fidelma smiled gently. There was a hint of a shrug in the position of her shoulders.

'The abbot takes his position as father of his flock very seriously. He would want to know more details of this tragedy before he could be assured that he need not concern himself. As the matter is so clear to you, perhaps you will explain it to me?'

Father Febal gazed at the religieuse, hearing for the first time the note of cold determination in her soft tones.

He was aware that Sister Fidelma was not merely a religieuse but a qualified advocate of the Brehon Law courts of the five kingdoms. Furthermore, he knew that she was the young sister of King Colgú of Cashel himself, otherwise he might have been more brusque in his responses to the young woman. He hesitated a moment or two and then shrugged indifferently.

'The facts are simple. My assistant, Father Ibor, a young and indolent man, went missing the day before yesterday. I had known for some time that there had been something troubling him, something distracting him from his priestly duties. I tried to talk to him about it but he refused to be guided by me. I came to the church that morning and found that the golden crucifix from our altar and the silver chalice, with which we dispense the communion wine, were both missing. Once I found that Father Ibor had also vanished from our small community here, it needed no great legal mind to connect the two events. He had obviously stolen the sacred objects and fled.'

Sister Fidelma inclined her head slowly.

'Having come to this conclusion, what did you do then?'

'I immediately organised a search. Our little church here is attended by Brother Finnlug and Brother Adag. I called upon them to help me. Before entering the order, Finnlug was master huntsman to the Lord of Maine, an excellent tracker and huntsman. We picked up the trail of Ibor and followed it to the woods nearby. We were only a short distance into the woods when we came across his body. He was hanging from the branch of a tree with the cord of his habit as a noose.'

Sister Fidelma was thoughtful.

'And how did you interpret this sight?' she asked quietly.

Father Febal was puzzled.

'How should I interpret this sight?' he demanded.

Fidelma's expression did not change.

'You tell me that you believe that Father Ibor stole the crucifix and chalice from the church and ran off.'

'That is so.'

'Then you say that you came across him hanging on a tree.'

'True again.'

'Having stolen these valuable items and run off, why would he hang himself? There seems some illogic in this action.'

Father Febal did not even attempt to suppress a sneer.

'It would be as obvious to you as it was to me.'

'I would like to hear what you thought.' Fidelma did not rise to his derisive tone.

Father Febal smiled thinly.

'Why, Father Ibor was overcome with remorse. Knowing that we would track him down, realising how heinous his crime against the Church was, he gave up to despair and pronounced his own punishment. He therefore hanged himself. In fact, so great was his fear that we would find him still alive, he even stabbed himself as he was suffocating in the noose, the knife entering his heart.'

'He must have bled a lot from such a wound. Was there much blood on the ground?'

'Not as I recall.' There was distaste in the priest's voice as if he felt the religieuse was unduly occupied with gory details. 'Anyway, the knife lay on the ground below the body where it had fallen from his hand.'

Fidelma did not say anything for a long while. She remained gazing thoughtfully at the priest. Father Febal

151

glared back defiantly but it was he who dropped his eyes first.

'Was Father Ibor such a weak young man?' Fidelma mused softly.

'Of course. What else but weakness would have caused him to act in this manner?' demanded the priest.

'So? And you recovered both the crucifix and chalice from his person, then?'

A frown crossed Father Febal's features as he hesitated a moment. He made a curiously negative gesture with one hand.

Fidelma's eyes widened and she bent forward.

'You mean that you did not recover the missing items?' she pressed sharply.

'No,' admitted the priest.

'Then this matter is not at all clear,' she observed grimly. 'Surely, you cannot expect the abbot to rest easy in his mind when these items have not been recovered? How can you be so sure that it was Father Ibor who stole them?'

Fidelma waited for an explanation but none was forthcoming.

'Perhaps you had better tell me how you deem this matter is clear then?' Her voice was acerbic. 'If I am to explain this clarity to the abbot, I must also be clear in my own mind. If Father Ibor felt that his apprehension was inevitable and he felt constrained to inflict the punishment of death on himself when he realised the nearness of your approach, what did he do with the items he had apparently stolen?'

'There is one logical answer,' muttered Father Febal without conviction.

'Which is?'

'Having hanged himself, some wandering thief happened by and took the items with him before we arrived.'

'And there is evidence of that occurrence?'

The priest shook his head reluctantly.

'So that is just your supposition?' Now there was just a hint of derision in Fidelma's voice.

'What other explanation is there?' demanded Father Febal
in annoyance.

Fidelma cast a scornful glance at him.

'Would you have me report this to the abbot and inform
him that he need not worry? That a valuable crucifix and a
chalice have been stolen from one of his churches and a priest
has been found hanged but there is no need to worry?'

Father Febal's features grew tight.

'I am satisfied that Father Ibor stole the items and took his
own life in a fit of remorse. I am satisfied that someone then
stole the items after Ibor committed suicide.'

'But I am not,' replied Fidelma bitingly. 'Send Brother
Finnlug to me.'

Father Febal had risen automatically in response to the
commanding tone in her voice. Now he hesitated at the vestry
door.

'I am not used . . .' he began harshly.

'I am not used to being kept waiting,' Fidelma's tone was
icy as she cut in, turning her head away from him in
dismissal. Father Febal blinked and then banged the door
shut behind him in anger.

Brother Finnlug was a wiry-looking individual; his sinewy
body, tanned by sun and wind, proclaimed him to be more a
man used to being out in all sorts of weather than sheltering
in the cloisters of some abbey. Fidelma greeted him as he
entered the vestry.

'I am Fidelma of . . .'

Brother Finnlug interrupted her with a quick, friendly
grin.

'I know well who you are, lady,' he replied. 'I saw you
and your brother, Colgú the King, many times hunting in the
company of my Lord of Maine.'

'Then you know that I am also an advocate of the courts
and that you are duty bound to tell me the truth?'

'I know that much. You are here to inquire about the tragic

death of Father Ibor.' Brother Finnlug was straightforward and friendly in contrast to his superior.

'Why do you call it a tragic death?'

'Is not all death tragic?'

'Did you know Father Ibor well?'

The former huntsman shook his head.

'I knew little of him. He was a young man, newly ordained and very unsure of himself. He was only here about a month.'

'I see. Was he the newest member of the community? For example, how long has Father Febal been here?'

'Father Febal has been priest here for seven years. I came here a year ago and Brother Adag has been here a little more than that.'

'I presume that the members of your little community were on good terms with one another?'

Brother Finnlug frowned slightly and did not reply.

'I mean, I presume that there was no animosity between the four of you?' explained Fidelma.

Finnlug's features wrinkled in an expression which Fidelma was not able to interpret.

'To be truthful, Father Febal liked to emphasise his seniority over us. I believe he entered the Church from some noble family and does not forget it.'

'Was that attitude resented?'

'Not by me. I was in service to the Lord of Maine. I am used to being given orders and to obeying them. I know my place.'

Was there a slight note of bitterness there? Fidelma wondered.

'If I recall rightly, the Lord of Maine was a generous man and those in his service were well looked after. It must have been a wrench for you to leave such an employer to enter religious life?'

Brother Finnlug grimaced.

'Spiritual rewards are often richer than temporal ones. But, as I say, I have been used to service. The same may be said for Brother Adag, who was once a servant to another lord. But he is somewhat of a simpleton.' The monk touched his forehead. 'They say such people are blessed of God.'

'Did Father Ibor get on well with Father Febal?'

'Ah, that I can't say. He was a quiet young man. Kept himself to himself. I do not think he liked Father Febal. I have seen resentment in his eyes.'

'Why would he be resentful? Father Febal was the senior of your community. Father Ibor should have recognised his authority without question.'

The monk shrugged.

'All I can say is that he was hostile to Father Febal's authority.'

'Why do you think that he stole the items from the church?' Fidelma asked the question sharply.

Brother Finnlug's expression did not alter.

He simply spread his arms.

'Who can say what motivates a person to such actions? Who can know the deep secrets of men's hearts?'

'That is what I am here to discover.' Fidelma replied dryly. 'Surely, you must have an idea? Even to hazard a guess?'

'What does Father Febal say?'

'Does it matter what he says?'

'I would have thought that he was closer to Father Ibor than either Brother Adag or myself.'

'Closer? Yet you said there was hostility between them.'

'I did not mean close in the manner of friends. But they were priests together. Of similar social backgrounds, unlike Adag and me. As Brothers of this community, our task was more like that of servants in this church rather than the equals of Fathers Febal and Ibor.'

'I see.' Fidelma frowned thoughtfully. 'I am sure the abbot will be distressed to learn that this is the way your community is governed. We are all servants of God and all one under His Supreme Power.'

'That is not exactly the Faith which Father Febal

espouses.' Now there was clearly bitterness in his voice.

'So you do not know why Ibor might have stolen the items?'

'They were items of great value. They would never be poor on the proceeds of that wealth.'

'*They?*'

'I mean, whoever stole the items.'

'You have a doubt that Father Ibor stole them, then?'

'You are sharp, Sister. Alas, I do not have the precise way with words that you do.'

'Why do you think Father Ibor hanged himself having fled with these valuable items?'

'To avoid capture?'

'Your reply is in the form of a question. You mean that you are not sure of this fact either?'

Brother Finnlug shrugged.

'It is difficult for me to say. I cannot understand why a priest should take his life in any event. Surely no priest would commit such a sin?'

'Would you say that you cannot be sure that Father Ibor took his life?'

Brother Finnlug was startled.

'Did I say that?'

'You implied it. Tell me, in your own words, what happened during the last two days. Had there been any tension between Ibor and Febal or anyone else?'

Finnlug set his jaw firmly and stared at her for a moment.

'I did hear Father Ibor arguing the night before he disappeared.'

Fidelma leant forward, encouragingly.

'Arguing? With Father Febal?'

Brother Finnlug shook his head.

'I cannot be sure. I passed his cell and heard his voice raised. The other voice was quiet and muffled. It was as if Father Ibor had lost his temper but the person he was arguing with was in control.'

'You have no idea who this other person was?'

'None.'

'And you heard nothing of the substance of the argument?'

'I caught only a few words here and there.'

'And what were these words?'

'Nothing that makes sense. Ibor said: "It is the only way". Then he paused and after the other person said something, he replied, "No, no, no. If it has to end, I shall not be the one to end it". That was all I heard.'

Fidelma was quiet as she considered the matter.

'Did you interpret anything from these words, especially in the light of what subsequently happened?'

Brother Finnlug shook his head.

The door of the vestry suddenly opened and Father Febal stood on the threshold, his features wearing a peculiar look of satisfaction. He was clearly a man who had heard some news which pleased him.

'We have found the thief who took the crucifix and chalice from Father Ibor,' he announced.

Brother Finnlug rose swiftly to his feet. His eyes flickered from Father Febal to Sister Fidelma. Fidelma saw something within his expression but could not quite interpret it. Was it fear?

'Bring the thief forth,' she instructed calmly, remaining seated.

Father Febal shook his head.

'That would be impossible.'

'Impossible?' asked Fidelma with a dangerous note to her voice.

'The thief is dead.'

'You'd best explain,' Fidelma invited. 'In detail. Does this thief have a name?'

Father Febal nodded.

'Téite was her name.'

There was a deep intake of breath from Brother Finnlug.

'I take it that you knew her, Brother Finnlug?' Fidelma turned her head inquiringly.

'We all did,' replied Father Febal shortly.

'Who was she?'

'A young girl who lived not far from our community in the forest. She was a seamstress. She sewed garments and laundered clothes for us.'

'Where was she found and how was she identified as the thief?'

'Her cabin is within a short distance of where we found Father Ibor,' explained the priest. 'I understand from Brother Adag that she had picked up some garments from the community and when she did not return with them this morning, as she had arranged, Brother Adag went to her cabin and found her . . .'

Fidelma raised a hand to silence him.

'Let Brother Adag come forth and tell me his story in his own words. It is proper that I hear this matter at first hand. You and Brother Finnlug may wait outside.'

Father Febal looked uncomfortable.

'I think that you had better be warned, Sister.'

'Warned?' Fidelma's head came up quickly to stare at the priest.

'Brother Adag is slightly simple in nature. In many ways his mind has not matured into adulthood. His role in our community is to do simple manual tasks. He . . . how shall I explain it? . . . has a child's mind.'

'It might be refreshing to speak with one who has remained a child and not developed the contrived attitudes of an adult,' Fidelma smiled thinly. 'Bring him hither.'

Brother Adag was a handsome youth but clearly one who was used to taking orders rather than thinking for himself. His eyes were rounded and seemed to hold an expression of permanent innocence; of inoffensive naïveté. His hands were calloused and showed that he was also a man used to manual work.

'You found the body of the woman, Téite, in her cabin, so I am told?'

158

The young man drew his brows together as if giving earnest consideration to the question before answering.

'Yes, Sister. When she did not arrive here at midday, with some garments which she had collected yesterday and promised to deliver, Father Febal sent me to fetch them. I went to her cabin and she was lying stretched on the floor. There was blood on her clothing. She had been stabbed several times.'

'Ah? So Father Febal sent you to her cabin?'

The youth nodded slowly.

'How old was this woman, Téite? Did you know her?'

'Everyone knew her, Sister, and she was eighteen years and three months of age.'

'You are very exact.' Fidelma smiled at his meticulous diction, as if he considered each word almost before he uttered it.

'Téite told me her age and, as you ask me for it, I told you.' It was a simple statement of fact.

'Was she pretty?'

The youth blushed a little. He dropped his eyes.

'Very pretty, Sister.'

'You liked her?' pressed Fidelma.

The young man seemed agitated. 'No. No, I didn't.' He protested. His face was crimson.

'Why ever not?'

'It is the Father's rule.'

'Father Febal's rule?'

Brother Adag hung his head and did not reply.

'Rule or not, you still liked her. You may tell me.'

'She was kind to me. She did not make fun like the others.'

'So, what persuaded you that she had stolen the crucifix and chalice from Father Ibor?'

The young brother turned an ingenuous look upon her.

'Why, the chalice was lying by the side of her body in the cabin.'

Fidelma hid her surprise.

'The chalice only?' She swallowed hard. 'Why would someone enter her cottage, kill her and leave such a valuable item by the body?'

Brother Adag clearly did not understand the point she was making. He said nothing.

'What did you do after you found the body?' she continued after a pause.

'Why, I came to tell Father Febal.'

'And left the chalice there?'

Brother Adag sniffed disparagingly.

'I am not stupid. No, I brought it with me. Father Febal has been searching for it these last two days. I brought it back to Father Febal for safekeeping. I even searched for the crucifix but could not find it there.'

'That is all, Adag. Send Father Febal in to me,' Fidelma instructed the youth.

The priest entered a moment later and sat down before Fidelma without waiting to be asked.

'A sad tale,' he muttered. 'But at least the matter should be cleared up to your satisfaction now. You may return to give your report to the abbot.'

'How well did you know this woman, Téite?' asked Fidelma, without commenting.

Father Febal raised his eyebrows a moment and then sighed.

'I have known her since she was a small girl. I went to administer the last rites when her mother died. Téite had barely reached the age of choice then. However, she had a talent with a needle and therefore was able to make a good living. She has lived within the forest these last four years to my knowledge and often repaired or made garments for our community.'

'Did Father Ibor know her?'

Febal hesitated and then gave an odd dismissive gesture with his hand.

'He was a young man. Young men are often attracted to young women.'

Fidelma glanced at the priest curiously.

'So Father Ibor was attracted to the girl?' she asked with emphasis.

'He was in her company more than I found to be usual. I had occasion to reprimand him.'

'Reprimand him? That sounds serious.'

'I felt that he was neglecting his duties to be with the girl.'

'Are you telling me that there was a relationship between Father Ibor and this girl?'

'I am not one to judge such a matter. I know only that they were frequently in one another's company during the past few weeks, almost since the time he arrived at our little community. I felt that he was ignoring his obligation to his community. That is all.'

'Did he resent your admonition?'

'I really have no idea whether he resented my telling him or not. That was not my concern. My concern was to bring him to an awareness of what was expected of him in this community.'

'You did not have an argument about it?'

'An argument? I am . . . I *was* his superior and when I told him of my concern that should have been an end to the matter.'

'Clearly it was not an end to it,' observed Fidelma.

Father Febal gave her an angry look.

'I do not know what you mean.'

'The events that have unfolded since you told Father Ibor that he was spending too much time with Téite have demonstrated that it was not an end to the matter,' Fidelma pointed out coldly. 'Or do you have some other interpretation of these events?'

Father Febal hesitated.

'You are right. You are implying that the two of them were in the plot to steal the artefacts from the church and, having done so, Father Ibor was overcome with remorse and killed himself . . .' The priest's eyes suddenly widened. 'Having killed the girl first,' he added.

Fidelma stroked the side of her nose with a forefinger reflectively.

'It is an explanation,' she conceded. 'But it is not one that I particularly favour.'

'Why not?' demanded the priest.

'The hypothesis would be that the young priest was so enamoured of the girl that they decided to run away, stealing the valuable objects as a means of securing themselves from want and poverty. We would also have to conclude that, having reached as far as the girl's cabin, the young priest is overcome with remorse. He quarrels with the girl and stabs her to death. Then, leaving the precious chalice by her body, yet curiously hiding the crucifix, he wanders into the forest and, after travelling some distance, decides he is so distressed that he hangs himself. Furthermore, while hanging, while suffocating to death, he is able to take out a knife and stab himself through the heart.'

'What is wrong with that surmise?'

Fidelma smiled thinly.

'Let us have Brother Adag back here again. You may stay, Father Febal.'

The ingenuous young monk stood looking from Fidelma to Father Febal with an unstudied innocence.

'I am told that it was you who saw Téite when she came to the community yesterday?'

The boy was thoughtful.

'Yes. It is my task to gather the clothes that need washing or mending and prepare a bundle for Téite.'

'And this you did yesterday morning?'

'Yes.'

'Téite collected them? These were garments for sewing?'

'And two habits for washing. Father Febal and Brother Finnlug had given me . . . They had been torn and one bloodied in the search for Father Ibor.'

'Let me be sure of this,' interrupted Fidelma. 'Téite collected them yesterday morning?'

Brother Adag looked across at Father Febal, dropped his eyes and shifted his weight from one foot to another.

'Yes, yesterday morning.'

'You are sure that she collected them *after* the search had been made for Father Ibor then?'

'Yes. Father Ibor was found the day before.'

'Think carefully,' snapped Father Febal, irritated. 'Think again.'

The young monk flushed and shrugged helplessly.

Father Febal sniffed in annoyance.

'There you are, Sister, you see that little credit may be placed on this simpleton's memory. The clothes must have been taken before we found Father Ibor.'

The young monk whirled around. For a moment Fidelma thought that he was going to attack Father Febal for both hands came up, balled into clenched fists. But he kept them tight against his chest in a defensive attitude. His face was red and there was anger in his eye.

'Simple I may be but at least I cared for Téite.' There was a sob in his voice.

Father Febal took an involuntary step backwards.

'Who did not care for Téite?' Fidelma prompted gently. 'Father Ibor?'

'Of course he did not care. But she cared for him. She loved him. Not like . . .'

The youth was suddenly silent.

'I would take no notice of this boy's foolishness, Sister,' Father Febal interposed blandly. 'We all know what happened.'

'Do we? Since we are talking of people being attracted to this young girl, was Brother Finnlug attracted to her?'

'Finnlug?' Brother Adag grimaced dismissively. 'He has no time for women.'

Father Febal looked pained. 'Brother Finnlug has several faults. Women were certainly not one of them.'

'Faults?' pressed Fidelma with interest. 'What faults does he have then?'

'Alas, if only he had the gift of spirituality we would be

compensated. He was of use to us only in his ability to hunt and gather food for our table. He is not suited to this religious life. Now, I think we have spoken enough. Let us call a halt to this unhappy affair before things are said that may be regretted.'

'We will end it only when we discover the truth of the matter,' replied Fidelma firmly. 'Truth is never to be regretted.' She turned to the youth. 'I know you liked the girl, Téite. Yet now she is dead and has been murdered. Father Febal's rule does not apply now. You owe it to your feelings for her to tell us the truth.'

The boy stuck out his chin.

'I am telling the truth.'

'Of course, you are. You say that Father Ibor did not like Téite?'

'He did not love her as I did.'

'And how did Téite feel about Ibor?'

'She was blinded by Father Ibor's cleverness. She thought that she loved him. I overheard them. He told her to stop . . . stop pestering, that was his word . . . stop pestering him. She thought that she loved him just as Father Febal thought that he loved her.'

The priest rose angrily.

'What are you saying, boy?' he thundered. 'You are crazy!'

'You cannot deny that you told her that you loved her,' Brother Adag replied, not intimidated by the priest's anger. 'I overheard you arguing with her on the day before Father Ibor died.'

Father Febal's eyes narrowed. 'Ah, now you are not so stupid that you forget times and places and events. The boy cannot be trusted, Sister. I would discount his evidence.'

'I loved Téite and can be trusted!' cried Brother Adag.

'I did not love her . . .' Father Febal insisted. 'I do not love anyone.'

'A priest should love all his flock,' smiled Fidelma in gentle rebuke.

'I refer to the licentious love of women. I merely looked after Téite when her mother died. Without me she would not have survived.'

'But you felt, perhaps, that she owed you something?'

Father Febal scowled at her.

'We are not here to speak of Téite but the crime of Father Ibor.'

'Crime? No, I think that we are here to speak of a crime committed against him rather than by him.'

Father Febal paled.

'What do you mean?'

'Téite was murdered. But she was not murdered by Father Ibor. Nor was she responsible for stealing the crucifix or chalice, the latter of which was found so conveniently by her body.'

'How have you worked this out?'

'Send for Brother Finnlug. Then we may all discuss the resolution of this matter.'

They sat in the small vestry facing her: Father Febal, Brother Finnlug and Brother Adag. Their faces all wore expressions of curiosity.

'I grant that people behave curiously,' began Fidelma. 'Even at the best of times their behaviour can be strange. But I doubt that they would behave in the manner that is presented to me.'

She smiled, looking at each of them in turn.

'What is your solution to this matter?' sneered the priest.

'Certainly it would not be one where the murder victim appears alive and well after the murderer has hanged himself.'

Father Febal blinked. 'Adag must be mistaken.'

'No. Father Ibor and the artefacts vanished the day before yesterday? You immediately raised the alarm. Brother Finnlug tracked Ibor through the forest and you found him hanging from a tree. Isn't that right?'

'Quite right.'

165

'Had he killed Téite, as is now being suggested, before he hanged himself, she could not have come to the community yesterday noon to pick up the garments that needed sewing.'

'Why do you discount the fact that Adag might be confused about the day?'

'Because he gave Téite two habits that had been torn and bloodied in the search for Father Ibor, those worn by you and Finnlug when you found him hanging on the tree. Doubtless they will be found in her cabin to prove the point.' Fidelma paused. 'Am I to presume that no one thought to tell the girl that Ibor had just been discovered having hanged himself? She did think she was in love with him.'

'I did not see the girl,' Father Febal replied quickly. 'Brother Adag did.'

'And Brother Adag admits that he loved Téite,' added Brother Finnlug cynically.

The young man raised his head defiantly. 'I do not deny it. But she didn't return my love; she loved Father Ibor who rejected her.'

'And that made you angry?' asked Fidelma.

'Yes. Very angry!' replied Brother Adag vehemently.

Brother Finnlug turned to gaze at his companion in suspicion.

'Angry enough to kill them both?' he whispered.

'No,' Fidelma replied before Brother Adag could put in his denial. 'Ibor and Téite were not killed in anger, but in cold blood. Weren't they, Brother Finnlug?'

Brother Finnlug turned sharply to her, his eyes suddenly dead.

'Why would I know that, Sister Fidelma?'

'Because you killed them both,' she said quietly.

'That's nonsense! Why would I do that?' exploded the monk, after a moment's shocked silence.

'Because when you stole the crucifix and chalice from the church, you were discovered by Father Ibor. You had to kill him. You stabbed him in the heart and then took the body to the forest where you concocted a suicide by hanging. Then you realised the knife wound could not be hidden and so you left the knife lying by his body. As if anyone, hanging by a cord from a tree, would be able to take out a knife and stab themselves in the heart. How, incidentally, was the poor man able to reach the branch to hang himself? No one has reported to me any means whereby he could have climbed up. Think of the effort involved. The body was placed there by someone else.'

She gazed at Father Febal who was deep in thought. He shook his head, denying he could offer an explanation.

Fidelma returned her gaze to Brother Finnlug.

'You concocted an elaborate plan to deceive everyone as to what had truly happened.'

There was a tension in the vestry now.

'You are insane,' muttered Brother Finnlug.

Fidelma smiled gently.

'You were huntsman to the Lord of Maine. We have already discussed what a generous man he was to those in his service. None went in want, not even when the harvest was bad. When I asked you what reason you had to leave such a gainful employer, you said it was because of your spiritual convictions. Do you maintain that? That you rejected the temporal life for the spiritual?'

Father Febal was gazing at Brother Finnlug in bemusement. The monk was silent.

'You also revealed to me, unwittingly, perhaps, your resentment at the structure of this community. If it was a spiritual life you wanted, this was surely not it, was it?'

Father Febal intervened softly.

'The truth was that Finnlug was dismissed by the Lord of Maine for stealing and we took him in here.'

'What does that prove?' demanded Finnlug.

'I am not trying to prove anything. I will tell you what you did. You had initially hoped to get away with the robbery. The motive was simple, as you told me; the sale of those precious artefacts would make you rich for life. That would appease your resentment that others had power and riches but you did not. As I have said, Ibor discovered you and you stabbed him and took his body to the forest. When you returned, you realised that you had his blood on your clothing.

'The theft was now discovered and Father Febal sought your help. The blood was not noticed. Maybe you put on a cloak to disguise it. You, naturally, led him to Father Ibor's body. Everything was going as you planned. Father Ibor had been blamed for the theft. Now Father Febal was led to believe that Ibor must have killed himself in a fit of remorse. Even the fact that Ibor had been stabbed was explained. The fact there was little blood on the ground did not cause any questions. You, meanwhile, could pretend that the blood-stains on your cloak were received in the search for Ibor. Perhaps you, Finnlug, came up with the idea that the missing crucifix and chalice had been taken by some robber.

'The following day, Téite, unaware, came to collect the sewing and washing. Adag had gathered it as usual, including your habit, the bloodstained one. You had not meant the girl to have it. You hurried to her cottage to make sure she did not suspect. Perhaps you had made your plan even before you went there? You killed her and placed the chalice by her side. After all, the crucifix was such as would still give you wealth and property. It was known that Téite and Ibor had some relationship. Everyone would think the worst. All you had to do was return and bide your time until you could leave the community without arousing suspicion.'

Brother Finnlug's face was white.

'You can't prove it,' he whispered without conviction.

'Do I need to? Shall we go and search for the crucifix? Will you tell us where it is . . . or shall I tell you?' She stood up decisively as if to leave the room.

Brother Finnlug groaned, raising his hands to his head.

'All right, all right. It is true. You know it is still hidden in my cell. It was my chance to escape . . . to have some wealth, a good life.'

Father Febal walked slowly with Fidelma to the gate of the complex of buildings which formed the community.

'How did you know where Brother Finnlug had hidden the crucifix?' he asked.

Sister Fidelma glanced at the grave-looking priest and suddenly allowed a swift mischievous grin to flit across her features.

'I didn't,' she confessed.

Father Febal frowned.

'How did you know then . . .? Know it was Finnlug and what he had done?' he demanded.

'It was only an instinct. Certainly it was a deduction based on the facts, such as they were. But had Brother Finnlug demanded that I prove my accusation, I do not think I would have been able to under the strictures of the proceedings of a court of law. Sometimes, in this business of obtaining proof, more depends on what the guilty person thinks you know and believes that you can prove than what you are actually able to prove. Had Brother Finnlug not confessed, I might not have been able to clear up this business at all.'

Father Febal was still staring at her aghast as she raised her hand in farewell and began to stride along the road in the direction of Cashel.

Holy Blood

'Sister Fidelma! How came you here?'

The Abbess Ballgel, standing at the gate of the Abbey of Nivelles, stared at the dusty figure of the young religieuse with open-mouthed surprise.

'I am returning home to Kildare, Ballgel,' replied the tall, slimly built figure, a broad smile of greeting on her travel-stained features. 'I have been in Rome awhile and where else should I come when passing through the land of the Franks on my way to the coast?'

To the surprise of two elderly religieuses standing nearby, the Abbess Ballgel and Sister Fidelma threw their arms around one another and hugged each other with unconcealed joy.

'It is a long time,' observed the abbess.

'Indeed, a long time. I have not seen you since you departed Kildare and left the shores of Éireann to come to this place. Now I am told that you are the abbess.'

'The community elected me to that honour.'

Sister Fidelma became aware that the two sisters who accompanied the abbess were fretting impatiently. She was surprised at their grim faces and anxiety. Abbess Ballgel caught her swift examination of her companions. The group had been leaving the abbey when Fidelma had come upon them.

'I am afraid that you have chosen a bad moment to arrive, Fidelma. We are on our way to the Forest of Seneffe, a little way down the road there. You didn't come by that route, did you?'

Fidelma shook her head.

'No. I came over the hills from Namur where I arrived by boat along the river.'

'Ah!' The abbess looked serious and then she forced a smile. 'Go in and accept our hospitality, Fidelma. I hope to be back before nightfall and then we will talk and catch up on each's other's news.'

Fidelma drew her brows together, sensing a preoccupation in the abbess's voice and manner.

'What is the matter?' she demanded. 'There is something vexing you.'

Ballgel grimaced.

'You had ever a keen eye, Fidelma. A report has just arrived that one of our sisters has been found murdered in the Forest of Seneffe, and another member of our community is missing. We are hurrying there now to discover the truth of this report. So go and rest yourself from your travels and I will join you later.'

Fidelma shook her head quickly.

'Mother Abbess,' she said softly, 'it has been a long time and perhaps you have forgotten. I spent eight years studying law under the Brehon Morann. I have an aptitude for solving conundrums and investigating mysteries. Let me come with you and I will lend you what talent I have to resolve this matter.'

Fidelma and Ballgel had been novices together in the Abbey of Kildare.

'I remember your talent well, Fidelma. In fact, I have often heard your name spoken for we receive many travellers from Éireann here. By all means come with us.'

In fact, Ballgel looked slightly relieved.

'And you may explain the details of this matter as we go,'

172

Fidelma said, putting down her travelling bag within the gate of the abbey before joining the others.

They set off, walking side by side, with the two other religieuses bringing up the rear.

'Who has been reported murdered?' Fidelma began.

'I do not know. I know that early this morning Sister Cessair and Sister Della set off to the Abbey of Fosse. It is the seventeenth day of March and so they were taking the phial of the Holy Blood of Blessed Gertrude to the Brothers of Fosse for the annual blessing and . . .'

Fidelma laid a hand on her friend's arm.

'You are raising more questions than I can keep pace with, Ballgel. Remember that I am a stranger here.'

The abbess was apologetic. 'Let me start at the beginning then. Twenty-five years ago the ruler of this land, Peppin the Elder of Landen, died. His widow, Itta, decided to devote herself to a religious life and came here, to Nivelles, with her daughter, Gertrude. They built our abbey. When Itta died, the Blessed Gertrude became abbess.

'About that time two Brothers from Éireann, Foillan and Ultan, came wandering and preaching the word of God. They decided to stay and Gertrude granted them lands a few miles from here in Fosse, the other side of the forest of Seneffe. Foillan and Ultan gathered many Irish religious there and some were attracted to our abbey as well. It is said that the Blessed Foillan prophesied that Abbess Gertrude, because she so loved and encouraged the Irish missionaries, would die on the same day that the Blessed Patrick died. And it happened as he said it would seven years ago today.'

Abbess Ballgel grew silent for a while until Fidelma encouraged her to continue.

'So Foillan proved to be a prophet?'

'He did not live to see his prophecy fulfilled for he died four years before his beloved Gertrude. He and his three companions were travelling from his Abbey of Fosse through the very same forest that we are entering – the forest of Seneffe – when they were set upon by robbers and murdered. Their bodies were so well hidden in the forest that it took three months before anyone stumbled across them. Foillan's brother Ultan then became the abbot.

'When the Blessed Gertrude died it was agreed between the two abbeys that, as she was the benefactor of both, each anniversary of her death, a phial of her holy blood, taken from her at death to be held behind the high altar at our abbey, would be taken to the Abbey of Fosse and blessed by the abbot in service with his community and then returned here. This was the task which Sister Cessair and Sister Della set out to fulfil this morning.'

'How did you hear that a sister had been murdered in the forest?'

'When midday came, the time of the service at Fosse, and no members of our community had arrived with the holy blood, Brother Sinsear from the Fosse abbey set out to see what delayed them. He found the dead body of one of the sisters by the roadside. He came straightaway to tell us and then immediately returned to alert the community at Fosse.'

'But you do not know which of the poor sisters was killed?'

The abbess shook her head.

'Brother Sinsear was too agitated to say, but merely told our gatekeeper the news before returning.'

By now they had entered the tall, dark brooding forest of Seneffe. The track was fairly straight, though at times it twisted around rocky outcrops, avoiding streams to find a ford in a more accessible place. The afternoon sun was obliterated by the heavy foliage and the day grew cold around them. Fidelma realised that the highway proved an ideal ambush spot for any robbers and it did not surprise her to hear that lives had been lost along this roadway.

Although Irish religious went out into the world unarmed to preach the Faith, most of them were taught the art of *troid-sciathagid* or battle through defence – a method of defending oneself without the use of weapons. Not many religious, thus prepared, fell to bands of marauding thieves and robbers. Clearly from their names, the two sisters had been Irish and must have known some rudiments of the art for it was the custom to have such knowledge before being allowed to take the holy word from the shores of Éireann into the lands of the strangers.

Now they walked silently and swiftly along the forest track, eyes anxiously scanning for any dangers around them.

'Is it not a dangerous path for young sisters to travel?' observed Fidelma after a while.

'No more so than other places,' her friend replied. 'Do not let the death of Foillan colour your thinking. Since his death a decade ago, the robbers were driven from these parts and there have been no further incidents.'

'Until now,' Fidelma added grimly.

'Until now,' sighed Ballgel.

A moment or two later, they rounded a clump of trees which the path had skirted. Not far away they saw a group of religious. There were four or five and they had a cart with them, harnessed to an ass. They clustered under a gnarled oak whose branches formed a canopy over the pathway, so low that one might almost reach up and grab the lower branches. It made this particular section of the forest path even more gloomy and full of shadows.

A tall, florid man, wearing a large gold cross, and clearly one of authority, saw Abbess Ballgel and came hurrying forward.

'Greetings, Mother Abbess. This is a bad business, a profane business.' He spoke in Latin but Fidelma could hear his Frankish accent.

'Abbot Heribert of Fosse,' Ballgel whispered to Fidelma just out of earshot.

'Where is the body?' Ballgel came straight to the point, also speaking in Latin.

Abbot Heribert looked uncomfortable.

'I would prepare yourself . . .' he began.

'I have seen death before,' replied Abbess Ballgel quietly.

He turned and indicated the far side of the oak tree.

Ballgel moved forward in the direction of his hand, followed by Fidelma.

The woman was tied to the oak tree facing away from the path, almost in mockery of a crucifixion. There was blood everywhere. Fidelma screwed her features up in distaste. The woman, who was dressed in the habit of a religieuse, had been systematically mutilated about the face.

'Cut her down!' cried the sharp tone of the Abbess Ballgel. 'At once! Do not leave the poor girl hanging there!'

Two of the monks went forward grimly.

'Who is it?' Fidelma asked. 'Do you recognise her?'

'Oh yes. We have only one sister with hair as golden as that. It is young Sister Cessair. God be merciful to her soul.' She genuflected.

Fidelma pursed her lips thoughtfully. She watched as two male religious cut down the body.

'Wait!' Fidelma called and, turning to the abbess, she said quickly, 'I would examine the body carefully and with some privacy.'

Ballgel raised her eyes in surprise.

'I do not understand.'

'This is a bizarre matter. It might be that she has been . . . brutalised.'

Ballgel passed a hand across her brow as if bewildered but she understood what Fidelma meant.

She called to the monks to set the body down on the ground before the cart and then asked Abbot Heribert to withdraw his men to a respectful distance while Fidelma made her investigation.

Fidelma knelt by the body, noticing that the shade of the oak tree stopped the sun's rays from drying the ground. It was muddy and the mud had been churned by the cart and the footprints of those trampling round. Her attention was momentarily distracted by indentations of two feet at one point which were far deeper than the others, to the extent that water had formed in the hollows. Nevertheless, she ignored the mud and bent over the body. She turned and motioned the Abbess Ballgel to come closer.

'If you will observe and witness my examination, Ballgel,' she called over her shoulder. 'You will observe that the sister's face has been severely mutilated with a knife. The skin has been deliberately marked with a sharp blade, disfiguring it, as if the purpose were to destroy the features of this young girl.'

Ballgel forced herself to look on and nodded, suppressing a soft groan of anguish.

Fidelma bent further to her work before pausing, satisfied as to her physical examination. Then she turned her attention to the small leather *marsupium* which hung at the dead sister's waist. It was not secured with the leather thong that usually fastened such a purse and it was empty.

Fidelma rose to her feet. Next she went to the tree from which the body had been taken and began to look about. With a gasp of triumph she bent down a picked up a torn scrap of paper. There was no writing but a few curious short lines drawn on it. Fidelma frowned and placed it in her own *marsupium*.

Her keen eye then caught a round stone on the ground. It was bloody and pieces of hair and skin were stuck to it.

'What is it?' demanded Abbess Ballgel coming forward.

'That is the instrument with which Cessair was killed,' Fidelma explained. 'Her death was caused by her skull being smashed in and not through the blade of the knife that destroyed her features. At least this was no attack by robbers.'

'How can you be so certain?'

'We have observed that the girl was not sexually molested in any way. Yet this was an attack of hate towards the sister.'

Ballgel stared at her friend in amazement.

177

'How can you say it was an attack of hate?'

'Let us discount the idea of robbers. The purpose of a thief is to steal. It is true that some thieves have even been known to sexually assault Sisters of the faith. There was no attempt at theft here. The Sister's crucifix of silver still hangs around her neck. It was not a sexual assault. What is left of the motivation which would cause someone to smash her skull, tie her to a tree and mutilate her features? There is surely only hatred left?'

'The Holy Blood of the Blessed Gertrude is not in her *marsupium*,' Ballgel pointed out. 'I have been looking all around for the phial. That is valuable; but above all, where is Sister Della?'

Fidelma grimaced.

'The holy blood may be valuable to you, yes. Not to a thief. There would be no purpose in stealing that if one wanted money.'

'Do thieves and robbers need a purpose?'

'All people need a purpose, even those whom we deem mad follow a logic, which may not be our logic but one of their own creation with its own rules. Once one deciphers the code of that logic then it is as easy to follow as any.'

'And what of Sister Della?'

Fidelma nodded. 'There is the real mystery. Find her and we may find the missing phial. Has a search been made for her?' She asked the question of the abbot.

Abbot Heribert looked sourly at Fidelma.

'Not yet. And who are you?'

'Sister Fidelma is a qualified advocate of our legal courts,' explained Abbess Ballgel hurriedly, seeing the look of derision on the abbot's face.

'Do women have such a status in your country?' he demanded in astonishment.

'Is that so strange?' Fidelma replied irritably. 'Anyway, we waste time. We must find Sister Della for she may be in danger. If Sister Cessair was not robbed, and was not attacked for sexual motives, the alternative is that she was killed from some personal motive which, judging from the savagery of the attack, shows a depth of malice that makes me shudder. Who could have been so angered by her that they would attempt to destroy her beauty? It is as if she were attacked by a jealous lover, for it is known that hate and love are two sides of the same coin.'

Fidelma suddenly saw Abbot Heribert's eyes widened a fraction. She saw him glance swiftly at Ballgel and then drop his gaze.

'Why does the mention of a lover have some special meaning for you?' she demanded.

It was Abbess Ballgel who answered for him.

'Sister Cessair did have a . . . a liaison,' she said quietly.

'It was disgusting!' grunted Abbot Heribert.

'A curious choice of word.' Fidelma's eyes narrowed. 'Disgusting in what way?'

'Abbot Heribert is a firm believer in the concept of celibacy,' explained Ballgel.

'Celibacy is by no means universally approved of by the Church,' Fidelma pointed out. 'There are many double houses where religious of both sexes live and raise their children to the service of God. What is disgusting about that?'

'Paul of Tarsus spoke firmly in favour of celibacy and many other Church Fathers have done so. There are those of us who argue that only through celibacy do we have the power to spread the Faith.'

'I am not here to discuss theology, Heribert. Are you telling me that Cessair was in love with a religieux from your Abbey of Fosse?'

'God forgive him,' Heribert lowered his head piously.

'Only him?' Was there sarcasm in Fidelma's voice. 'Surely forgiveness is universal? Who was this monk?'

'Brother Cano,' replied Ballgel. 'He was a young monk who arrived from Éireann only a few weeks ago. It seems that he and Sister Cessair met and were immediately attracted by one another.'

'And this relationship was disapproved of?'

'It did not matter to me,' Ballgel said hastily. 'Our culture does not forbid such relationships as you have pointed out. Even Kildare, where we studied, was a mixed house.'

'But it mattered to Abbot Heribert,' Fidelma swung round on the tall Frankish prelate.

'Of course it mattered. My Abbey of Fosse is for men of the Faith only. I follow the strict rule of celibacy and expect all members of my community to do the same. I warned Brother Cano several times to cease this disgusting alliance. Abbess Ballgel knew my views. It does not surprise me that this woman of loose morals has paid a bitter price.'

Fidelma raised her eyebrows in surprise.

'That is also an interesting statement. Are you given to much passion over this matter, Father Abbot?'

Heribert frowned suspiciously at her.

'What do you mean?'

'I merely make an observation. Does it worry you that I comment on the passionate tones by which you denounce this poor Sister?'

'I believe in the teachings of Paul of Tarsus.'

'Yet it is not the rule of the Church. Nor, indeed, does the Holy Father denounce those who reject celibacy. It is not even a rule of our Faith.'

'Not yet. But the ranks of those of us who believe in the segregation of men and woman and the rule of celibacy are increasing. One day the Holy Father will have to pay us heed. Already he has suggested that celibacy is the best way forward . . .'

'Until that happens, it is not a rule. Very well, I understand your position now. But we have a murder to be solved. Where is this Brother Cano?'

Abbot Heribert shrugged.

'I understand from brother Sinsear that Brother Cano left

the abbey this morning and was last seen heading along this
road. Perhaps he meant to meet Sister Cessair?'

Abbess Ballgel groaned softly.

'If Cano was coming to meet Sister Cessair . . . if he
could do this to her . . . we must find Sister Della.'

Fidelma gave her a reassuring smile.

'No one has said that Cano did this as yet,' she observed
quietly. 'However, it seems that, as well as the missing
Sister, we also have a missing Brother to account for.
Perhaps we will find one with the other. Where is this
Brother Sinsear?'

A religieux who was standing nearby coughed nervously
and took a hesitant step towards her. He was a pale-faced
young man, hardly more than an adolescent. His features
were taut and he appeared in the grip of strong emotions.

'I am Sinsear.'

Fidelma regarded his flushed, anxious face.

'You appear agitated, Brother.'

'I work with Brother Cano in the gardens of our abbey,
Sister. I am his friend. I knew that he had a . . .' he glanced
nervously at his abbot, '. . . a passion for Sister Cessair.'

'A passion? You do not have to bandy words, Brother.
Was he in love with her?'

'I only knew that they met at regular times in the forest here
because of Father Abbot's disapproval of their relationship.'

Abbot Heribert's brows drew together in anger but
Fidelma held up a hand to silence him.

'Go on, Brother Sinsear. What are you saying?'

'They had a special meeting spot in a glade not a far
distance from here. A woodsman's hut. It occurs to me, in
the circumstances, that the hut might be examined.'

'You should have spoken up sooner, Brother,' snapped
Abbot Heribert. 'Cano may have fled by now. I see no point
in seeking him in that hut.'

'You are presuming that he is guilty of this deed, Heribert,'
Fidelma rebuked him. 'Yet I think we should investigate this

hut. Do you know the way to it, Brother Sinsear?'

'I think so. There is a small path leading off this track about fifty metres in that direction.' He pointed towards Fosse, and on the far side of the track to the oak tree where Cessair had been found.

'How far into the forest?'

'No more than three hundred metres.'

'Then lead the way. Father Abbot, you may send the rest of the Brothers of your community to escort the Sisters and the body of Cessair back to the Abbey of Nivelles.'

Heribert made to object and then did her bidding.

Brother Sinsear turned pale eyes on Fidelma.

'Could Cano really have done such a terrible deed? Oh God, to maltreat such grace and beauty! Why did she not give her love to one who would appreciate such exquisite . . .'

Abbot Heribert interrupted him.

'Let us get a move on, Brother Sinsear. I expect it will be a waste of time. If Cano killed her then he will not be hiding in a forest hut but will have left the area by now.'

'You are also forgetting the missing Sister Della,' Fidelma pointed out. 'And it is wrong to assume Cano's guilt.'

'Yes, yes,' Heribert snapped. 'Have it your own way.'

With the young Brother Sinsear leading the way, clutching at a newly cut hawthorn stick, they trod a well-worn path through the great forest.

Eventually they came on a little glade, a pleasant spot through which a small stream meandered. By it stood a woodsman's crude hut. The door was shut and there was no sign of life.

Fidelma raised her hand and brought them to a halt on the edge of the glade. As they neared the door of the hut, Fidelma's keen eyes surveyed it quickly. The first thing she noticed was bloodstains on the door jamb and there were several palm prints on the door as if someone had, with bloodied hands, pushed it open. Blood was also on a piece of wood near the door.

They heard a sobbing sound from within.

'Brother Cano!' Sinsear suddenly called. 'The abbot and I are here.'

There was a silence. The sobbing suddenly halted.

'Sinsear?' came a hesitant male voice. 'Thank God! I need help.'

There was another sound now. A feminine cry which sounded as if it were stifled almost immediately.

Fidelma glanced at her companions.

'Stay back. I shall go in first.' She turned and raised her voice. 'Brother Cano? I am Fidelma of Cashel. I have come to help you. I am coming in.'

There was no response.

Slowly Fidelma leant forward, placing her hand near the bloodied imprint and pushed against the door. It swung open easily.

At the far end of the woodsman's hut she saw a young man clad in religious robes, kneeling on the floor. His hair was dishevelled, his eyes red and cheeks stained as if from weeping. He held a piece of bloodstained cloth in his hands. Before him lay the prone figure of a girl. Her eyes were opened and she appeared conscious but her clothes were covered in blood.

Fidelma heard a sound behind her and swung round. She saw Abbot Heribert and the others trying to squeeze behind her and swiftly waved them back.

'Stay there!' she snapped. There was such a power in her voice that they paused. 'I will speak with Cano and Sister Della first.'

Fidelma turned and took a step into the hut.

'I am Sister Fidelma,' she repeated. 'May I attend to Sister Della?'

'Of course,' the young man seemed bewildered.

Fidelma knelt by his side. He had been trying to cleanse her wounds.

'Lie still,' she said, as she examined the wound of the young religieuse. It was to the back of the head. Sister Della

183

had been clubbed in the same fashion as Sister Cessair. Unlike the blow delivered to Cessair's skull, it had not broken the bone. There was, however, a nasty swelling.

'Am I dying, Sister?' The girl's voice was faint.

'No. In a moment we will get you back to the abbey so that you may be properly attended. What can you tell me about the attack on Sister Cessair and yourself?'

'Little enough.'

'A little in these circumstances may mean a lot,' encouraged Fidelma.

'Alas, the little is nothing. Sister Cessair and I were bringing the phial of the Holy Blood of Blessed Gertrude to the Abbey of Fosse. We were walking through the woods. I remember . . .' she paused and groaned. 'I did not hear anyone behind us for we were talking together and . . .' She held up a hand to her head and groaned. 'There came a sharp blow and then I can remember nothing until I came to, lying on the path with a blinding pain in my head. I thought I was alone. I could see no one. I began to look around and then, then I saw Cessair . . .'

She gave a heartrending sob.

'What then?' prompted Fidelma gently.

'I could do nothing for her, except try to get help. I came here and . . .'

'You came here?' Fidelma interrupted quickly. 'Why come to this woodsman's hut? Why not go on to the Abbey of Fosse or back to Nivelles?'

'I knew Cano would be here.' The girl groaned again.

'She knew that I had arranged to meet Cessair here on the journey from Nivelles to Fosse,' interrupted Cano defiantly. 'I am not ashamed of it.'

Fidelma ignored him and smiled down at the girl.

'Rest awhile. It will not be long before we have you safe and your wound attended.'

Only then did she turn to Cano.

'So you were waiting here for Cessair?'

'Cessair and I loved one another. We often met here because Abbot Heribert was vehement against us.'

'Tell me about it.'

'There is not much to tell. I arrived at Fosse about a month ago to join the community. Although there are several Irish religious here and in Nivelles, it is a strange land. They are more inclined to celibacy than we are in Éireann. They do not have the number of mixed houses that we do. Abbot Heribert was fanatical for the rule of celibacy; even though there is no such proscription in the church, he makes it a rule in his abbey. I think I would have left long ago had I not met Cessair.'

'When did you and Cessair meet?'

'The week after I came here. It was Brother Sinsear who introduced me when we were taking produce from Fosse to Nivelles.'

'Brother Sinsear introduced you?'

'Yes. As a gardener, Sinsear often took produce between the two abbeys. He knew many of the religieuses at Nivelles.'

'Did Cessair have any enemies that you knew of?'

'Only Abbot Heribert, when he discovered our relationship.' Cano's voice was bitter. From the doorway, Fidelma heard Heribert's expression of anger.

'Why didn't you leave and move on to a mixed house?'

'We planned to but Abbess Ballgel counselled Cessair against it.'

Fidelma frowned.

'Why would she be against such a plan?'

Cano shrugged.

'She was . . . protective to Cessair. She felt Cessair was too young.'

'More protective than to her other charges?'

'I do not know. All I know is that we were desperate and planning to leave here.'

Fidelma waited a while. Then she said abruptly: 'Did you kill Cessair?'

The young monk raised a tear-stained face to her and there was a haunted look in his eyes.

'How can you ask such a question?'

'Because I am a *dálaigh*, an advocate of the law,' replied Fidelma. 'It is my duty to ask.'

'I did not.'

'Tell me what happened this morning, then.'

'I knew that Cessair and Della were bringing the phial to Fosse for the annual blessing. So we arranged to meet here.'

'Surely that would mean a delay in the bringing of the phial to Fosse? The service was at midday.'

'Cessair was going to persuade Della to take the phial on to Fosse while she joined me here. We only meant to meet briefly to make some arrangements and then Cessair would hasten after Della, pretending she had broken her sandal on the road.'

'What arrangements were you going to make?'

'Arrangements to leave this place. Perhaps to go back to Ireland.'

'I see. So you arrived here . . .?'

'And here I waited. I thought Cessair was late and was about to go down to the main track to see if there was a sign of her when Della came stumbling into the hut. She was almost hysterical and told me what had happened then she passed out. I could not leave her alone and have been trying to return her to consciousness ever since. It is only a moment ago that she regained her senses.'

Fidelma turned to Della.

'Do you agree with this account?'

The girl had raised herself on an elbow: she still looked pale and shaken.

'So far as I am able. I do not remember much at all.'

'Very well. Then I think we should get you to the abbey where you may have the wound tended.' She glanced at Cano who was twisting his hands nervously. Then she remembered something.

'Do you have the phial of blood, Sister Della? The Holy Blood of the Blessed Gertrude?'

Della frowned and shook her head.

'Cessair carried it in her *marsupium*.'

'I see,' replied Fidelma thoughtfully, before turning to the others and waving them forward.

'We will carry Sister Della to Fosse,' she told them. 'There are a few more questions that I wish to ask but we should ensure that Sister Della gets proper treatment for her wound.'

The church and community of Fosse was not as spectacular as some of the abbeys which Fidelma had encountered in her travels. She reminded herself that it was barely twenty years old. It was not more than a collection of timber houses around a large, rectangular wooden church.

Sister Della was immediately taken to the infirmary while the abbot led the abbess and Fidelma to the refectory for refreshments. Brother Sinsear and Brother Cano were told to go to their cells and await the abbot's call.

Abbess Ballgel was the first to break the uneasy silence that had fallen between them. She had seen Fidelma's work before while they had been together at the Abbey of Kildare.

'Well, Fidelma, do you see a solution to this horror? And where is the Holy Blood of Gertrude?'

'Let us summarise what we know. We can eliminate certain things. Firstly, the concept that this action was committed by robbers. I have already given one main reason, that is the mutilation of Cessair. That was done from hate. Secondly, we have the testimony from Della who says that she was walking along talking with Cessair and did not hear or see anything until she was struck from behind.'

'You mean, if there had been robbers waiting in ambush then she would have seen something of them?'

'Just so. The very idea of even a single person creeping unobserved behind someone walking in a forest is, I find, rather a difficult one to accept.'

Abbess Ballgel frowned quickly.

'You claim that Sister Della is lying?'

'Not necessarily. But think of it in this way; think of a forest path strewn with dead leaves, twigs and the like. An animal might move quietly over such a carpet but can a human? Could a man or woman creep up so quickly behind someone walking along then strike them before they knew it?'

'Then we must question the girl further,' snapped Heribert, 'and force her to confess.'

Fidelma looked at him in disapproval.

'Confess to what?'

'Why, the killing of the other girl,' replied Heribert.

Fidelma gave a deep sigh.

'There is another more plausible explanation why Sister Della did not hear her assailant creep up behind her.'

The abbot frowned in anger.

'What game are you playing? First you say one thing and then you say another. I do not follow.'

The Abbess Ballgel intervened as she saw Fidelma's facial muscles go taut and her eyes change colour.

'Fidelma is a qualified advocate used to these puzzles. I suggest we allow her to follow her path of reasoning.'

The abbot sat back, his face set in a sneer.

'Proceed, then.'

'Before I come back to that point, let us proceed along another route. The savagery with which Sister Cessair was attacked, the fact that her features were mutilated, the fact that Sister Della was left unmarked except for the blow that laid her unconscious, means that Cessair was, indeed, singled out particularly in this attack. She was, as I said before, attacked out of some great malice towards her.'

'It is logical, Fidelma,' agreed the abbess.

'Then we must consider who had such a hatred of Cessair.'

She paused and allowed them to consider her proposal in silence.

'Well, we can eliminate almost everyone,' the abbess smiled briefly.

'How so?'

'Brother Cano was her lover. Sister Della was her closest friend in the abbey. Cessair made no enemies . . . except . . .'

She suddenly hesitated.

'Except?' encouraged Fidelma gently.

The abbess had dropped her eyes.

It was Abbot Heribert who flushed with anger.

'Except me, you mean?' He rose to his feet. 'What are you implying? Because I uphold the teaching of celibacy? Because I forbid any liaison with women among the members of my community? Because I urged the abbess to forbid Sister Cessair to see Brother Cano as I had forbidden him to meet with her? Are these things to be thrown at me in accusation that I murdered her?'

'Did you?'

Fidelma asked the question so quietly that for a long time it seemed that the abbot had not heard her.

'How dare you!'

'I dare because I must,' replied Fidelma calmly. 'Keep your bluster to yourself, Abbot. We are here discover the truth not to engage in games of vanity.'

Heribert went red in the face. He was inarticulate with rage.

The Abbess Ballgel leant forward.

'Abbot Heribert, we are simply intelligent people trying to resolve a problem. Our pride and self-regard should not impinge on that process for we are seeking the truth and the truth alone.'

Abbot Heribert blinked.

'I resent being accused . . .'

'I did not accuse you, Heribert,' Fidelma replied. 'Your unthinking pride did so. But, since you have raised this matter yourself, I put it to you that you certainly had no liking for Cessair.'

He stared at her and then shrugged.

'I have made that evident. No. I disliked her for she was a distraction to Brother Cano. Indeed, she was a distraction to all the young men in my community. I have even seen young men like Brother Sinsear moonstruck in her presence.'

'My mentor, the Brehon Morann of Tara, used to say: it is easier to become a monk in one's old age,' sighed Fidelma.

Abbess Ballgel hid a smile.

'Anyway,' Fidelma continued, 'as abbot you were expecting Sisters Cessair and Della to arrive at Fosse at noon or so I am led to believe?'

'Not precisely. I was expecting two sisters of Abbess Ballgel's community to arrive but I did not know who they would be. Had I known one was going to be Sister Cessair . . .'

'What would you have done?'

'I should have stopped her coming to mislead Brother Cano further into temptation's way.'

'Cano was misled?' queried Fidelma. 'I thought he was in love with Cessair?'

The abbot stirred uncomfortably.

'Women are the temptresses by which the saintly fall from grace.'

He did not meet Fidelma's flashing anger. But, Fidelma, realising it was impossible to overcome the misogynist prejudice, decided to ignore the remark.

'Ballgel, why did you choose Cessair and Della to bring the phial of blood for the service this morning?'

'Why?'

'Someone knew that Cessair was going to be walking along that forest track.'

The eyes of the abbess widened.

'Why, it was Sister Della who came to me last night and asked if she be allowed to take the phial for the blessing. She also asked me if she could choose a companion to accompany her.'

'You did not know that she would choose Cessair?'

'As a matter of fact,' smiled the abbess, 'I presumed that she would. They have been inseparable companions.'

'You knew that she would choose Cessair to accompany her through the forest of Seneffe even though the abbot disapproved of Cessair? Isn't that strange?'

'Not at all. I am like you, Fidelma. I refuse to be dictated to as to who I can send here or there.'

Abbot Heribert's mouth set in a grim line. He was clearly displeased but did not say anything.

'So Sister Della was the only other person who knew Cessair would go with her, apart from yourself, Ballgel?'

Abbess Ballgel looked carefully at her friend.

'You will remember, Fidelma,' she said softly, 'that you arrived at Nivelles only a short time after Brother Sinsear had brought us the dreadful news.'

Fidelma smiled sympathetically.

'I do remember. And you need hardly remind me that you would have had no time to have done the deed. Besides, it would be very difficult for an abbess to absent herself from her abbey for the time needed to do carry out this murder. I also presume that you would have had no motive either?'

Before Ballgel could respond, Abbot Heribert interrupted.

'It would similarly be difficult for an abbot to absent himself from his abbey,' he said shortly.

'I had not forgotten, Heribert,' Fidelma said solemnly. 'Tell us, as a matter of record, where you were about noon?'

Abbot Heribert shrugged.

'I will play the game to the end,' he said heavily. 'Today, being the anniversary of the death of the Blessed Gertrude, we have a midday Angelus followed by a service of remembrance, not only for Gertrude but in memory of the Blessed Foillan whom she allowed to build our abbey. The phial of the holy blood is brought to the abbey just before the midday Angelus bell is sounded.

'At ten minutes before midday I was standing with several brothers awaiting the appearance of the two sisters, who usually carry the phial from Nivelles. I did not know who they would be. When midday came and the bell was tolled, I thought that the only thing to do was proceed with the service, although without the phial.'

'Did you not send anyone to look for the Sisters?'

'I was informed that Brother Sinsear had already left to escort the Sisters through the forest. So I did not need to.'

'I see. Go on.'

'Well, we performed the service and when it was over there was still no sign of the Sisters nor of Brother Sinsear.'

'Brother Sinsear had come straight to Nivelles to alert us,' pointed out Ballgel.

'It was some time before Brother Sinsear returned,' agreed Heribert, 'and told us the appalling news and we immediately set out to the forest. We had barely reached there when you arrived.'

'I see. Will you send for Brother Sinsear?'

It was moments before they were joined by the young monk. The youth made an effort to overcome the nervous twisting of his hands by placing them behind his back.

'It is a terrible business,' he began, breaking the silence.

'I know that you are upset,' Fidelma smiled gently. 'After all, it is your close friend who stands in some danger. The finger of suspicion points in his direction.'

'Brother Cano might be possessed of a temper but he would never . . . never . . .'

'He was quick tempered?' Fidelma interrupted.

Brother Sinsear hung his head.

'I should not have said that. I meant . . .'

'It is true,' observed Abbot Heribert. 'I have rebuked him a couple of times for his turbulent moods.'

'Well, all I want from you, Brother Sinsear, are the details about today. I understand that you left the abbey go to in search of the two Sisters bringing the phial of holy blood? At what time was this?'

'Some time before midday, I think. Yes, it was half an

hour before the midday Angelus bell sounded because that was when the phial was due to be at the abbey.'

'Were you instructed to do so?'

Brother Sinsear shook his head.

'No. But knowing Cessair . . . well, I knew she would be in no hurry.'

There was a brief silence.

'You *knew* that one of the two sisters would be Cessair?' pressed Fidelma. 'How did you know?'

'Why, Brother Cano told me. We had few secrets. He left to go to the woodsman's hut where he and Cessair usually met. I knew that this would delay them bringing the phial to the abbey. That was why I set off in good time to meet them and encourage them to hurry. Alas, I was too late.'

'You found Cessair dead?'

'I did. She was tied to the tree even as you saw her.'

'And Sister Della?'

'There was no sign of her. So I hurried straight to Nivelles to alert Abbess Ballgel.'

'Why did you do that?' Fidelma asked.

'Why?'

'There were other options. Why not rush back to Fosse and alert the Abbot Heribert?'

Sinsear grimaced.

'It is well known that Nivelles is closer to that point in the forest than is Fosse. I thought it more expedient to bring the news to Nivelles and then return to alert Fosse.'

'Have you been friends with Cano from the time he arrived in Fosse?'

'He was assigned to help me in the gardens and we became friends.'

'Yet you knew Cessair before Cano arrived?'

'I have met Cessair and Della as well as many others of the sisters of Nivelles. There is much intercourse between the abbeys. You see, I am employed in the gardens and my job is to take fruit and vegetables to Nivelles once a week.'

'Brother Sinsear is perfectly correct,' interrupted Heribert. 'Members of our community often go to Nivelles to help them with the heavy building work and the upkeep of their fields and crops. In fact, Brother Sinsear took produce to Nivelles only yesterday afternoon. Ah, and didn't Brother Cano accompany you?'

Brother Sinsear flushed and nodded reluctantly.

Fidelma pursed her lips thoughtfully.

'There is a further question that I must now ask Sister Della. Please wait for me here.'

In the infirmary, Sister Della, although pale-faced and weak, was looking much improved.

'Sister Della,' Fidelma began without preamble. 'There is only one question I need ask you. Why did you especially ask to be allowed to take the phial of holy blood to Fosse today?'

'Sister Cessair asked me to.'

'Cessair, eh? Then it was not your idea?'

'No. Neither was it her idea, to be truthful. She knew that there would be some argument with the abbot who disliked her and was reluctant to go. However, Brother Cano had especially asked her to come . . .'

'How had he asked? Had he not seen her yesterday?'

'No. He sent a message, for there is always someone coming or going between our two abbeys. He sent a note to Cessair asking her to come early to the hut so that he could spent a few moments with her to discuss their future.'

'Did you approve of her meetings with Cano?'

'I was Cessair's friend. I know that there is no stopping the stupidities that love brings with it. And I thought it was only one question that you wished to ask?'

'So it was. Is this the note?' She pulled out the piece of torn paper from her *marsupium*.

Sister Della glanced at it and shrugged.

'I do not read Ogham,' she said. 'But I think it is part of the note. Cano and Cessair used the ancient form of Irish writing to write cryptic notes to one another.'

Fidelma turned back to the refectory.

'I think I have the solution to this mystery,' she announced as Abbess Ballgel and Abbot Heribert gazed up as she re-entered the refectory.

'Who then is guilty?' demanded Heribert.

'Ask Brother Cano to come here. You will remain, Brother Sinsear.'

'Brother Cano,' Fidelma began when the young man arrived, 'the future looks bleak for you.'

Cano grimaced in resignation.

'The future is empty for me,' he corrected. 'Without Cessair my life is indeed an abyss filled with pain.'

'Why did you ask Cessair to meet you today?'

'I have told you already. So that we could plan to go away together and find a mixed house where we could live and work and, God willing, raise our children in His service.'

'Whose idea was that?'

'Mine.'

'I thought that someone else might have suggested it to you as a solution to your problems,' Fidelma said quietly.

Cano frowned.

'It matters not who suggested it. That was the purpose of our rendezvous.'

'It does matter. Wasn't it Brother Sinsear who suggested that you should plan to leave here?'

'Perhaps. Sinsear has been a good friend. He saw that there was no future for us here.'

'You went with Brother Sinsear to Nivelles last evening to take garden produce. Why didn't you speak with Cessair then?'

'We arrived during the evening service and as there was no excuse to delay at Nivelles, I wrote Cessair a note in Ogham suggesting the meeting. I knew that Cessair could read the ancient Irish writing so I put the instructions in that note and left it with the gatekeeper.'

'Yes. It all fits now,' Fidelma sighed. She turned to the young brother. 'Sinsear, would you mind handing Abbess Ballgel the phial of holy blood from your *marsupium*? The abbess has been fretful about it ever since she realised that it was missing.'

Brother Sinsear started, his face white. As if in a dream he opened his waist purse and handed it over.

'I found it on the ground . . . I meant to give it to you before . . .'

Fidelma shook her head sadly.

'One of the most terrible passions is love turned to hatred because of rejection. A lover who sees the object of their love with a rival can sometimes be transformed into a fiend incarnate.'

Brother Cano looked astounded.

'Cessair did not reject me,' he exclaimed. 'I tell you again, I did not kill her. We planned to go away together.'

'It is Sinsear to whom I refer,' replied Fidelma. 'It was Sinsear whose love had turned to a rage that wanted to hurt and mutilate her.'

Sinsear was staring at her open-mouthed.

'Sinsear here had been in love with Cessair for a long time. Being young and unable to articulate his love, he worshipped her from afar, dreaming of the day when he could summon up courage to declare himself. Then Cano arrived. At first the two were good friends. Then Sinsear introduced Cano to his love. Horror! Cano and Cessair fell truly in love. Day by day, Sinsear found himself watching their passion, and his jealousy grew to such a peak at what he saw as Cessair's rejection of him, that his mind broke with the anguish. He would revenge himself on Cessair with such a vengeance that hell did not possess.'

Sinsear's face was drained of all emotion now.

'He suggested to Cano that he invite Cessair to a rendez-vous in the hut and gave him the pretext of discussing a means of leaving the abbeys. Then he left Fosse in plenty of time to climb the old oak, hiding among the low hanging branches, to await the arrival of Cessair and her companion. That was why Sister Della did not hear anyone approach them from behind. He jumped down. I saw the indentation of where he landed. He landed just behind Della and felled her with a blow before she knew it. Am I right?'

Sinsear did not respond.

'Perhaps then he revealed his twisted love to Cessair? Perhaps he begged her to go with him. Did she react in horror, did she laugh? How did she treat this frenzied would-be lover? We only know how it resulted. He struck her several blows on the head and then, in a gruesome ritual, which serves to demonstrate his immaturity, he decided to punish her beauty by which she had beguiled him by mutilating her face with a knife. Whether he tied her first to the tree or not, we do not know unless he tells us. But I have no doubt that she was dead by then.

'Something made him pick up the phial of holy blood and his religious training took the better of him, for instead of leaving it in Cessair's purse, he put it in his own for safe-keeping. Knowing the missing phial was irrelevant, I could not account for its disappearance before.

'Perhaps then he heard Sister Della coming to. He turned and raced on to Nivelles to raise the alarm. He believed that Sister Della would probably go to Fosse to raise the alarm which is why he chose Nivelles.'

Abbot Heribert was staring at Sinsear, seeing the truth of Fidelma's accusation confirmed in his cold features.

'How did you first suspect him?' he asked.

'Many reasons can be mentioned if you think back over the events. But, according to his story, Sinsear went along the path in search of Cessair and Della. He found Cessair dead and tied to the tree. He claimed that he had reached the point after Della had disappeared. But how could he have seen the body tied to the tree when it was on the far side of the tree to the path he was travelling?

'Even allowing for the fact that he somehow might have spotted something that made him suspicious, that he was so distraught that he did not think to cut her down and see if he could revive her, why did he run on to Nivelles?'

'For help. He wished to raise the alarm and, as he pointed out when you asked, Nivelles was closer than Fosse to the place. It is logical.'

'There was an even closer place to seek help,' Fidelma pointed out. 'Why not go there? He knew that Brother Cano was waiting in the woodsman's hut just a few hundred metres away. Had he been innocent, he would have rushed to seek Cano and get immediate help.'

The scream made them freeze.

Sinsear had drawn a knife and made a thrust at Brother Cano. He was babbling incoherently.

Cano reacted by striking out in self-defence, felling the young monk with a blow to the jaw.

'Now you can punish him by whatever laws apply here,' Fidelma told Abbot Heribert. She turned to the abbess. 'And we, Ballgel, shall escort poor Sister Della back to Nivelles. We have much to talk about . . .' She paused and glanced sadly at Brother Cano who was now sitting quietly, his head in his hands.

'Even the ancients were acutely aware of the role of emotions causing the symptoms of mental illness. *Aegra amans* – the lover's disease – can make people lose all reason. Even the most mature people can go mad, and to the young and immature love can destroy the soul as well as the mind.'

Our Lady of Death

❧

T he awesome moaning of the wind blended chillingly
with the howling of wolves. They were nearby, these
fearsome night hunters. Sister Fidelma knew it but could not
see them because of the cold, driving snow against her face.
It came at her in clouds; clouds of whirling, ice-cold, tiny
pellicles. It obliterated the landscape and she could scarcely
see beyond her arm's length in front of her.

Had it not been for the urgency of reaching Cashel, the
seat of the kings of Muman, she would not have been
attempting the journey northwards through these great, forbidding peaks of Sléibhte an Comeraigh. She bent forward in
the saddle of her horse, which only her rank as a *dálaigh* of
the law courts of the five kings of Ireland entitled her to have.
A simple religieuse would not be able to lay claim to such a
means of transportation. But then Fidelma was no ordinary
religieuse. She was a daughter of a former king of Cashel, an
advocate of the law of the *Fenechus* and qualified to the level
of *Anruth*, one degree below the highest qualification in
Ireland. The wind drove the snow continuously against her. It
plastered the strands of red hair that spilled from her *cubhal*,
or head-dress, against her pale forehead. She wished the
wind's direction would change, even for a moment or two,
for it would have been more comfortable to have had the
wind at her back. But it was constantly raging from the north.

The threatening howl of the wolves seemed close. Was it her imagination or had it been gradually getting closer as she rode the isolated mountain track? She shivered and once more wished that she had stopped for the night at the last *bruidhen* or hostel in order to await more clement weather. But the snow storm had set in and it would be several days before conditions improved. Sooner or later she would have to tackle the journey. The message from her brother, Colgú, had said her presence was needed urgently for their mother lay dying. Only that fact brought Fidelma traversing the forbidding tracks through the snowbound mountains in such intemperate conditions.

Her face was frozen and so were her hands as she confronted the fierce wind-driven snow. In spite of her heavy woollen cloak, she found her teeth chattering. A dark shape loomed abruptly out of the snow nearby. Her heart caught in her mouth as her horse shied and skittered on the trail for a moment. Then she was able to relax and steady the beast with a sigh of relief, as the regal shape of a great stag stared momentarily at her from a distance of a few yards before recklessly turning and bounding away into the cover of the white curtain that blocked out the landscape.

Continuing on, she reached what she felt must be the crest of a rise and found the wind so fierce here that it threatened to sweep her from her horse. Even the beast put its head down to the ground and seemed to stagger at the icy onslaught. Masses of loose powdery snow drifted this way and that in the howling and shrieking of the tempest.

Fidelma blinked at the indistinct blur of the landscape beyond.

She felt sure she had seen a light. Or was it her imagination? She blinked again and urged her horse onwards, straining to keep her eyes focused. She automatically pulled her cloak higher up around her neck.

Yes! She had seen it. A light, surely!

She halted her horse and slipped off, making sure she had

the reins looped securely around her arm. The snow came up to her knees, making walking almost impossible, but she could not urge her mount through the drifting snow without making sure it was safe enough first. After a moment or two she came to a wooden pole. She peered upwards. Barely discernible in the flurries above her head hung a dancing storm lantern.

She stared around in surprise. The swirling snow revealed nothing. But she was sure that the lantern was the traditional sign of a *bruidhen*, an inn, for it was the law that all inns had to keep a lantern burning to indicate their presence at night or in severe weather conditions.

She gazed back at the pole with its lantern, and chose a direction, moving awkwardly forward in the deep, clinging snow. Suddenly the wind momentarily dropped and she caught sight of the large, dark shadow of a building. Then the blizzard resumed its course and she staggered, head down, in the direction of the building. More by good luck than any other form of guidance, she came to a horse's hitching rail and tethered her beast there, before feeling her way along the cold stone walls towards the door.

There was a sign fixed there but she could not decipher it. She also saw, to her curiosity, a ring of herbs hanging from the door, almost obliterated in their coating of snow.

She found the iron handle, twisted it and pushed. The door remained shut. She frowned in annoyance. It was the law that a *brugh-fer*, an innkeeper, had to keep the door of his inn open at all times, day and night and in all weathers. She tried again.

The wind was easing a little now and its petulant crying had died away to a soft whispering moan.

Irritated, Fidelma raised a clenched fist and hammered at the door.

Did she hear a cry of alarm or was it simply the wailing wind?

There was no other answer.

She hammered, angrily this time.

Then she did hear a noise. A footstep and a harsh male cry.

'God and his saints stand between us and all that is evil! Begone foul spirit!'

Fidelma was thunderstruck for a moment. Then she thrust out her jaw.

'Open, innkeeper; open to a *dálaigh* of the courts; open to a Sister of the Abbey of Kildare! In the name of charity, open to a refugee from the storm!'

There was a moment's silence. Then she thought she heard voices raised in argument. She hammered again.

There came the sound of bolts being drawn and the door swung inwards. A blast of warm air enveloped Fidelma and she pushed hurriedly into the room beyond, shaking the snow from her woollen cloak.

'What manner of hostel is this that ignores the laws of the Brehons?' she demanded, turning to the figure that was now closing the wooden door behind her.

The man was tall and thin; a gaunt, pallid figure of middle-age, his temples greying. He was poorly attired and his height was offset by a permanent stoop. But it was not that which caused Fidelma's eyes to widen a fraction. It was the horror on the man's face; not a momentary expression of horror but a graven expression that was set deep and permanently into his cadaverous features. Tragedy and grief stalked across the lines of his face.

'I have a horse tethered outside. The poor beast will freeze to death if not attended,' Fidelma snapped, when the man did not answer her question but simply stood staring at her.

'Who are you?' demanded a shrill woman's voice behind her.

Fidelma swung round. The woman who stood there had once been handsome. Now age was causing her features to run with surplus flesh, and lines marked her face. Her eyes stared, black and apparently without pupils, at Fidelma. She had the feeling that here was a woman whom, at some awesome moment in her life, the pulsating blood of life had frozen and never regained its regular ebb and flow. What surprised her more was that the woman held before her a tall ornate crucifix. She held it as if it were some protective icon against the terror that afflicted her.

She and the man were well matched.

'Speak! What manner of person are you?'

Fidelma sniffed in annoyance.

'If you are the keepers of this inn, all you should know is that I am a weary traveller in these mountains, driven to seek refuge from the blizzard.'

The woman was not cowed by her haughty tone.

'It is not all we need to know,' she corrected just as firmly. 'Tell us whether you mean us harm or not.'

Fidelma was surprised.

'I came here to shelter from the storm, that is all. I am Fidelma of Kildare,' replied the religieuse in annoyance. 'Moreover, I am a *dálaigh* of the courts, qualified to the level of *Anruth* and sister to Colgú, *tánaiste* of this kingdom.'

The grandiloquence of her reply was an indication of the annoyance Fidelma felt, for normally she was not one given to stating more than was ever necessary. She had never felt the need to mention that her brother, Colgú, was heir-apparent to the kingdom of Cashel before. However, she felt that she needed to stir these people out of their curious mood.

As she spoke she swung off her cloak, displaying her habit, and she noticed that the woman's eyes fell upon the ornately worked crucifix which hung from her neck. Did she see some expression of reassurance in those cold unfeeling eyes?

The woman put down her cross and gave a bob of her head.

'Forgive us, Sister. I am Monchae, wife to Belach, the innkeeper.'

Belach seemed to be hesitating at the door.

'Shall I see to the horse?' he asked hesitantly.

'Unless you want it to freeze to death,' snapped Fidelma, making her way to a large open fire in which sods of turf were singing as they caused a warmth to envelop the room. From the corner of her eyes she saw Belach hesitate a moment longer and then, swinging a cloak around his shoulders, he took from behind the door a sword and went out into the blizzard.

Fidelma was astonished. She had never seen an ostler take a sword to assist him in putting a horse to stable before.

Monchae was pushing the iron handle on which hung a cauldron across the glowing turf fire.

'What place is this?' demanded Fidelma as she chose a chair to stretch out in front of the warmth of the fire. The room was low beamed and comfortable but devoid of decorations apart from a tall statuette of the Madonna and Child, executed in some form of painted plaster; a gaudy, alabaster figurine. It dominated as the centre display at the end of a large table where, presumably, guests dined.

'This is Brugh-na-Bhelach. You have just come off the shoulder of the mountain known as Fionn's Seat. The River Tua is but a mile to the north of here. We do not have many travellers this way in winter. Which direction are you heading?'

'North to Cashel,' replied Fidelma.

Monchae ladled a cup of steaming liquid from the cauldron over the fire and handed it to her. Although the liquid must have been warming the vessel, Fidelma could not feel it as she cupped her frozen hands around it and let the steaming vapour assail her nostrils. It smelled good. She sipped slowly, her sense of taste confirming what her sense of smell had told her.

She glanced up at the woman.

'Tell me, Monchae, why was the door of this hostel barred? Why did I have to beg to be admitted? Do you and your husband, Belach, know the law of hostelkeepers?'

Monchae pressed her lips together.

'Will you report us to the *bó-aire* of the territory?'

The *bó-aire* was the local magistrate.

'I am more concerned at hearing your reasons,' replied Fidelma. 'Someone might have perished from the cold before you and your husband, Belach, opened your door.'

The woman looked agitated, chewing her lip as if she would draw blood from it.

The door opened abruptly, with a wild gust of cold air, sending snowflakes swirling across the room and a stream of icy wind enveloping them.

Belach stood poised a moment in its frame, a ghastly look upon his pale features, and then, with a sound which resembled a soft moan, he entered and barred the door behind him. He still carried the sword as a weapon.

Fidelma watched him throw the bolts with curiosity.

Monchae stood, both hands raised to her cheeks.

Belach turned from the door and his lips were trembling.

'I heard it!' he muttered, his eyes darting from his wife to Fidelma, as though he did not want her to hear. 'I heard it!'

'Oh Mary, mother of God, save us!' cried the woman, swaying as if she would faint.

'What does this mean?' Fidelma demanded as sternly as she could.

Belach turned, pleading to her.

'I was in the barn, bedding down your horse, Sister, and I heard it.'

'But what?' cried Fidelma, trying to keep her patience.

'The spirit of Mugrán,' wailed Monchae suddenly, giving way to a fit of sobbing. 'Save us, Sister. For the pity of Christ! Save us!'

Fidelma rose and went to the woman, taking her gently but firmly by the arm and leading her to the fire. She could see that her husband, Belach, was too nervous to attend to the wants of his wife and so she went to a jug, assessed its contents as *corma*, a spirit distilled from barley, and poured a little into a cup. She handed it to the woman and told her to drink.

'Now what is all this about? I cannot help you unless you tell me.'

Monchae looked at Belach, as if seeking permission, and he nodded slowly in response.

'Tell her from the beginning,' he muttered.

Fidelma smiled encouragingly at the woman. 'A good place to start,' she joked lightly. But there was no humorous response on the features of the innkeeper's wife.

Fidelma seated herself before Monchae and faced her expectantly.

Monchae paused a moment and then began to speak, hesitantly at first and then more quickly as she gained confidence in the story.

'I was a young girl when I came to this place. I came as a young bride to the *brugh-fer*, the innkeeper, who was then a man named Mugrán. You see,' she added hurriedly, 'Belach is my second husband.'

She paused, but when Fidelma made no comment, she went on.

'Mugrán was a good man. But often given to wild fantasies. He was a good man for the music, an excellent piper. Often he entertained here in this very room and people would come far and wide to hear him. But he was a restless soul. I found that I was doing all the work of running the inn while he pursued his dreams. Mugrán's younger brother, Cano, used to help me but he was much influenced by his brother.

'Six years ago our local chieftain lit the *crois-tara*, the fiery cross, and sent his rider from village to village, raising the clans to send a band of fighting men to fight Guaire of Connacht in the service of Cathal Cú cen Máthair of Cashel. One morning Mugrán announced that he and young Cano were leaving to join that band of warriors. When I protested, he said that I should not fear for my security. He had placed in the inn an inheritance which would keep me from want. If anything happened to him then I would not be lacking for anything. With that, he and Cano just rose and left.'

Even now her voice was full of indignation.

'Time passed. Seasons came and went and I struggled to keep the inn going. Then, when the snows of winter were clearing, a messenger came to me who said a great battle had been fought on the shores of Loch Derg and my man had been slain in it. They brought me his bloodstained tunic as token. Cano, it seemed, had been killed at his side, and they brought me a bloodstained cloak as proof.'

She paused and sniffed.

'It is no use saying that I grieved for him. Not for my man, Mugrán. We had hardly been together for he was always searching out new, wild schemes to occupy his fancy. I could no more have tethered his heart than I could train the inn's cat to come and go at my will. Still, the inn was now mine, and mine by right as well as inheritance, for had I not worked to keep it while he pursued his fantasies? After the news came, and the *bó-aire* confirmed that the inn was mine since my man was dead by the shores of the far-off loch, I continued to work to run the inn. But life was hard, it was a struggle. Visitors along these isolated tracks are few and come seldom.'

'But what of the inheritance Mugrán had left in the inn that would keep you from want?' asked Fidelma, intrigued and caught up in the story.

The woman gave a harsh bark of laughter.

'I searched and searched and found nothing. It was just one of Mugrán's dreams again. One of his silly fantasies. He probably said it to keep me from complaining when he left.'

'Then what?' Fidelma pressed, when she paused.

'A year passed and I met Belach.' She nodded to her husband. 'Belach and I loved one another from the start. Ah, not the love of a dog for the sheep, you understand, but the love of a salmon for the stream. We married and have worked together since. And I insisted that we re-named this inn Brugh-na-Bhelach. Life has been difficult for us, but we have worked and made a living here.'

Belach had moved forward and caught Monchae's hand in his. The symbolism assured Fidelma that Monchae and Belach were still in love after the years that they had shared together.

'We've had five years of happiness,' Belach told Fidelma. 'And if the evil spirits claim us now, they will not steal those five years from us.'

'Evil spirits?' frowned Fidelma.

'Seven days ago it started,' Monchae said heavily. 'I was out feeding the pigs when I thought I heard the sounds of music from up on the mountain. I listened. Sure enough, I heard the sound of pipe music, high up in the air. I felt suddenly cold for it was a tune, as I well remember, that Mugrán was fond of playing.

'I came into the inn and sought out Belach. But he had not heard the music. We went out and listened but could hear nothing more than the gathering winds across the mountains that betokened the storms to come.

'The next day, at the noon hour, I heard a thud on the door of the inn. Thinking it a traveller who could not lift the latch. I opened the door. There was no one there . . . or so I thought until I glanced down. At the foot of the door was . . .' Monchae genuflected hastily. 'At the foot of the door was a dead raven. There was no sign of how it met its death. It seemed to have flown into the door and killed itself.'

Fidelma sat back with pursed lips.

She could see which way the story was going. The sound of music, a dead raven lying at the door. These were all the portents of death among the rural folk of the five kingdoms. She found herself shivering slightly in spite of her rational faith.

'We have heard the music several times since,' interrupted Belach for the first time. 'I have heard it.'

'And whereabouts does this music come from?'

Belach spread one hand, as if gesturing towards the mountains outside.

'High up, high up in the air. All around us.'

'It is the lamentation of the dead,' moaned Monchae. 'There is a curse on us.'

Fidelma sniffed.

'There is no curse unless God wills it.'

'Help us, Sister,' whispered Monchae. 'I fear it is Mugrán come to claim our souls, a vengeance for my love for Belach and not for him.'

Fidelma gazed in quiet amusement at the woman.

'How did you reckon this?'

'Because I have heard him. I have heard his voice, moaning to me from the Otherworld, crying to me. "I am alone! I am alone!" he called. "Join me, Monchae!" Ah, how many times have I heard that ghostly wail?'

Fidelma saw that the woman was serious.

'You heard this? When and where?'

'It was three days ago in the barn. I was tending the goats that we have there, milking them to prepare cheese when I heard the whisper of Mugrán's voice. I swear it was his voice. It sounded all around me.'

'Did you search?' Fidelma asked.

'Search? For a spirit?' Monchae sounded shocked. 'I ran into the inn and took up my crucifix.'

'I searched,' intervened Belach more rationally. 'I searched, for, like you Sister, I look for answers in this world before I seek out the Otherworld. But there was no one in the barn, nor the inn, who could have made that sound. But, again like you Sister, I continued to have my doubts. I took our ass and rode down into the valley to the *bóthan* of Dallán, the chieftain who had been with Mugrán on the shores of Loch Derg. He took oath that Mugrán was dead these last six years and that he had personally seen the body. What could I do further?'

Fidelma nodded slowly.

'So only you, Monchae, have heard Mugrán's voice?'

'No!' Belach interrupted again and surprised her. 'By the apostles of Patrick, I have heard the voice as well.'

'And what did this voice say?'

'It said: "Beware, Belach. You walk in a dead man's shoes without the blessing of his spirit." That is what it said.'

'And where did you hear this?'

'Like Monchae, I heard the voice speak to me within the barn.'

'Very well. You have seen a dead raven, heard pipe music from far off and heard a voice which you think is that of the spirit of Mugrán. There can still be a logical explanation for such phenomena.'

'Explanation?' Monchae's voice was harsh. 'Then explain this to me, Sister. Last night, I heard the music again. It awoke me. The snow storm had died down and the sky was clear with the moon shining down, reflecting on the snow, making it as bright as day. I heard the music playing again.

'I took my courage in my hands and went to the window and unfixed the shutter. There is a tiny knoll no more than one hundred yards away, a small snowy knoll. There was a figure of a man standing upon it, and in his hands were a set of pipes on which he was playing a lament. Then he paused and looked straight at me. "I am alone, Monchae!" he called. "Soon I will come for you. For you and Belach." He turned and . . .'

She gave a sudden sob and collapsed into Belach's embrace.

Fidelma gazed thoughtfully at her.

'Was this figure corporeal? Was it of flesh and blood?'

Monchae raised her fearful gaze to Fidelma.

'That is just it. The body shimmered.'

'Shimmered?'

'It had a strange luminescence about it, as if it shone

with some spectral fire. It was clearly a demon from the Otherworld.'

Fidelma turned to Belach.

'And did you see this vision?' she asked, half expecting him to confirm it.

'No. I heard Monchae scream in terror; it was her scream which awoke me. When she told me what had passed, I went out into the night to the knoll. I had hoped that I would find tracks there. Signs that a human being had stood there. But there were none.'

'No signs of the snow being disturbed?' pressed Fidelma.

'There were no human tracks, I tell you,' Belach said irritably. 'The snow was smooth. But there was one thing . . .'

'Tell me.'

'The snow seemed to shine with a curious luminosity, sparkling in an uncanny light.'

'But you saw no footprints nor signs of anyone?'

'No.'

The woman was sobbing now.

'It is true, it is true, Sister. The ghost of Mugrán will soon come for us. Our remaining time on earth is short.'

Fidelma sat back and closed her eyes a moment in deep thought.

'Only the Living God can decide what is your allotted span of life,' she said in almost absent-minded reproof.

Monchae and Belach stood watching her uncertainly as Fidelma stretched before the fire.

'Well,' she said at last, 'while I am here, I shall need a meal and a bed for the night.'

Belach inclined his head.

'That you may have, Sister, and most welcome. But if you will say a prayer to our Lady . . .? Let this haunting cease. She needs not the deaths of Monchae and myself to prove that she is the blessed mother of Christ.'

Fidelma sniffed in irritation.

'I would not readily blame the ills of the world on the Holy Family,' she said stiffly. But, seeing their frightened faces, she relented in her theology. 'I will say a prayer to Our Lady. Now bring me some food.'

Something awoke Fidelma. She lay with her heart beating fast, her body tense. The sound had seemed part of her dream. The dropping of a heavy object. Now she lay trying to identify it. The storm had apparently abated, since she had fallen asleep in the small chamber to which Monchae had shown her after her meal. There was a silence beyond the shuttered windows. An eerie stillness. She did not make a further move but lay, listening intently.

There came to her ears a creaking sound. The inn was full of the moans of its ageing timbers. Perhaps it had been a dream? She was about to turn over when she heard a noise. She frowned, not being able to identify it. Ah, there it was again. A soft thump.

She eased herself out of her warm bed, shivering in the cold night. It must be well after midnight. Reaching for her heavy robe, she draped it over her shoulders and moved stealthily towards the door, opening it as quietly as she could and pausing to listen.

The sound had come from downstairs.

She knew that she was alone in the inn with Monchae and Belach and they had retired when she had, their room being at the top of the stairs. She glanced towards it and saw the door firmly shut.

She walked with quiet, padding feet, imitating the soft walk of a cat, along the wooden boards to the head of the stairs and peered down into the darkness.

The sound made her freeze a moment. It was a curious sound, like something soft but weighty being dragged over the bare boards.

She paused, staring down the well of the stairs into the main room of the inn where the eerie red glow of the dying embers of the fire cast shadows which chased one another in the gloom. Fidelma bit her lip and shivered. She wished that she had a candle to light her way. Slowly, she began to descend the stairs.

She was halfway down when her bare foot came into contact with a board that was loose. It gave forth a heavy creak which sounded like a thunderclap in the night.

Fidelma froze.

A split second later she heard a scuffling noise in the darkness of the room below and then she was hastening down the rest of the stairs into the gloom.

'If anyone is here, identify yourself in the name of Christ!' she called, making her voice as stern as she could, and trying to ignore the wild beating of her heart.

There was a distant thud and then silence.

She peered around the deserted room of the inn, her eyes darting here and there as the red shadows danced across the walls. She could see nothing.

Then . . . there was a sound behind her.

She whirled round.

Belach stood on the bottom stair, his wife, Monchae, peering fearfully over his shoulder.

'You heard it, too?' he whispered nervously.

'I heard it,' confirmed Fidelma.

'God look down on us,' sighed the man.

Fidelma made an impatient gesture.

'Light a candle, Belach, and we will search this place.'

The innkeeper shrugged.

'There is no purpose, Sister. We have heard such noises before and made a search. Nothing is ever found.'

'Indeed,' echoed his wife, 'why search for temporal signs from a spectre?'

Fidelma set her jaw grimly.

'Why would a spectre make noises?' she replied. 'Only something with a corporeal existence makes a noise. Now give me a light.'

Reluctantly, Belach lit a lamp. The innkeeper and his wife stood by the bottom of the stairs as Fidelma began a careful search of the inn. She had barely begun when Monchae gave a sudden shriek and fell forward onto the floor.

Fidelma hurried quickly to her side. Belach was patting her hands in a feeble attempt to revive her senses.

'She's fainted,' muttered the man unnecessarily.

'Get some water,' instructed Fidelma, and when the water had been splashed against the woman's forehead and some of it nursed between her lips, Monchae blinked and opened her eyes.

'What was it?' snapped Fidelma. 'What made you faint?'

Monchae stared at her a moment or two, her face pale, her teeth chattering.

'The pipes!' she stammered. 'The pipes!'

'I heard no pipes,' Fidelma replied.

'No. Mugrán's pipes . . . on the table!'

Leaving Belach to help Monchae to her feet, Fidelma turned, holding her candle high, and beheld a set of pipes lying on the table. There was nothing remarkable about them. Fidelma had seen many of better quality and workmanship.

'What are you telling me?' she asked, as Monchae was led forward by Belach, still trembling.

'These are Mugrán's pipes. The pipes he took away with him to war. It must be true. His ghost has returned. Oh, saints protect us!'

She clung desperately to her husband.

Fidelma reached forward to examine the pipes.

They seemed entirely of this world. They were of the variety called *cetharchóire*, meaning four-tuned, with a chanter, two shorter reed-drones and a long drone. A simple pipe to be found in almost any household in Ireland. She pressed her lips tightly, realising that when they had all retired for the night there had been no sign of any pipes on the table.

'How are you sure that these are the pipes of Mugrán?' she asked.

'I know them!' The woman was vehement. 'How do you know what garment belongs to you, or what knife? You know its weave, its stains, its markings . . .'

She began to sob hysterically.

Fidelma ordered Belach to take the woman back to her bed.

'Have a care, Sister,' the man muttered, as he led his wife away. 'We are surely dealing with evil powers here.'

Fidelma smiled thinly.

'I am a representative of the greater power, Belach. Everything that happens can only occur when under His will.'

After they had gone, she stood staring at the pipes for a while and finally gave up the conundrum with a sigh. She left them on the table and climbed the stairs back to her own bed, thankful it was still warm for she realised, for the first time, that her feet and legs were freezing. The night was truly chill.

She lay for a while thinking about the mystery which she had found here in this desolate mountain spot and wondering if there was some supernatural solution to it. Fidelma acknowledged that there were powers of darkness. Indeed, one would be a fool to believe in God and to refuse to believe in the Devil. If there was good, then there was, undoubtedly, evil. But, in her experience, evil tended to be a human condition.

She had fallen asleep. It could not have been for long. It was still dark when she started awake again.

It took a moment or two for her to realise what it was which had aroused her for the second time that night.

Far off she could hear pipes playing. It was a sweet, gentle sound. The sound of the sleep-producing *súan-traige*, the beautiful, sorrowing lullaby.

'*Codail re suanán saine . . .*'

'Sleep with pleasant slumber . . .'

Fidelma knew the tune well, for many a time had she been lulled into drowsiness as a child by its sweet melody.

She sat up abruptly and swung out of bed. The music was real. It was outside the inn. She went to the shuttered window and cautiously eased it open a crack.

Outside the snow lay like a crisp white carpet across the surrounding hills and mountains. The sky was still shrouded with heavy grey-white snow clouds. Even so, the nightscape was light, in spite of the fact that the moon was only a soft glow hung with ice crystals that produced a halo around its orb. One could see for miles. The atmosphere was icy chill and still. Vapour from her breath made bursts of short-lived clouds in the air before her.

It was then that her heart began to hammer as if a mad drummer was beating a warning to wake the dead.

She stood shock still.

About a hundred yards from the inn was a small round knoll. On the knoll stood the figure of a lonely piper and he was playing the sweet lullaby that woke her. But the thing that caused her to feel dizzy with awe and apprehension was the fact that the figure shimmered as if a curious light emanated from him, sparkling like little stars against the brightness of the reflecting snow.

She stood still, watching. Then the melody trailed off and the figure turned its head in the direction of the inn. It gave vent to an awesome, pitiful cry.

'I am alone! I am alone, Monchae! Why did you desert me? I am alone! I will come for you soon!'

Perhaps it was the cry that stirred Fidelma into action.

She turned, grabbed her leather shoes and seized her cloak, and hurried down the stairs into the gloomy interior of the main room of the inn. She heard Belach's cry on the stair behind her.

'Don't go out, Sister! It is evil! It is the shade of Mugrán!'

She paid no heed. She threw open the bolts of the door

and went plunging into the icy stillness of the night. She ran through the deep snow, feeling its coldness against her bare legs, up towards the knoll. But long before she got there, she realised that the figure had disappeared.

She reached the knoll and paused. There was no one in sight. The nocturnal piper had vanished. She drew her cloak closer around her shoulders and shivered. But it was the night chill rather than the idea of the spectre that caused her to tremble.

Catching her breath against the icy air, she looked down. There were no footprints. But the snow, on careful inspection, had not lain in pristine condition across the knoll. Its surface was rough, ruffled as if a wind had blown across it. It was then she noticed the curious reflective quality of it. She bent forward and scooped a handful of snow in her palm and examined it. It seemed to twinkle and reflect as she held it.

Fidelma gave a long, deep sigh. She turned and retraced her steps back to the inn.

Belach was waiting anxiously by the door. She noticed that he now held the sword in his hand.

She grinned mischievously.

'If it were a spirit, that would be of little assistance,' she observed dryly.

Belach said nothing, but he locked and bolted the door behind Fidelma as she came into the room. He replaced the sword without comment as she went to the fire to warm herself after her exertion into the night.

Monchae was standing on the bottom step, her arms folded across her breast, moaning a little.

Fidelma went in search of the jug of *corma* and poured out some of the spirit. She swallowed and then took a wooden cup to Monchae and told her to drink it.

'You heard it? You saw it?' The wife of the innkeeper wailed.

Fidelma nodded.

Belach bit his lip.

'It is the ghost of Mugrán. We are doomed.'

'Nonsense!' snapped Fidelma.

'Then explain that!' replied Belach, pointing to the table.

There was nothing on the table. It was then Fidelma realised what was missing. She had left the pipes on the table when she had returned to bed.

'It is two hours or so until sunrise,' Fidelma said slowly. 'I want you two to return to bed. There is something here which I must deal with. Whatever occurs, I do not wish either of you to stir from your room unless I specifically call you.'

Belach stared at her with white, taut features.

'You mean that you will do battle with this evil force?'

Fidelma smiled thinly.

'That is what I mean,' she said emphatically.

Reluctantly, Belach helped Monchae back up the stairs, leaving Fidelma standing in the darkness. She stood still, thinking for a while. She had an instinct that whatever was happening in this troubled, isolated inn, it was building up towards its climax. Perhaps that climax would come before sunrise. There was no logic to the idea but Fidelma had long come to the belief that one should not ignore one's instincts.

She turned and made her way towards a darkened alcove at the far end of the room in which only a deep wooden bench was situated. She tightened her cloak against the chill, seated herself and prepared to wait. Wait for what, she did not know. But she believed that she would not have to wait for long before some other manifestation occurred.

It was only a short time before she heard the sounds of the pipe once more.

The sweet, melodious lullaby was gone. The pipes were now wild keening. It was the hair-raising lament of the *gol-traige*, full of pain, sorrow and longing.

Fidelma held her head to one side.

The music was no longer outside the old inn but seeming to echo from within, seeping up under the floorboards, through the walls and down from the rafters.

She shivered but made no move to go in search of the sound, praying all the while that neither Monchae nor Belach would disobey her instructions and leave their room.

She waited until the tune came to an end.

There was silence in the old building.

Then she heard the sound, the sound she had heard on her first waking. It was a soft, dragging noise. Her body tensed as she bent forward in the alcove, her eyes narrowed as she tried to focus into the darkness.

A figure seemed to be rising from the floor, upwards, slowly upwards on the far side of the room.

Fidelma held her breath.

The figure, reaching its full height, appeared to be clutching a set of pipes beneath its arm. It moved towards the table in a curious limping gait.

Fidelma noticed that, now and again, as the light of the glowing embers in the hearth caught it, the figure's cloak sparkled and danced with a myriad pinpricks of fire.

Fidelma rose to her feet.

'The charade is over!' she cried harshly.

The figure dropped the pipes and wheeled around, seeking to identify the speaker. Then it seemed to catch its breath.

'Is that you, Monchae?' came a sibilant, mocking whisper.

Then, before Fidelma could prepare herself, the figure seemed to fly across the room at her. She caught sight of light flashing on an upraised blade and instinct made her react by grasping at the descending arm with both hands, twisting her body to take the weight of the impact.

The figure grunted angrily as the surprise of the attack failed.

The collision of their bodies threw Fidelma back into the alcove, slamming her against the wooden seat. She grunted in pain. The figure had shaken her grip loose and once more the knife hand was descending.

'You should have fled while you had the chance, Monchae,' came the masculine growl. 'I had no wish to harm you or the old man. I just wanted to get you out of this inn. Now, you must die!'

Fidelma sprang aside once more, feverishly searching for some weapon, some means of defence.

Her flaying hand caught against something. She dimly recognised it as the alabaster figure of the Madonna and Child. Automatically, her fingers closed on it and she swung it up like a club. She struck the figure where she thought the side of the head would be.

She was surprised at the shock of the impact. The alabaster seemed to shatter into pieces, as she would have expected from a plaster statuette, but its impact seemed firm and weighty, causing a vibration in her hand and arm. The sound was like a sickening smack of flesh meeting a hard substance.

The figure grunted, a curious sound as the air was sharply expelled from his lungs. Then he dropped to the floor. She heard the sound of metal ringing on the floor planks as the knife dropped and bounced.

Fidelma stood for a moment or two, shoulders heaving as she sought to recover her breath and control her pounding emotions.

Slowly she walked to the foot of the stairs and called up in a firm voice.

'You can come down now. I have laid your ghost!'

She turned, stumbling a little in the darkness, until she found a candle and lit it. Then she went back to the figure of her erstwhile assailant. He lay on his side, hands outstretched. He was a young man. She gave a soft intake of breath when she saw the ugly wound on his temple. She reached forward and felt for a pulse. There was none.

She looked round curiously. The impact of a plaster statuette could not have caused such a death blow.

Fragments and powdered plaster were scattered in a large area. But there, lying in the debris was a long cylindrical tube of sacking. It was no more than a foot high and perhaps one inch in diameter. Fidelma bent and picked it up. It was heavy. She sighed and replaced it where she had found it.

Monchae and Belach were creeping down the stairs now.

'Belach, have you a lantern?' asked Fidelma, as she stood up.

'Yes. What is it?' demanded the innkeeper.

'Light it, if you please. I think we have solved your haunting.'

As she spoke she turned and walked across the floor to the spot where she had seen the figure rise, as if from the floor. There was a trap-door and beneath it some steps which led into a tunnel.

Belach had lit the lamp.

'What has happened?' he demanded.

'Your ghost was simply a man,' Fidelma explained.

Monchae let out a moan.

'You mean it is Mugrán? He was not killed at Loch Derg?'

Fidelma perched herself on the edge of the table and shook her head. She stooped to pick up the pipes where the figure had dropped them on the table.

'No; it was someone who looked and sounded a little like Mugrán as you knew him. Take a look at his face, Monchae. I think you will recognise Cano, Mugrán's younger brother.'

A gasp of astonishment from the woman confirmed Fidelma's identification.

'But why, what . . .?'

'A sad but simple tale. Cano was not killed as reported at Loch Derg. He was probably badly wounded and returned to this land with a limp. I presume that he did not have a limp when he went away?'

'He did not,' Monchae confirmed.

'Mugrán was dead. He took Mugrán's pipes. Why he took so long to get back here, we shall never know. Perhaps he did not need money until now, or perhaps the idea never occurred to him . . .'

'I don't understand,' Monchae said, collapsing into a chair by the table.

'Cano remembered that Mugrán had some money. A lot of money he had saved. Mugrán told you that if he lost his life, then there was money in the inn and you would never want for anything. Isn't that right?'

Monchae made an affirmative gesture. 'But as I told you, it was just Mugrán's fantasy. We searched the inn every-where and could find no sign of any money. Anyway, my man, Belach, and I are content with things as they are.'

Fidelma smiled softly.

'Perhaps it was when Cano realised that you had not found his brother's hoard that he made up his mind to find it himself.'

'But it isn't here,' protested Belach, coming to the support of his wife.

'But it *was*,' insisted Fidelma. 'Cano knew it. But he didn't know where. He needed time to search. How could he get you away from the inn sufficiently long to search? That was when he conceived a convoluted idea to drive you out by pretending to be the ghost of his brother. He had his brother's pipes and could play the same tunes as his brother had played. His appearance and his voice made him pass for the person you once knew, Monchae, but, of course, only at a distance with muffled voice. He began to haunt you.'

'What of the shimmering effect?' demanded Belach. 'How could he produce such an effect?'

'I have seen a yellow clay-like substance that gives off that curious luminosity,' Fidelma assured them. 'It can be scooped from the walls of the caves west of here. It is called *mearnáil*, a phosphorus, a substance that glows in the gloom. If you examine Cano's cloak you will see that he has smeared it in this yellowing clay.'

'But he left no footprints,' protested Belach. 'He left no footprints in the snow.'

'But he did leave some tell-tale sign,' Fidelma pointed out. 'You see, he took the branch of a bush and, as he walked backwards away from the knoll, he swept away his footprints. But while it does disguise the footprints, one can still see the ruffled surface of the snow where the bush has swept over its top layer. It is an old trick, taught to warriors, to hide their tracks from their enemies.'

'But surely he could not survive in the cold outside all these nights?' Monchae said. It was the sort of aspect which would strike a woman's precise and practical logic.

'He did not. He slept in the inn, or at least in the stable. Once or twice he tried to search the inn while you lay asleep. Hence the bumps and sounds that sometimes awakened you. But he knew, however, that he could only search properly if he could move you out.'

'He was here with us in the inn?' Belach was aghast.

Fidelma nodded to the open trap-door in the floor.

'It seemed that he knew more of the secret passages of the inn than either of you. After all, Cano was brought up here.'

There was a silence.

Monchae gave a low sigh.

'All that and there was no treasure. Poor Cano. He was not really evil. Did you have to kill him, Sister?'

Fidelma compressed her lips for a moment.

'Everything is in God's hands,' she said in resignation. 'In my struggle, I seized the statuette of Our Lady and struck out at Cano. It caught him on the temple and fragmented.'

'But it was only alabaster. It would not have killed him, surely?'

'It was what was inside that killed him. The very thing he was looking for. It lies there on the floor.'

'What is it?' whispered Monchae, when Belach reached down to pick up the cylindrical object in sackcloth.

'It is a roll of coins. It is Mugrán's treasure. It acted as a bar of metal to the head of Cano and killed him. Our Lady had been protecting the treasure all these years and, in the final analysis, Our Lady meted out death to him that was not rightful heir to that treasure.'

Fidelma suddenly saw the light creeping in through the shutters of the inn.

'And now day is breaking. I need to break my fast and be on my way to Cashel. I'll leave a note for your *bó-aire* explaining matters. But I have urgent business in Cashel. If he wants me, I shall be there.'

Monchae stood regarding the shattered pieces of the statuette.

'I will have a new statuette of Our Lady made,' she said softly.

'You can afford it now,' replied Fidelma solemnly.

Acknowledgements

'Tarnished Halo' – originally published in *Midwinter Mysteries 5*, edited by Hilary Hale (UK: Little, Brown, 1995)

'The Horse that Died for Shame' – originally published in *Murder at the Races*, edited by Peter Haining (UK: Orion, 1995)

'At the Tent of Holofernes' – originally published in *Ellery Queen's Mystery Magazine* (USA: December, 1998)

'A Scream from the Sepulchre' – originally published in *Ellery Queen's Mystery Magazine* (USA: May, 1998)

'Invitation to a Poisoning' – originally published in *Past Poisons*, edited by Maxim Jakubowski (UK: Headline, 1998)

'Those that Trespass' – originally published in *Chronicles of Crime*, edited by Maxim Jakubowski (UK: Headline, 1999)

'Holy Blood' – originally published in *Great Irish Stories of Murder and Mystery*, edited by Peter Haining (UK: Souvenir Press, 1999)

'Our Lady of Death' – originally published in *Dark Detectives*, edited by Steve Jones (USA: Fedogan & Bremer, 1999)